CASE CLOSED

MYSTERY IN THE MANSION

P9-DDG-032

THE CASE CLOSED SERIES

LAUREN MAGAZINER

CASE CLOSED

MYSTERY IN THE MANSION

PICK YOUR PATH,

CRACK THE CASE

KATHERINE TEGEN BOOKS
An Imprint of HarperCollins Publishers

Katherine Tegen Books is an imprint of HarperCollins Publishers.

Case Closed: Mystery in the Mansion
Copyright © 2018 by Lauren Magaziner
All rights reserved. Printed in the United States of America.
No part of this book may be used or reproduced in any manner
whatsoever without written permission except in the case of brief
quotations embodied in critical articles and reviews. For information address HarperCollins Children's Books, a division of
HarperCollins Publishers, 195 Broadway, New York, NY 10007.
www.harpercollinschildrens.com

Library of Congress Cataloging-in-Publication Data
Names: Magaziner, Lauren, author.
Title: Mystery in the mansion / Lauren Magaziner.
Description: First edition. | New York : Katherine Tegen Books,
    an imprint of HarperCollins Publishers, [2018] | Series: Case
    closed ; 1 | "Pick Your Path, Crack the Case!" | Summary: Carlos
    and his friends must uncover who is sending death threats to a
    wealthy eccentric or Carlos's mother may lose her business, and
    the reader decides which clues they will follow.
Identifiers: LCCN 2017034681 | ISBN 978-0-06-267628-3
Subjects: LCSH: Plot-your-own stories. | CYAC: Mystery and
    detective stories. | Buried treasure—Fiction. | Friendship—
    Fiction. | Plot-your-own stories. | BISAC: JUVENILE
    FICTION / Interactive Adventures. | JUVENILE FICTION /
    Mysteries & Detective Stories.
Classification: LCCPZ7.M2713 Mys 2018 | DDC [Fic]—dc23
    LC record available at https://lccn.loc.gov/2017034681

Typography by Andrea Vandergrift
21 22 23   BRR   11
❖
First paperback edition, 2019

To Brianne Johnson, who gave this book life.
And to Ben Rosenthal, who found its heart.
25-15-21   20-23-15   1-18-5   20-8-5   2-5-19-20 . . .
3-1-19-5   3-12-15-19-5-4

RRRRRRRIIIIIIIINNNGGGGGGGG!!!!
RRRIIINNNGGGGGG!!!!

Mom's alarm clock goes off for the second time this morning. It rattles through my wall.

"Ugh," I groan as I roll over. I'm soaked in sweat. Every day this summer, I've been waking up like this. We can't afford to use our air conditioner anymore. Now that it's the beginning of July, a fan just doesn't cut it.

RRRRRIIIIIINNNGGGGG!

I hit my hand on the wall. "Mom! Shut off your alarm!"

Then I roll out of bed and stumble to the bathroom. My breath is really bad this morning, so I scrub my teeth. I not-so-accidentally "forgot" to brush last night, because let's be honest: toothpaste tastes gross. Usually Mom nags me to brush, but she was so busy preparing for her case today that she didn't bother to do it.

Mom co-owns a detective agency, but it's not doing so hot. In fact . . . it stinks more than my breath. Six months ago, my mom had a case that flopped, and her agency had to pay a lot of money for damages. They also took a hit to their reputation; they haven't had any new business since. But she *finally* got a new case—and a big one too! A million-billion-zillionaire named Guinevere LeCavalier is being sent death threats by a mystery person, and she hired Mom to help find the criminal! Mom is going to interview Mrs. LeCavalier for the first time this morning.

RRRRRIIIIIINNNGGGGG!

Is that Mom's alarm . . . again? That's odd. It usually only takes her one snooze before she pops out of bed like a jack-in-the-box.

I shuffle across the hall and knock on Mom's door. "Mom? Are you awake?" I crack the door open and peek inside.

"ACHOO!" She sneezes.

I walk in and sit by her bed. "Uh . . . Mom? Are you feeling okay?"

"I'b sick!"

"Sick! You can't be sick! Not today!" This job is important—to both of us!

"Carwos," Mom says to me. "Pwease call my pardner and tell him I'b sick."

"What?"

"Send Cowe! Put Cowe on de case!" Cole is Mom's business partner, who is up to his neck in another case—*his* first case in months too. I get nervous thinking about what will happen if Mom's company goes bankrupt. And Cole can't handle two cases at once. It's hard enough that Mom and Cole don't even have assistants to help them investigate.

"But Mom . . . Cole can't take the Guinevere LeCavalier case. Doesn't he have another case to solve?"

"He'll hab to do bof!" Mom says, her nose dripping with snot.

"Mooooooom!" I shake the bed. "Get up, get up, get up! You have to take this case! You can't afford not to!" My sweat-soaked pajama shirt suddenly feels grosser than ever. But I try not to think about how sticky it is as I lean over Mom. "Come . . . on!" I grunt, yanking her by the wrists and pulling her up into a sitting position. But she flops back down.

"Wheeeee! How'djya make de room spin?" she says. Then she coughs again and groans. "Pwomise me you'll caw Cowe wight now, Carwos! Pwease! I don't want to woose dis case eiber."

"I . . ."

"Carwos!" Mom says, reaching for a tissue. "Pwease!"

"Okay, fine. I'll go call him."

I slowly walk back out of the room, kicking my feet the whole way—and to my surprise, my best friend, Eliza, is sitting at the kitchen table.

3

But I guess I shouldn't be too surprised. Whenever Eliza comes over, she always walks right in without knocking. She's been my best friend since we were in preschool. She lives in my neighborhood, two streets over.

Lately, it's almost embarrassing having her over to my place, a dusty one-story house with peeling wood panels on the walls and shaggy carpet. Since my mom's agency took a nosedive, we haven't been able to fix up all the things that keep going wrong with our house: the leaky faucet, the clogged bathroom sink, the malfunctioning dishwasher, the broken vacuum cleaner. And I don't want her to notice that we've had to cut back on a lot of things, like air-conditioning and expensive groceries. We even had to sell a bunch of our lamps, books, and furniture, just to get by.

I don't want her over here. I don't want her noticing. But I haven't said anything, and Eliza is used to keeping me company every summer. At home and at day camp, another thing we couldn't afford anymore.

Camp starts in two weeks, and Eliza still doesn't know I'm not going yet. Every time she talks about all the fun we're going to have, I feel like shriveling up. I'm not excited to be stuck at my house all alone while she does all the sports and games we used to do together. But I'm trying not to think about it. Until she leaves,

I'm going to spend as much time with her as I can.

"Eliza! When did you get here?"

"Just a second ago. I let myself in."

"Oh," I say, and I slump down on the chair next to her. I know I need to call Mom's partner right now, but I really, really don't want to do it.

Eliza's eyes narrow as she looks at me. "What's wrong, Carlos?"

I sigh. "Mom wants me to call the detective agency and tell Cole to go."

"Go where?"

"Mom was supposed to investigate the Guinevere LeCavalier case—"

"That old lady in the rich part of town?"

I nod. "Yeah. She's been receiving death threats. Mom's too sick to work, though. And Cole's way too busy. But if they don't take this case . . ." I look away from Eliza. But I can still feel her staring at me. I wish I could just crawl into a hole right now. Or a ditch. Or a pit. (I'm not picky.)

Honestly, I'd rather crawl into a sewer full of poop than talk about our money problems.

Eliza puts her hand on my arm. "What aren't you telling me, Carlos? You're hiding something."

"It's nothing," I say to my feet.

Eliza frowns, and I start calling Cole.

This stinks. This case could have put Las Pistas Detective Agency back on the map . . . it would have turned things around for Mom. For both of us.

I pause in the middle of dialing. "*We* should go."

"What?" Eliza says.

"YEAH!" shouts a muffled voice from under the couch.

"Oh no," I groan. "Not Frank!"

Frank is Eliza's little brother, and he always tags along with Eliza and me. He's six years old, and Eliza says Frank is short for Frankenstein's Monster. But she's the only one who's allowed to say anything mean about him. She even gets mad at *me* when I call him annoying.

I walk over to the couch. Frank's head is underneath it, but the rest of him isn't. His butt is wiggling high in the air.

"Frank! You're not even hiding! I can see you."

Frank crawls out of his hiding spot. "I found a nickel!" he says. "And a button! And a piece of fuzz. Can I eat it?" He looks to Eliza.

"No, you can*not* eat random fuzz!" she says, turning around to gag.

The second she turns away, Frank pops the fuzz into his mouth and grins at me.

"Wait, go back," Eliza says to me. "You want to take on Guinevere LeCavalier's case?"

"Carwos?" Mom shouts from her bedroom. "What's

going on ou—ah—*achoooooo!*"

"Nothing, Mom!" I shout. "Just Eliza and Frank!"

Then I turn to Eliza and whisper so my mom doesn't hear. "We have to. My mom needs us. You think we can do it, right?"

Eliza smiles. "Three kids are about equal to the size and mass of one adult."

I don't know what she's talking about, but Eliza is smart. In fact, she's the smartest person I know.

"So, you're in?" I say to her, wiping off some sweat that's dripping out of my hair. Guinevere LeCavalier *would* pay a lot of money if we solved her case. And we could certainly use the money.

And together we *could* solve it, and save my mom's agency. Eliza is a genius. She could figure out anything that needs figuring out. And Frank is really good at finding things—maybe he could find some clues. The only weak link is me, because I have no idea what I'd bring to the team.

"Of course I'm in," Eliza replies. "You know that!"

"Me too!" Frank hollers.

I have the best friend—and the best best friend's little brother—in the world.

Guinevere LeCavalier's house is in the nicest part of town, in a neighborhood called River Woods. Only there is no river and no woods. It's kind of an open field with a bunch of houses the size of the White House. Usually the only time I ever come to River Woods is for Halloween. Rich people give out the best candy.

We wander around looking for the house number 1418, Mrs. LeCavalier's address, according to Mom's files. But so far no luck. Eliza and Frank are checking the other side of the street, while I look at the ones on this side. I pass a big blue mansion, then a white one, then a brown one. None of them are right. I ignore Frank as he shouts, "THIS ONE! NO, THIS ONE! NO, *THIS* ONE!" He shouts just to shout.

"Carlos?" Eliza suddenly says. "Look at this."

Eliza nods toward a house that's kind of yellowish and has big white columns all along the outside—and a weird lawn with hedges shaped like Yorkie dogs.

"Uh . . . is that it?"

"No," Eliza says. "Look at the window next to the front door."

I squint toward the window, but it's hard to see with the sun glaring in my face. But then—I see it. Or *her*. There's a woman in the window, and she's spying on us with binoculars.

I shudder. "Is she watching *us*?"

Eliza shrugs.

"Well, who is she?"

"P. Schnozzlepoop," Frank says, peering at the mailbox.

"P. Schnozzle*ton*," Eliza corrects.

"I got bored in the middle of reading that word," Frank admits, "so I made up the rest."

I try not to roll my eyes.

Eliza gasps. "She's gone!"

The window blinds are down now. I wonder if the woman is peeking through them, still spying. "But who *is* P. Schnozzleton?" I ask Eliza. "Is that her?"

Eliza looks nervous as she says, "I don't know. That was *very* weird."

Across the street, we finally find 1418—Guinevere LeCavalier's house. The driveway is long and twisty like a gummy worm, and at the end of it is a big BIG *ENORMOUS* gray stone house. It's got four chimneys and a zillion windows, and it's so nice it's hard to look at it without feeling all lumpy in my throat. I wish Mom and I could live in a house even a quarter as nice as this one. Or I'd even settle for a house with two stories. Or a house with a fireplace. Or a house that didn't smell weird. Or a house with affordable air-conditioning.

Mom says money doesn't grow on trees, but maybe she's wrong. Because Guinevere LeCavalier seems to have found one giant money oak.

"Carlos?" Eliza says. "Should we go in?"

I can't let Eliza know what I'm feeling. And I can't afford to think about money right now—it won't help me solve this mystery. I just have to concentrate on the clues. And then my mom will have the big break she needs to boost her agency.

As my Little League coach says, I have to keep my head in the game! "Come on," I say to Eliza, and run toward the door, cutting across the grass to save time.

"Excuse me!" says a voice, and a man comes running from a toolshed near the side of the house. "What are you *doing?*" he calls from halfway across the yard. He's tall and thin, with messy blond hair, bright blue eyes, and a dimple in his chin.

"No, no, no!" the man cries, walking over to us by tiptoeing along the mulch. "I just mowed the lawn to perfection! Don't tread all over it with your shoes! You'll flatten out the grass!"

"Ooops!" Eliza squeaks. "Sorry!"

"It's okay." The man sighs. "I didn't mean to yell at you kids. You didn't know any better."

"Who are—?" I start to say, but Frank interrupts.

"Excuuuuuuse meeeeeeeee!" he shouts, pointing at the man. "Your chin is in the shape of a butt." Then Frank bursts into hysterical giggles.

The man cracks a smile. "My name is Otto Paternoster. I'm Mrs. LeCavalier's landscaper."

"What's a land caper?" Frank asks.

"I help her maintain her beautiful gardens and lawn. I plant vegetation, pluck weeds . . ."

Otto continues talking, but my eyes glaze over and I tune out what he says. I can do this with a lot of adults, especially my teachers.

"But this is probably boring you kids," I hear Otto say.

"What? No!" Eliza says. "It's very interesting!" But I can tell she's lying because she turns pink. Eliza is such a bad liar.

"What are you kids up to?" Otto says. "Are you family of Mrs. LeCavalier?"

"No," Eliza says.

"We're defectives!" Frank says, puffing out his chest.

"Detectives," Eliza corrects.

"Detectives? What—why—"

"We're here to figure out who has been sending Mrs. LeCavalier death threats. Do you know anything about this?" Eliza asks.

Otto's eyes grow wide. His irises are like two blue saucers. "No! This is the first time I'm hearing about this! What's going on? What kind of threats? Is she in danger?"

I can't discuss the details of my case with a perfect stranger. That's like . . . rule number one of detective work.

"Don't worry, Mr. Otto, sir," I say. "Everything is under control."

Then I grab Eliza's and Frank's arms and drag them to Guinevere LeCavalier's ironclad front door.

"Is it weird to be excited?" Eliza whispers as I ring the doorbell.

A towering man opens the door. He's wearing a fancy suit that looks too tight for his big body—especially around the arms and shoulders. The man has speckled gray hair with a bald patch on the top of his head, and his eyes droop like a basset hound's.

"Yes?" the man says, scowling at us like somebody put a plate of poo under his nose.

"Hello, sir," I begin. "We're detectives from—"

"HELLOOOOOOOOO!" sings a booming voice. Behind the giant man, an old lady floats down the stairs. Her hair is a silvery white, and her face is thin and crinkly. She's wearing pearls and diamonds and rubies and sapphires and more diamonds and purple gems and green gems—she looks like a human Christmas tree. "Move aside, Smythe," the old woman demands, and the man glares.

"Hello," I say. "Are you Guinevere LeCavalier?"

"Well, aren't you a precious plum?" she says. "I could just eat you right up!" She looks dangerously close to pinching our cheeks. Why do adults always love to pinch and squeeze and slobber-kiss kids? Gross!

I smile. "We're the detectives from Las Pistas Detective Agency."

"You are much smaller than I thought you'd be."

Before I can think of what to say, Frank says, "HUMPH! You're a meanie!"

"We are . . . uh . . . very sensitive because we look much younger than we are," Eliza jumps in, and even *I* don't believe her.

"I promise, we'll solve your case, though," I say firmly. "Trust us."

Guinevere raises an eyebrow. "Perhaps you can prove you're adult enough to handle this case. Hmmm . . . what is it adults do?"

"Work at a job you hate," the man grumbles from beside her.

"Pay taxes?" Eliza says.

"Worry a lot?" I suggest.

"Be boring?" Frank replies.

"Get colonoscopies?" Eliza says.

"Wear matching socks!" Frank yells.

"That sounds adult enough for me!" Guinevere says. "Come on in. *Smythe!*" she screams, even though he is standing right next to her. "Prepare the tea!"

Inside, Guinevere LeCavalier's house is even *more* fancypants. The walls are encrusted with jewels. The windows are made of stained glass. The ceilings are fifteen feet tall. She even has a ballroom. And multiple staircases.

"What's up there?" I say as we pass the third staircase.

Guinevere LeCavalier waves her hand. "Oh, nothing. Just my grand bedroom, my late husband's study, Smythe's quarters, three bathrooms, and Ivy's bedroom."

"Who is Ivy?" Eliza asks.

Guinevere pauses for a moment, and Frank runs smack into her butt. "GROSS!" he says with a grin. He *loves* gross things.

"Ivy is my daughter," Guinevere says.

"Oh!" I say. "Does she live here?"

"She moved away. She lives with her *husband* now, in Wichita." Her voice is cold. "Ivy's coming tomorrow, though. To visit me."

"Do you see her often?" Eliza asks.

"No," Guinevere says. She folds her arms and pouts.

We pass through a library, where a bookshelf is toppled and books are everywhere. There's red writing on the wall, but it's too far away to read.

Guinevere quickly brushes past the room without a word, and Frank marches right behind her. I start to follow, but I notice Eliza is moving closer to the red, swoopy cursive on the far wall, like she wants to read the death threat. The crusty paint looks close to blood from where I'm standing.

"Come on, Eliza!" I hiss. "If we lose Guinevere, we

can be lost forever in this house."

I grab Eliza's hand and drag her into the next room, where Guinevere is tapping her foot expectantly.

"About time!" she says.

"ABOUT TIME!" Frank copies, tapping his foot too.

We pass through a billiard room, a lounge, a family room, a living room, a great room, and a den. Honestly, I don't know what the difference is between any of these rooms. Each one is grander than the last, with arched ceilings, old tapestries, marble walls, wide windows, and hardwood floors.

At last we get to a dining room, and the butler, Smythe, comes in with a tray of teacups, a teapot, milk, sugar, honey, and a bowl of jelly beans.

Guinevere pours a half a cup's worth of jelly beans into her tea and begins stirring madly.

Let me repeat that: she put *jelly beans* in her *tea*.

"So, now," Guinevere says. "What are your names?"

"I'm Carlos," I say, "and this is my best fri—I mean, my colleague Eliza. And another detective, Frank."

"And you three will solve my case?"

"We're the best detectives the agency has to offer." And seeing as we're the *only* detectives it could offer, it's not technically a lie.

Guinevere takes a sip of tea. "Mmmmm, jelly beany." She sighs.

Eliza leans forward, eyes squinty. I know that face. It means she's thinking very hard. "Why don't you start with the first threat? When did you receive it?"

"About two months ago," Guinevere says. "I got a threatening letter in the mail. No return address. No stamps."

"Interesting," Eliza says.

"Interesting how?" Guinevere asks.

"You mean *boring*!" Frank cries, and I kick him under the table.

Eliza ignores Frank. "Well, the lack of fingerprints means that the criminal was wearing gloves. But more importantly, it means he or she is smart. And the fact that the letter didn't go through the mail means the threat was hand delivered. Someone had to come to your mailbox and deliver it in person. He—or she— was in town. And since the threats have continued, he or she is probably *still* in town."

"Impressive," Guinevere says. "I can see why the agency sent you."

Eliza gives a shy grin. I smile too, only I can't stop thinking about how much smarter she is than me, and how I don't have any special skills to offer this case, and how much Mom needs the money. And suddenly I'm not smiling at all.

Eliza looks at me for approval, and I flash her a

thumbs-up when Guinevere LeCavalier looks away to shovel more jelly beans into her tea. "Yes, Eliza is one of the top detectives on staff," I tell Guinevere. Then I glare at Frank, who has started falling asleep on the table.

"So do you think I'm in danger?" Guinevere says, shaking so much that her tea sloshes over the top. "My lawyer seems to think I'm in grave danger."

"Your lawyer?" Eliza says.

"Oh yes," Guinevere says. "Attorney Joe Maddock. Best in town. He charges an arm and a leg—well, really, more like two arms, two legs, a torso, and a head. He's been swinging by the house often, ever since the threats started, so I've been writing him a lot of checks recently. But if he's the most expensive lawyer in town, he must be the best, right?"

"Uh, sure," I say.

"I am very afraid," Guinevere says. "This nasty affair has thrown off my whole groove! And I would meet the letter's demands if that would just make this all go away! But the demands are impossible. . . ."

"What were the demands?" Eliza and I ask simultaneously.

"The criminal wants me to share the location of my late husband's treasure."

"Treasure!" Frank perks up. "What treasure?"

17

"Wouldn't I like to know!" Guinevere LeCavalier pinches her eyebrows together like she's thinking really, really hard. "The thing is," she says, "I have no idea where or what the treasure is. My husband died five years ago, and he left me a treasure in his will. The problem is, I can't find it. You see, he only left me one clue, which was supposed to lead me to more clues, but I can't figure it out. He was very odd. I keep thinking if I find the treasure, this would all be over. I could hand it to the criminal, and maybe they would just go away before anyone gets hurt."

"Hurt?" I gulp. "You think the criminal will actually go through with the death threat?"

Guinevere nods, and her many necklaces jangle. "Perhaps. The first threat was very . . . chilling."

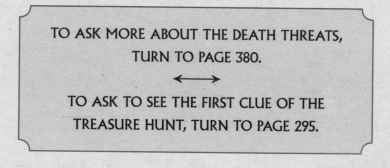

TO ASK MORE ABOUT THE DEATH THREATS, TURN TO PAGE 380.

←——→

TO ASK TO SEE THE FIRST CLUE OF THE TREASURE HUNT, TURN TO PAGE 295.

WE NEED TO search Ivy's room. She is, after all, the prime suspect. Well, *a* prime suspect. Or maybe she's just a suspect.

We dash up to Ivy's room. There are a lot of bedrooms in the house, but we know this one's hers because it's got a couple of suitcases in it. She still hasn't unpacked from when she arrived this morning.

We shut the door behind us. I grab one suitcase, Eliza grabs the other, and Frank starts trying on Ivy's fancy hats. He prances in front of the mirror, giggling like mad.

My suitcase is full of clothes—summer dresses, tank tops, shorts, socks, and even underwear. Ewwwwww! I close the suitcase back up and go to help Eliza sift through hers. That one is filled completely with papers.

"What is this?" I ask, holding one up to the light. It's full of numbers, and it looks like gibberish to me.

"Financial records," Eliza gasps. "Ivy is having money problems!"

"Money problems!" I choke. "But what does that mean?"

"She has a motive," Eliza says. "She really needs the treasure—"

We both stop dead. The doorknob is turning.

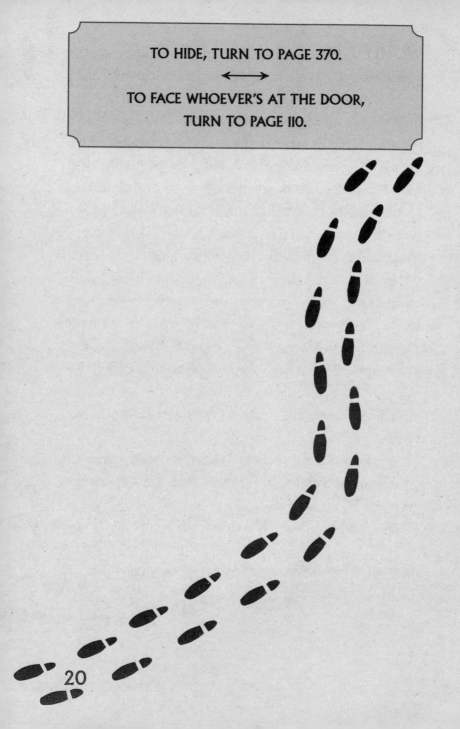

TO HIDE, TURN TO PAGE 370.

←——→

TO FACE WHOEVER'S AT THE DOOR,
TURN TO PAGE 110.

20

THERE'S JUST NO reasoning with Smythe. We have to make a break for it.

"Run!" I shriek.

All three of us run at Smythe, who is so surprised he doesn't know which one of us to go after. Frank leaps by his left side, Eliza spins into the house with a pirouette on his right, and I slide through his legs—just like I slide into home on my baseball team each year.

Once we're in the house, there's no stopping—we can't let Smythe catch us.

"Kids!" he hollers after us, chasing us with a spatula. "I'll call the cops!"

But we run much faster than he does.

"HIDE AND GO SEEK! HIDE AND GO SEEK!" Frank shouts as we dash through the grand ballroom. Then we scamper down the hall, and the wooden floor squeaks under our sneakers. We climb the stairs, and Frank's muddy shoes track dirt on the white runner (oops). Then we hop down the tapestry-covered hall like bunnies. Then we soar through a stone archway. And BAM!

Our path is a dead end.

The room we're standing in is circular—two stories tall, no windows, and the whole wall is lined with books, like a mini library. There's also a ladder to get to the books that are too tall to reach by tiptoe. The desk is right in the center of the room, made of dark red wood with some sort of shiny polish. It looks like a desk made of glazed red-velvet doughnuts. This must've been Mr. LeCavalier's study.

"Why did we stop?" cries Frank. "Let's go!"

THUMP.

THUMP.

THUMP.

Big thudding footsteps are headed our way, and I know Smythe is in the hallway we just came from. There's no way out of this room without running right into Smythe! We're trapped. Cornered.

"Hide!" I tell Eliza and Frank.

Frank curls himself onto a half-empty bookshelf, but Eliza stays put and shakes her head.

"We need to meet Smythe. Head-on. It's time to talk to him."

"No," I insist. "Hide!"

"No! *Talk!*" she says.

"Hide!"

"Talk!"

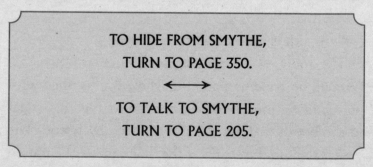

TO HIDE FROM SMYTHE,
TURN TO PAGE 350.

←→

TO TALK TO SMYTHE,
TURN TO PAGE 205.

I ENTER THE password *Art Blue Book Hare Sad* into the keyboard underneath the doorknob, and the door swings open, revealing a plain hallway, totally unlike anything I've seen in Guinevere LeCavalier's house before. The floors and walls are both made of reddish wood, and nothing hangs on any of the walls. It's way too plain. I guess she doesn't care if the staff lives with nice stuff.

I take a step into the hall, and I realize it's ten degrees hotter in this wing of the house, too. Maybe Guinevere doesn't pump AC through parts of the house she doesn't go in? But that seems pretty unfair to poor Smythe.

Maybe that's why he's so grumpy. I definitely know how that feels—living without air-conditioning makes *me* grumpy!

Frank leaps ahead and stops at the last door on the right. "Found it!" He gestures to the door. When I catch up to him, I see that the door has a nameplate: SAMUEL S. SMYTHE.

I pump my fist silently, and Eliza grins. Then she puts a hand over Frank's mouth to make sure he doesn't accidentally shout.

I push the door open, ever so slightly.

Clomp.

A big, floor-shaking step comes from inside the room, and the door swings open.

23

"What are you doing?" fumes Smythe, his droopy eyes red with rage.

Eliza stammers. "I just—we just—"

"This is my room! You cannot come in here without my permission, and I give you no such permission!"

Shoot shoot shoot!

Run! my brain suddenly shouts. *Runnnnnnnnnnn!*

I grab Eliza and Frank by the hands, back out of the staff's hallway, and leave Smythe roaring behind us.

Eliza is trembling from fear, but poor Frank is on the verge of tears. "That was scarier than *everything*."

"No kidding," I say, patting Frank on the back.

My heart is still beating wildly. I lean against one of Guinevere's fancy tapestries and wipe my sweaty hands on the cloth.

Eliza and Frank are both looking to me, so I have to pull it together. "Next time," I say, my voice a little shakier than I want it to sound, "let's make sure the person whose room we want to search isn't *in* the room."

"Speaking of," Eliza says, "we could try searching Ivy's room right now. . . ."

"Noooooooooo," Frank whines. "Not again!"

"We *have* to find more clues, Fra—"

KABOOM!

A huge crash echoes down the hallway—so loud it's

24

like the house is caving in. The noise is followed by an earsplitting, hair-raising shriek. A woman's voice! Could Guinevere be in trouble?

Frank squeals and hugs Eliza's legs for comfort. For the first time, I worry about danger . . . and wonder if maybe we shouldn't have taken this case.

Should we follow the noise? On the one hand, the best detectives *would* monitor a crash.

But on the other hand, maybe the best detectives would take advantage of a distraction like this to go search a suspect's room. This might be our *only* chance to search Ivy's room for clues.

TO FOLLOW THE NOISE,
TURN TO PAGE 174.

←——→

TO SEARCH IVY'S ROOM,
TURN TO PAGE 19.

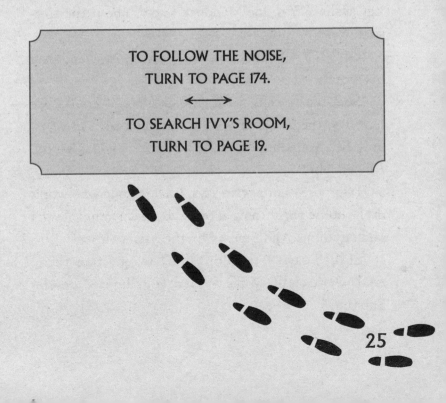

"WHO ELSE KNOWS about the treasure?" I ask.

"Well, there's me," she says. "And my daughter, Ivy, as I said. And Smythe, my butler of thirty years. Under my employment for *ages*. Although . . ."

I lean forward. "Although?"

She looks around to make sure Smythe isn't lurking nearby before she squeaks, "He *has* been grouchy lately. Even more than usual." She shakes her head. "But no, no, it's not him. I trust him completely!" she says, sounding very firm about it.

Eliza and I exchange a look.

"Who else? Ah! My lawyer," continues Guinevere LeCavalier. "Yes, Joe Maddock knows about the treasure, too."

"GUILTY!" Frank cries, and I clamp my hand over his mouth.

"So," Eliza recaps, with a quick glare at Frank, "we have Ivy, the daughter who you haven't seen in years; Smythe, your butler; and Maddock, your lawyer. Anyone else?"

"I suppose," Guinevere says, "that anyone who works in the house *might* know about it. But I certainly haven't said anything. And I trust Smythe hasn't either."

"Still," I say. "It wouldn't hurt to question them. And who exactly works around your house? Besides Smythe?"

"Well, the only other person who is around regularly is my landscaper, Otto. He's been redoing all my flowers and bushes. My husband used to take care of that, and since he passed, I'm afraid I've let the weeds sprout for far too long! We have a terrible infestation!" She pauses. "Is . . . is any of this a help to you?"

"Yes!" I say.

"Utterly," Eliza says.

"Milk comes from udders, you know!" Frank says.

"Before you go," Guinevere LeCavalier says, "I must warn you about my . . . strange house. There are some rooms and secret passageways that are locked and can only be opened by solving a puzzle. You be careful, now."

"We will," Eliza says. I know she *loves* the sound of puzzles. And Frank loves the sound of secret passageways and locked rooms.

We stand up from the table and excuse ourselves.

Eliza squeals when we get into the hallway. "I'm so glad we did this! I love mysteries, and this one is juicy!"

She's too giddy about death threats, I think. "I'm glad you're excited, but it's not a book, Eliza," I remind her. "It's real."

She grins.

"So where do we start?" I ask her.

"We start by questioning our suspects. We have two things to consider: motive and means."

I should know more about detective work, especially after watching Mom solve a few cases. "Motive and means? What's that?"

"Motive—who has a reason to commit the crime? Means—who is physically able to commit the crime? So the criminal is going to be someone who wants—or needs—the treasure. Badly. That's the motive. And the means is the ability to set up the threats. The culprit obviously needs access to the house to pull this off."

"So we have to figure out who needs the treasure. And which of them was able to do the threats. Right?"

Eliza nods.

"Let's play house," Frank says.

"We don't have time to play house right now," Eliza says, taking him by the hand. "We can play later."

"Okay," Frank says. "But only if I'm the llama."

"There aren't any llamas in house, Frank," I say.

"There is in *my* house! And unicorns too!"

I ignore Frank. Last thing I want is for him to throw a tantrum when I tell him the bad news about the existence of unicorns. . . .

Suddenly a man comes strutting down the hall like he's *very important*. He's carrying a briefcase and, boy, does he smell awful!

He is coated in about five layers of cologne. His odor is so sharp and so strong—it's like he took a bath in cleaning solution. Blech.

I cough and put my sleeve to my nose, trying to breathe through my shirt.

"MADDOCK!" I whisper loudly. "I bet that's Maddock, the lawyer!"

"Should we talk to—" Eliza begins, and I don't even wait for her to finish the question before I wave Maddock down.

"Mr. Maddock, sir!" I shout, and the three of us run up to him.

Maddock is a middle-aged man with dark, greasy, slicked-back hair. His face is sharp and angular, with a chin so pointy he could carve an ice sculpture with it.

"Children," he says distastefully.

"If you don't mind, sir," Eliza says, "we have a few questions for you."

"I *do* mind," Maddock says. "I have nothing to say to children. Now run along and play."

"Hey!" I shout. "We have important questions for you!"

"YEAH, YOU BIG MEANIE!" Frank adds.

Maddock looks at his watch and sighs. "As much as I'd like to participate in your little game, kids, I have *real* work to do. And I don't have time for *this*."

"This isn't a *game*!" I say. "We've been hired to solve

Guinevere LeCavalier's case."

At this, Maddock raises his eyebrows at us. "Oh, really?" he says with an amused smirk. He leans against the wall, like he's trying to be cool. "And what is it you want from me?"

"We have questions. About what's been going on around here."

"Then perhaps you should be interviewing Smythe," Maddock says. "Guinevere LeCavalier's butler."

"Yes, we've met," Eliza says.

"And he's a big meanie, too!" Frank adds.

Maddock sneers. "He lives here with Mrs. LeCavalier. If you're curious about what's been going on around here, he would know. Not me. So go find *him*."

"We'll get to him later," I say. "You first. Now, what do you know about Guinevere LeCavalier's treasu—"

"Oh, look at the time!" Maddock says pointedly. "Listen, kids. This was entertaining at first, but I am no longer interested in your antics. I have very important things to be doing right now. I don't usually make house calls, you know. Good-bye."

He tightens up his tie and scurries down the hallway.

I squint after him. "Guilty behavior?"

"Who knows?" Eliza says. "He *did* seem like he was in an awful hurry to leave."

"We can follow him to see what he's up to—"

"YES! FOLLOW!" Frank squeals.

"Or," I continue, "we could try to interview Smythe. He *did* seem really grumpy."

"True," Eliza says. "Maddock's right about one thing—Smythe *does* have free rein of this house. Though . . . I wonder what 'important things' Maddock is doing. Why is he here? Why would he come to Mrs. LeCavalier's house instead of having her visit his office? Maybe he wants access to the house to set up threats. . . ."

Ah, I never thought of that. I feel useless compared to Eliza, but I have to shake off this feeling like I'll never measure up. This won't help my mom.

"So what now?" I ask Eliza.

"It's your mom's case, Carlos. So *you* make the decision. Do you want to question Smythe now? Or follow Maddock?"

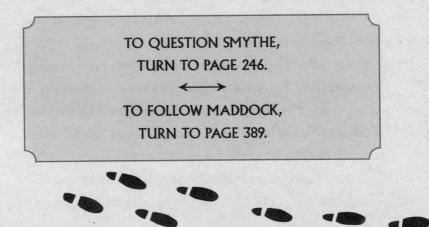

TO QUESTION SMYTHE,
TURN TO PAGE 246.

←→

TO FOLLOW MADDOCK,
TURN TO PAGE 389.

31

WHEN WE FINALLY arrive at my house, I run to the kitchen to pour myself a glass of water. I fill up three cups, and we all drink like we've been walking across the Sahara Desert.

"Ahhhh!" Frank sighs. Then he puts the empty cup on his head like a hat.

"Can we sleep over, Carlos?" Eliza asks.

"SLEEPOVER!" Frank shouts, and the cup flies off his head and rolls around on the ground. He picks it up, puts it over his mouth, and sucks his breath so hard that the cup sticks to his face.

"I can take the couch," Eliza says.

I survey my shabby house, and I can feel myself flush with humiliation. Lately I've been trying to get myself invited to Eliza's house instead of having her come here, and I know it's going to be especially bad tonight without the air-conditioning.

"Wellllllll," I say. "You don't have any pajamas or clothes for tomorrow."

"Yes, I do," Eliza says, opening her backpack. And to my surprise, she has a bunch of clothes wadded up in there—and two toothbrushes. "I already told Mom and Dad we're sleeping here. I just promised to call them after dinner to let them know I'm safe."

"Wellllllllll," I say again, "I have to ask my mom."

Eliza nods. "I just thought we could get an early start

tomorrow . . . and this way we can leave together right from here."

It's a trade-off:

1. Eliza and Frank stay at my embarrassing house (bad), but we get an earlier start on the case (good).
2. I send Eliza and Frank home and save myself a night of feeling ashamed about our money problems (good), but we get a late start tomorrow (bad).

I hide my face in my hands.

"What is it, Carlos?" Eliza asks.

"We . . . we don't have air-conditioning," I whisper, still not looking at her. Please don't ask why, please don't ask why.

There's a pause that feels like a *decade*. But then finally Eliza says, "We'll survive."

I escape as fast as I can, into Mom's room, before Eliza can say anything else. Mom is so buried under the covers that I can only see her eyes.

"Mom?"

"ACHOOOOO!"

"Are you okay?"

"I fin ib worb." Her words are all muffled from the covers over her head . . . *and* she sounds like she's got a crab pinching her nose.

"Um, can Eliza and Frank sleep over? It's just we had a really fun day, er, playing outside, and we don't want the fun to end." My face is burning up with the guilt of this lie. "But I promise they'll be quiet, and their parents are okay with it, and we won't come near your room, so we don't get sick—"

"Ib yorb romb queen?"

Still not sure what she's saying. But she clearly just asked me a question. "Uh . . . sure?"

"Den ib fye wib me." She coughs.

I stare at her. Was that a yes? Or a no?

She pulls her hand out from under the covers and flashes me a thumbs-up.

And to be honest, I'm disappointed that:

1. She's not sharp enough to catch me in a web of lies.
2. She's subjected Eliza and Frank to our horrible state of living. I miss Healthy Mom.

Later, I make dinner for all of us. Mac and cheese for me, Eliza, and Frank, and soup for my mom. I knock on her door and walk in with the bowl, but she's sleeping pretty heavily, so I leave it on her bedside table. I wonder . . . at what point do I have to call a doctor for her?

Eliza, Frank, and I don't talk about the mystery—just

in case Mom wakes up. She has ears like a bat. No, she has ears like a bat with *enormous* ears. And so we pass the time playing hide-and-go-seek with Frank. After all, the poor kid waited all day to play a game.

At nine, we all get ready for bed. Eliza takes the couch, Frank takes the plushy chair, and I sleep on the shaggy-carpeted floor. Once my head hits the ground, I drift off. I know there's a lot to think about with this case, but this was a long, hot day.

I WAKE UP to the sound of someone rattling around in the kitchen. "Mom?"

"No, it's just me," Eliza calls. "I'm making toast. It's the only thing I know how to make."

"And I'm helping!" Frank says.

I yawn and sit up.

Eliza puts a whole plate piled high with toast on the table. And without a word, we all sit down and start eating. As I nibble, I watch Frank with curiosity. He is rolling his bread into little balls, then popping the bread balls into his mouth like they're pieces of popcorn. He keeps doing this over and over and over.

"Save some for my mom!" I snap, and Frank spits the chewed-up pieces of bread onto his plate.

"Ooops!" he says.

I groan.

Eliza stands up and starts toasting another piece of bread for Mom. "I got it."

"Thanks," I say. "Mom likes it with margarine."

"No, not the toast!" Eliza says. "I mean . . . I think I've got it! The answer!"

I stand right up, fast as a rocket. "You know who did it?"

"No," Eliza says, "but I think I know where to go from here." She looks thoughtful and determined. "Don't you think it's weird how Ivy and Guinevere refuse to talk about their big fight all those years ago?"

"Yeah, I guess."

"Well, I just thought . . . maybe the key to this mystery is to figure out what happened back then," Eliza says, grabbing the crusty bread out of the toaster and slathering it with margarine.

I think about it for a second. It does make sense to figure out what happened between Guinevere and Ivy. But those details might not *necessarily* lead us to the answer. Maybe the past should . . . I dunno. Stay in the past.

"I don't know, Eliza," I say. "Maybe we should tail Ivy. Follow her around until she does something guilty. She *is* our lead suspect, after all."

Eliza shakes her head and moves my mom's piece of toast out of Frank's reach as he starts to lunge for it. "No, I'm certain about this, Carlos! There's something there—in Guinevere's past. And since Mr. LeCavalier's treasure is at the heart of this mystery, it might be worth looking into his past, too. History affects the future, and that's where we need to focus now. We have to dig deeper. That's the only way to figure this one out."

I'm still not sure. I feel like our best bet is to follow our prime suspect around and wait for a misstep. But I don't want to shoot down Eliza's idea. Maybe she's right. Isn't she usually?

TO FOLLOW IVY AROUND,
TURN TO PAGE 305.

←→

TO DIG DEEPER INTO THE LECAVALIERS' PAST,
TURN TO PAGE 224.

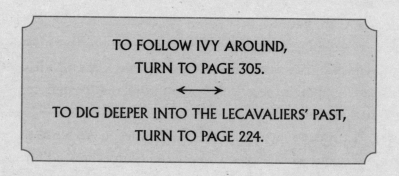

I UNPLUG WIRE A, and the whole room starts to shake. It rattles and rumbles and growls and grumbles, and I can hear all the books falling off the shelf in Mr. LeCavalier's fake study.

"EARTHQUAKE!" Frank shrieks.

I jump off the desk and grab on to Eliza and Frank, just in time for the walls to collapse, with lots of snaps and cracks.

Eliza squeaks, and I protectively cover her.

"LONDON BRIDGE IS FALLING DOWN!" Frank sings.

It's at least five minutes before the rumbling stops, and when it's finally safe to look up, I gasp. The walls and ceiling are all down, and we're practically sitting outside. In fact, there are *no* walls and *no* ceilings throughout the entire upstairs. We're just sitting on the floor, in the open air.

We stay put, too nervous to even move from our spots, just in case the floor decides to collapse beneath us. Eventually firemen come and pull us out of the wreckage, and we've destroyed half of Guinevere's mansion.

We tell Guinevere everything we found out about the culprit, but it doesn't matter. The second she pays us, she snatches the money right back out of our hands to repair the damages to her house. Boy, did that cost us!

CASE CLOSED.

ONCE WE FILL out the sudoku puzzle all the way, Patty's phone makes a *click!* sound.

WE'RE IN!

My heart pounds with excitement and I don't even hesitate: I open Patty's email right away, and . . . JACKPOT.

There are tons of emails, all from the same person: Joe Maddock.

"She has tons of emails from Maddock!" I say.

I click on a random email message:

> Dear Schnooky-Ooky-Lumpkins,
>
> To my pookie bear—shall I compare thee to a plate of nachos? Thou art more beautiful and delicious. Shall I compare thee to a lawyer's brief? Thou art more interesting by far. Shall I compare thee to chocolate cake? It's a tough call. But you know how much I adore desserts.
>
> My forever love, from the moment I saw your luscious locks, your abundant makeup, your distinctive waddle, I knew you must be MINE. I think about you all the time: the skip in your step, the curve of your lips, the sparkle in your eyes. Why, even right now, I'm thinking about your stout ankles. What sturdy ankles you have, my dumpling doodle.
>
> Every second we're apart is agony—perhaps

because I left my inhaler at your house last night, and I can barely breathe through this pollen! When you come over at four, please bring my inhaler, schnookums!

Affectionately yours,

Joe

"EWWWWWWWWW!" Frank shouts. "That was gross!"

"Open another," Eliza says eagerly. "Let's see how Patty responded to that email. Was she offended . . . or—"

"Or?" I say.

"Let's just see!"

I click on the next email.

My dearest snugglebunny honey-pie lovey-dovey shmoopsie,

Today, as I reflected upon your visage, I wrote down a very scholarly poem. (Please! Do not treat me any differently now that you know I'm a literary genius.)

There once was a man named Joe
Who made me feel all aglow.
He gave better smooches

Than all of my pooches

And that's why I call him my beau.

xoxo Patty

"What's a bee-ow?" I ask Eliza.

"It's pronounced 'bow,' like rainbow," she says, correcting my pronunciation. "And it means . . . boyfriend."

"Boyfriend!" I shout. "So Maddock and Patty! Patty and Maddock!"

Eliza nods. Frank gags.

"Are they working together?"

"Maybe," Eliza replies. "Maddock knows about the treasure, and Patty wants revenge. Together they could make the perfect crime duo. Patty has the motive, while Maddock has the means, with his access to the house."

"So they did it?" Frank asks, pulling on Eliza's arm.

"Frank! Stop!" Eliza says, wrenching her arm away from her brother. "They definitely have both motive and means. But . . . it doesn't prove they did it."

"It doesn't prove they *didn't*!" I grumble.

"We've gotten NOWHERE!" Frank groans, and he lies back down on the blacktop.

Silence falls between us. Well, not silence, exactly, as Otto comes around the house with the lawn mower. It is so loud I cover my ears. But still . . . when I think about our latest clue, I can't believe it! Patty and

42

Maddock . . . in a relationship! I'm thinking if they look guilty, and they seem guilty, then they're probably guilty. But I don't want to jump to conclusions. Good detectives are patient. We have to find conclusive evidence—something that proves they're the ones behind the threats.

"What are we waiting for?" I finally say. "Let's go follow Patty around!"

We run down Guinevere's driveway. Patty's yellow house is across the street, and her Yorkie hedges gleam in the afternoon sunlight.

It's hard to see into her windows, but as we get closer, I have a better view. At the left side of the house, Patty is standing near an open window.

"Let's go!" I say, and the three of us run across her yard and crouch beneath the window.

". . . can't find my cell phone, schmoopsie-poo. I must have left it in another purse or something. This is my house line." There's a pause. Then Patty says, "I memorized your number, of course." Pause. "Oh, she's in for the surprise of a lifetime tomorrow. I can't wait to see her face." Another pause. Then Patty says, "No! We have to go over the plan tonight." Pause. "Why? Because I'm afraid you're going to spoil everything. You have to be a good decoy."

Secret plans? Spoiling everything?

"Honey bunny, I have to hang up if I'm going to drive

over to your house right now. I just called to tell you I was running a few minutes late. Didn't want you to worry if you called my phone and couldn't reach me." Pause. "Yes, I love you too, schnookums."

Frank pretends to vomit.

And I agree.

Moments later, we hear the slam of the window above us closing. Eliza lets out a yelp.

"Sorry—the noise just frightened me."

I pull Eliza and Frank to their feet, and I gesture for them to follow me. Like a graceful gazelle, I leap across the yard and peer into another window. Patty's setting her home alarm system and leaving! Yay!

"Wait a second," Eliza says. "We can't investigate while she's gone—we don't know her alarm code."

A car engine rattles, and Patty's car pulls out of her driveway. I push Frank and Eliza behind a large Yorkie hedge, and we hide until Patty's car speeds down the street.

"On the plus side," Eliza says, "Patty said she and Maddock were planning for something tomorrow. If the plan has anything to do with Guinevere, at least we know it's not going to happen tonight."

"But it *will* happen tomorrow," I say with a gulp. And suddenly my hands are sweaty and my stomach feels all squirmy. One day left to crack this case. One day left to save my mom's agency.

"Carlos, at least we can go home knowing that Guinevere is safe . . . for now. . . ."

"Dum dum dummmmmmm!" Frank sings.

Even though I'm nervous about tomorrow, I feel proud of all the work we did today. We made awesome progress. Patty is up to something, and I'm going to follow her until I find out what.

By the time we get to my neighborhood, my stomach is growling, so I say a quick good-bye to Eliza and Frank and head inside.

I make myself a PB&J sandwich and scarf it down so fast that I barely taste it.

After that, I check on Mom. She's sitting up, eating a crusty piece of toast.

"Are you feeling better?" I ask her.

She shrugs. "I fink my fever's gone down, but I stew can't get outta bed."

"Stew?" I say. "Oh! *Still!*"

She smiles weakly.

I set a glass of water on her bedside table. "You should be drinking fluids, Mom." Which is exactly what she says to me whenever *I* get sick. "Do you need me to get you any medicine?"

"Ib good. But yourb sweet, hijo." She sneezes, then says, "Waddya do today wif Ewiza?"

My heart does a kick. "Oh, nothing interesting," I lie.

Then I pepper the lie with a truth so that she doesn't catch on. "I miss summer camp."

"Oh, Carwos, I know. I'm sowwy." Beneath her Rudolph-red nose, she is genuinely upset.

Great. Now I feel *extra* guilty for making her feel bad. My face is all hot and my stomach feels queasy. I think the guilt of lying is finally getting to me. The only thing I'm missing is the Pinocchio nose.

I really hate lying to Mom. And I've never told her a lie this big before. But I have to remember that I'm doing a good thing here. It's the only way to save her job, her agency, fix our money problems. Once we solve the mystery, I'll tell her. I *swear* I will.

Still, even a silent promise doesn't make me feel that much better.

"Carwos?" Mom sniffles. "You shouldn't be in hewe. Germs awe evewywhere."

"Just . . . feel better soon, okay, Mom?"

"Fank you, sweetheart. Wuv you," she says, and then I feel so terrible for sneaking around behind her back that I almost confess everything right there.

Keep it together, I think. For Mom.

I slip out of the room, feeling worse—and more determined—than ever.

DAY THREE

I WAKE UP, ridiculously excited. Today's the day I get to follow Patty Schnozzleton around! I shower, change, and eat as fast as possible. Then I peek my head into Mom's room to find she's still sleeping.

When I'm ready to go, I call Eliza's house and have to wait five minutes while their mom watches them as they cross the street. Mrs. Thompson always does this. Which I think is funny, because she'd probably go *bananas* if she knew that Eliza and Frank were really solving a murder threat investigation—instead of playing in the neighborhood, like she thinks.

Suddenly there's a knock on my door, and Eliza and Frank peer in.

"Ready to go?" I say, quickly slipping out of my house.

"YAY!" Frank shouts, and he jumps in the air with a pose like Superman about to zoom off. "One day, I'm really going to fly!" he announces.

"Frank's in a good mood this morning," Eliza says. She squints at me. "But you're not."

I wring my hands together. "I'm just nervous."

"About what?" Eliza says. "We'll do our best, and that's all anyone can ask of us."

Our best isn't good enough, I want to tell her. So much is on the line—my mom's livelihood is at risk. I know it's my fault for not telling Eliza what would happen to my mom if we failed, but still, I can't help thinking that Eliza has *no idea* how much this case even means to me.

"You're quiet. That's not like you, Carlos."

"Sorry." I try to shake all my worries away. Then, in a strangely cheerful voice, I say, "Let's talk about the clues."

In our half-hour walk, we discuss all the suspects, one by one.

PATTY AND MADDOCK: Are having an affair, could be working together, and have made some sort of plan for today. Have clear means and motive.

IVY: Has been in a big fight with her mom and seems to (suspiciously, maybe?) put the blame on a lot of other people. Has clear motive but unclear means (since she lives in Wichita).

OTTO: Has access to flowers (third death threat?), always suggests to us that we go home, and is kind of nosy. Has clear means but unclear motive.

SMYTHE: Is extraordinarily miserable for some reason, seems sulky and angry, and won't answer any of our questions or help us out in any way. Has clear means but unclear motive.

GUINEVERE LECAVALIER: Maybe faked the threats for attention? Unclear means, unclear motive. This is a *very* long shot, especially considering her reaction to the death threat yesterday.

So . . . we still have more investigating to do. And only half a day to do it. If we can't figure it out by noon, though, Eliza's going to call the police for backup. Just in case.

When we finally get to River Woods, everything is quiet and still. None of the neighbors are out and about. Otto isn't mowing the lawn, and Patty isn't peeking out from her blinds. But her car is parked in her driveway. I scan her windows, and I see her and Maddock KISSING. In front of a window! Are they *trying* to make their neighbors barf? Ugh!

"Should we check in with Guinevere?" Eliza asks.

I shake my head no. "We don't have time! We have to figure out what Patty's planning and stop her! And that involves going straight to Patty's house."

"But," Eliza says, "maybe they'll be expecting us at Guinevere's house. I think it's the responsible thing to do."

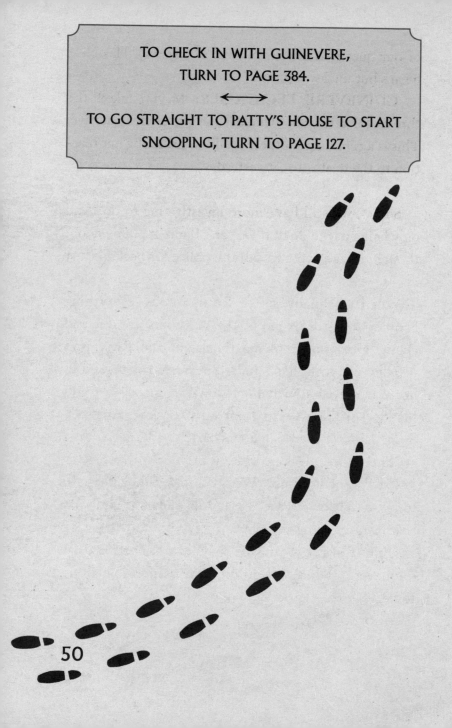

TO CHECK IN WITH GUINEVERE,
TURN TO PAGE 384.

←→

TO GO STRAIGHT TO PATTY'S HOUSE TO START
SNOOPING, TURN TO PAGE 127.

"CAN YOU TELL us more about your husband's treasure?"

Guinevere smiles. "Ahhhh! My husband was . . . *eccentric.* He was an engineer whose passion was logic and mathematics. One night, he told me that he had buried a treasure beneath the house, but only the worthy would be able to find it."

"What does that mean?" I ask.

"My husband set up a treasure hunt with clues and puzzles. Only to be solved by someone smart, like him."

Eliza squeals and claps her hands together. And I can't help but grin at her. There's *no one* smarter than Eliza. I bet she would love to solve Mr. LeCavalier's puzzles.

"Did your husband want you to find the treasure, Mrs. LeCavalier?" Eliza asks.

"Me?" Guinevere laughs so hard she spills her tea over her shoulder. "Heavens no! He didn't marry me for my brains, my dear! He married me for my looks!" She fluffs up her hair and bats her eyelashes.

"Ewwwwww!" Frank says out loud, and I kick him under the table.

"So, who's the treasure hunt for?" Eliza says, trying to draw attention away from Frank.

"Our Ivy is very smart. I'm sure he meant for her to find it."

"Your what?" I say.

"Ivy is our daughter. She's very intelligent."

"Oh, right. The one in . . ."

"Wichita. With her . . . *husband*." Guinevere frowns. "But she arrives tomorrow. Perhaps you'd like to meet her?"

"Absolutely," Eliza says.

TO ASK GUINEVERE ABOUT HER RELATIONSHIP WITH HER DAUGHTER, TURN TO PAGE 308.

←——→

TO ASK GUINEVERE WHO MIGHT BE SENDING THE THREATS, TURN TO PAGE 269.

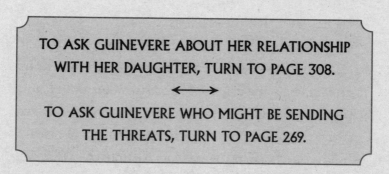

"I'LL TAKE THE garage and basement."

I zoom down the hall filled with the portraits of Patty and her dogs. I open every door I can find, looking for a staircase that leads down to the basement, but I find a closet, a dining room, and a dark sitting room.

At last I open a door to discover a creaky staircase leading down to an unfinished basement.

"CREEPY," Frank says over my shoulder.

I gulp. "Go play with the dogs, Frank."

But he shakes his head. "This looks like a job for SUPERFRANK!"

He leans forward to flick on a light, and I swear—I *swear*—I hear a bunch of spiders scuttling under old boxes.

I tiptoe downstairs and start opening boxes. They're full of dog stuff. Dog beds, dog brushes, dog toys, dog this, dog that, dog dog dog. Every new box I open makes the basement smell worse.

There are no new clues, so I head to the garage.

The whole garage is *covered* in cobwebs. It's like no one's cleaned the garage in a hundred years. I peek inside some storage cabinets against the wall. Boring. Just stores of toilet paper, paper towels, red paint, trash bags—

I pause. Something about red paint jogs my memory . . . and that's when I remember the second death threat. Someone painted that terrifying message on Guinevere's library wall. But what color was it?

I dig into my pocket and pull out the photo of the destroyed library. Just like I thought—the threat is written in ruby-red paint.

And here in Patty's garage?

Five cans of ruby-red paint.

I gasp and run into the house—I need to tell Eliza what I've found!

"Eliza!" I shout. "Eliza? Where are you?"

Frank tackles me around my middle. "Got your nose!" he shouts, even though his arms are *nowhere* near my nose.

"Not now, Frank! This is important! Eliza? Eliza!"

"I'm in the bedroom!" she calls. "And I think I found something!"

Frank and I bound up the stairs and wander through the narrow hallways, searching for the bedroom.

"Eliza?"

"Carlos!" she says, her voice carrying from two rooms down. When I run into the room, Eliza's sitting cross-legged on the velvety carpet, and she looks tiny next to the enormous king-sized canopy bed. The whole bedroom is gigantic and looks fit for royalty. I can't believe Patty sleeps in a room the size of my whole house.

I plop down next to Eliza, who puts a small lockbox in my lap.

"Are you okay, Carlos?"

"Fine," I respond, a bit too irritably.

Eliza winces. "I thought you'd be happy. I found this in Patty Schnozzleton's bedside drawer."

"I am happy," I lie. "I'm fine. Sorry."

"What is it?" Frank says. "A MILLION BUCKS?"

Eliza shakes her head. "I haven't opened it. It has one of those locks that requires a word to open it."

"A word?" Frank cries. "But there are a million gazillion words in the galaxy! We'll be here FOR-EVERRRRRRR."

Eliza grins like she's been waiting for one of us to say that. "Not forever. I found a sticky note under the lockbox. Take a look," she says, holding out the Post-it to me.

Patty, you forgetful goddess of a woman—

I look up and roll my eyes. "'Goddess of a woman'?" I say, trying not to barf.

"Keep reading!"

Here's a reminder of your password.

1. FLASH   2. BUTTER   3. PORK
   SPEED   FIRE   STICK
   STAR   TRAP   KARATE

Remember the words that are related to each of these.

I look at Eliza. "Huh?"

She smiles. "They're word associations. All three of these words are connected to another word . . . the *same* word. For example, if I said . . . um . . . *bag, stand,* and *before,* all of those words can be connected to the word *hand.* Because you have *handbag, handstand,* and *beforehand.* Make sense?"

"So with the first one," I say, looking back at the Post-it. "I guess it could be flashdance. Or flashback. Or flashlight. Or flashflood. Or photoflash."

"Now all we have to do is see if dance, back, light, flood, or photo can be combined with the front or end of the other words in the set. Whichever word works for all three is the first part of the password."

I stare back at the Post-it and get to work figuring it out.

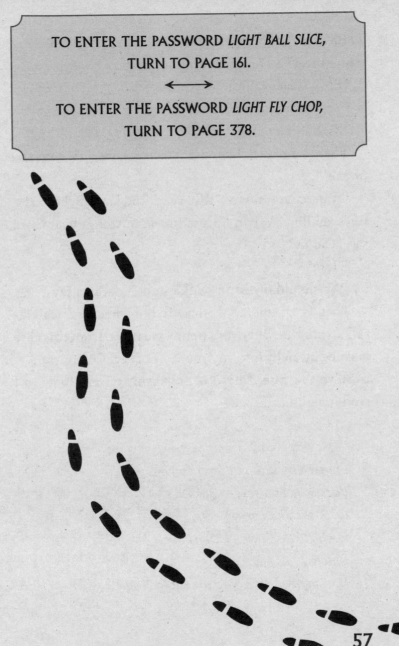

TO ENTER THE PASSWORD *LIGHT BALL SLICE*,
TURN TO PAGE 161.

←——————→

TO ENTER THE PASSWORD *LIGHT FLY CHOP*,
TURN TO PAGE 378.

57

THIS ST. IVES riddle is way too hard. I need more brainpower . . . *Eliza's* brainpower.

"Elizaaaaaaaaa!"

"Yes?" she shouts back.

"Riddle! Heeellllpppp!"

There's a pause. Then her voice echoes, "Pick up the phone!"

I wander around the office and find Patty Schnozzleton's landline. When I press the *on* button, I hear Eliza say, "Carlos?"

"Here!"

"We should invest in walkie-talkies," Eliza says.

That is a supercool idea, if only because walkie-talkies are fun. But every penny we make from this case is going straight into my mom's pocket. Of course . . . to solve the case, I have to solve this puzzle first, so I read it aloud to Eliza:

> "As I was going to visit St. Ives,
> I passed by seven different wives.
> Each wife had seven sacks,
> Each sack had seven cats,
> Each cat had seven kittens.
> Kittens, cats, sacks, wives,
> How many were going to visit St. Ives?"

* * *

58

When I finish, Eliza is giggling. No, more than giggling—she's full-on cracking up.

"What's so funny?"

"You've never heard of St. Ives before? It's an old nursery rhyme."

I don't say anything because my throat gets all lumpy. I don't have a lot of books at home—it's kind of a luxury we can't afford.

Eliza plows on like I didn't just go all silent on her. "Listen, Carlos. It's a classic riddle trick—they give you the answer right away, and all that stuff in the middle is supposed to distract you. And besides, the riddle says you're *passing by* all these things, not that they're coming *with* you to St. Ives."

"If they're not coming to St. Ives, then . . . then it's just me going?"

"Precisely," Eliza says. "Only one person is visiting St. Ives, and it's *you*!"

"Thanks, Eliza!" I say, hanging up the phone. Time to punch in the answer to this puzzle.

ADD THREE HUNDRED TO THE ANSWER OF THIS RIDDLE AND TURN TO THAT PAGE.

AS SOON AS we shout "TEN," the rectangles on the floor start to rumble. Then they split apart, twisting into a spiral staircase that leads down even farther! I feel like we're so deep underground that we're going to run into the earth's core at some point.

"Spinny stairs, yay!" Frank squeals.

I go first, then Frank, and Eliza last. As soon as we take a few steps down, we all marvel. This new room has glowing lights on the ceiling . . . like the sticker stars Eliza has in her outer-space-themed bedroom. But what's below the lights is what's really amazing. Or should I say: a-*maze*-ing.

A *huge* maze. With walls of tall stone. It looks never-ending. There seem to be three exits, but our staircase is dropping us right into the heart of the maze, far from all of them.

When we touch ground, we're in an area with stone statues of unicorns. And there's a map taped to one of the walls.

"We're in the center," I say.

"I wanna run in the maze," Frank whines.

"Soon," Eliza says as she traces different paths through the maze. "Three exits . . . but which one is right?"

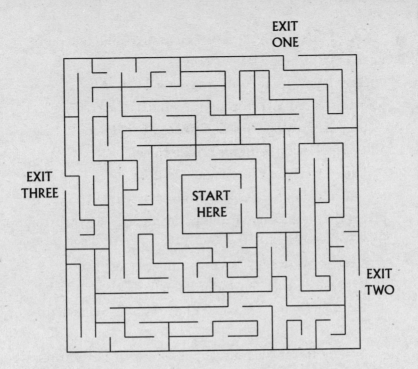

EXIT
ONE

EXIT
THREE

START
HERE

EXIT
TWO

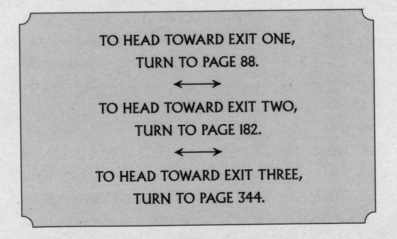

TO HEAD TOWARD EXIT ONE,
TURN TO PAGE 88.

←——→

TO HEAD TOWARD EXIT TWO,
TURN TO PAGE 182.

←——→

TO HEAD TOWARD EXIT THREE,
TURN TO PAGE 344.

"SO," I SAY, "Guinevere LeCavalier tells us you've been extra grumpy lately. Why?"

Smythe turns red. As red as a beet. As red as a tomato. As red as a stop sign. As red as the color red.

Smythe growls and leans toward us. He could beat all three of us up with his pinkie finger.

"How dare you," he sneers. "You . . . you! Prancing around this house! Sticking your snotty little noses in places they don't belong and pointing your greasy little fingers at me!"

I cower. "W-we just asked a simple question!"

"Get out of this house right now!"

"We don't work for you," Eliza says. "You can't fire us."

Smythe flexes his muscles. "Get out! If I ever catch you in here again, I'll—"

But I don't hear what he says because I run away. And so do Eliza and Frank. Smythe is so mad, he's going to EXPLODE, and we'll have intestine spaghetti all over us! We run quickly from the room, but Smythe tails us, chasing us out the front door. Then he slams the door in our faces.

Every day for a week, we try to sneak into Guinevere LeCavalier's house to investigate more, but Smythe blocks our every move. We can't get in. Guinevere thinks we are flaky, so she calls Mom's office to complain. And that is how Mom gets word of what we did.

Our punishment? We have to clean Guinevere LeCavalier's whole house with tiny toothbrushes. And worst of all, we have to listen to her sing off-tune opera the whole time!

Make it stop. MAKE IT STOP!

CASE CLOSED.

WE RUN BACK to Guinevere's house, let ourselves in the front door, and search all around for Smythe. We check inside room after room, but he's nowhere to be found. We zip through the hallways, our shoes squeaking as we run.

Suddenly Smythe towers over us, and his face scrunches up with anger.

"What are you children doing?" he snarls. "Who do you think will clean those scuff marks all over the floor?"

"Sorry," I say. "We were looking for you."

Smythe makes his hands into fists. I hope he's not thinking of punching us.

"What do you children want?"

"To ask you some questions," Eliza says, "about why you've been so grouchy lately."

I smack my head. *Eliza!*

Smythe's face gets so red that it's almost purple. His head looks like one giant grape about to burst. "Get out!"

"You can't kick us out," I say. "Guinevere hired us."

"I don't care!" Smythe roars. Spit flies from his mouth. "Leave!"

He looks so scary with his spit flying everywhere and his purple face and a vein popping out of his forehead. Frank looks like he's about to cry, and even Eliza's eyes fill with tears.

Smythe chases us out of the house and locks the door behind us. We spend all day trying to break back in, but he seals the place tight. Every time we run to another door or window, Smythe is on the other side, thwarting our every plan to get close to the case again.

Guilty behavior?

We'll never know.

CASE CLOSED.

MADDOCK SNEERS AT me. He is super mad. I have to get out of here! Plus, if I run, they'll chase me, allowing Eliza and Frank to escape.

I make a full one-eighty turn and start moving. I run so fast, I almost trip down the stairs, and I grab on to the bannister for support. But Maddock is faster—with his grown-up legs, he skips down three steps at a time and grabs me around the middle.

"LET! GO!"

At the sound of my voice, Eliza and Frank pop out of the laundry baskets and come to help.

I kick and scratch and flail as Maddock wrestles me to the ground . . . and, to add insult to defeat, he *sits* on me.

"There," he says. "You're not going anywhere. And *don't move!*" he says to Eliza and Frank at the top of the stairs. "Take one step, and I'll put all my weight on your friend here."

"This *isn't* all your weight?" I choke.

"It's about half," he says, and I cry out. If he decides to totally crush me, he could probably do it. "Honey bunny!" he calls at Patty Schnozzleton. "Call Guinevere LeCavalier! I want her to come over here and explain to me why these detectives were snooping in our house."

Patty blanches. "Do you think Guinevere told them to go after us?"

"She didn't!" Eliza says. "It was all our idea!"

"It doesn't matter," Maddock says. "I want her to come over to pick you up anyway."

Patty disappears down the hall, no doubt to phone Guinevere LeCavalier's house. I am so embarrassed, and not just because a grown man is sitting on top of me.

Within minutes, the doorbell rings, but when Patty opens the door, it's not Guinevere at all! It's Ivy and Smythe.

Ivy's hair is in rollers, and her eyes dart wildly around the foyer and the stairwell. "What are you doing, playing a wrestling game?" she cries.

"I'm not *playing*," I say angrily. Honestly, does it seem like fun to be crushed beneath two hundred pounds of icky lawyer?

Maddock finally rolls off me. I stand up with as much dignity as I can muster.

"Where have you been all morning? We've been waiting for you!" Ivy shrieks. She's shrill and hysterical, the total opposite of how she'd been during questioning yesterday, and I'm starting to wonder if I even know her at all. "We have an emergency!"

"Emergency? What emergency?" Eliza asks.

"My mother's been kidnapped!" Ivy says. "The culprit left a note, saying they've taken my mom along to help find the treasure! They say that at sunset they're going to . . . to . . ." She mimes drawing a line across her throat.

My stomach drops. This can't be real! "Kidnapped!" I gasp.

"Not kidnapped," Frank says. "She's been *adult-napped*."

"Sorry. Don't mind him," Eliza says with a nasty glower at Frank. Then she turns back to Ivy, saying gently, "How? When? What happened?"

Smythe scowls, and Ivy makes a choking noise. "You tell me! Do you have any working theories as to what's going on? Any lead suspects?"

TO SHARE SUSPICIONS ABOUT PATTY AND
MADDOCK, TURN TO PAGE 118.

←——————→

TO NOT ACCUSE ANYONE YET,
TURN TO PAGE 296.

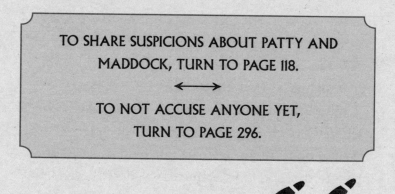

"WHAT'S UPSETTING? Please, can you tell us a bit more about the fight?"

Ivy dabs her eyes with a handkerchief. "Oh! I'm sorry, children! The memory is just too painful!"

She starts to blow into the handkerchief and cry, but it's totally fake. And believe me, I know *all about* fake crying. Frank does it all the time to get what he wants from Eliza and their parents.

"I'm done, children! I can't chat any longer."

"But what about—"

"I said *I'm done*," Ivy says, her cheeks flushed.

Suddenly I hear footsteps, and Guinevere LeCavalier opens the door to the sitting room.

"What's the matter, Ivy, my pumpkin?"

Ivy sniffs. "They! Won't! Leave! Me! Alone!" She fake-hyperventilates. "They're asking me questions like . . . like . . . like *I'm* the one who threatened you!"

Guinevere LeCavalier's eyes narrow on me. "Are you trying to *poison* our relationship?"

I shake my head no. So does Eliza. Frank—just to be opposite—nods.

Without a word, Guinevere LeCavalier walks over to a potted plant in the corner of the room. She picks it up by the base, brings it over to us, and dumps the plant on our heads. "I'll show *you* poison!" Guinevere shrieks. "That is poison ivy, and you have all been INFECTED!"

I don't know whether it's just in my head or whether it's real—but I suddenly feel so itchy I can't function. Frank, Eliza, and I start scratching ourselves all over. Our faces, our necks, our arms, our legs.

I can't help but feel like this is my fault; my rash questioning left us all with an actual rash. And now we're so painfully itchy scratchy prickly tickly uncomfortable that we can't continue working on this case.

CASE CLOSED.

I DECIDE TO search the garage right away. We can always talk to Patty Schnozzleton later.

We excuse ourselves from Patty, and she scurries down the driveway, back toward her house. Eliza, Frank, and I head in the opposite direction. We walk up the driveway and wander into the garage. For some privacy, we close the garage doors behind us.

It's ten degrees cooler in here, now that the sun isn't beating on us. There are two nice cars inside, and an area full of typical garage clutter: bikes, scooters, a lawn mower, a leaf blower, sleds, skis and poles, different kind of sports equipment, a big fridge, and a huge plastic cabinet with who knows what inside.

"In there!" I whisper, opening the door and crawling inside. It's deceptively big in here.

Eliza crawls in after me. "What are we looking for in here?"

Frank crawls in after her. "Narnia! The goat guy!"

I roll my eyes. "Frank, this is a *plastic* closet, not a wardrob—"

THUMP.

Suddenly it's pitch-black in the closet. The door must have closed behind us.

"Frank, can you kick that open again?"

Frank grunts, and his foot bangs against the door. "I can't! It's stuck!"

Ughhhhhhhhhhh! We groan as we push on the door all together, but it's unmovable. We bang on the door, but no one comes to help us.

Otto finds us two days later, and by that time Guinevere LeCavalier's treasure is long GONE. Mom loses *everything*—her business, all our money, her reputation, and her happiness. She gets a job as a snail farmer, which makes her really glum and pays even less than her detective work. We are forced to move out of our home—and into a one-room apartment that's the size of the plastic cubby we got stuck in. I wanted to get *close* to solving the mystery, but instead I got *closet*.

CASE CLOSED.

AT THIS POINT, it's probably a good idea if Ivy is caught up with the case. I tell her about all the suspects, from Maddock and Patty's relationship to Otto's nosing to Smythe's suspiciousness—and Smythe stiffens as we talk about him, his eyes narrowing to tiny, angry slits. Uh-oh. Maybe it's not such a good idea to discuss our suspicions about the suspects to their faces.

"Last," Eliza says, looking up at Ivy—into her startlingly blue eyes. "There's *you*."

"Eliza, wait! No!" I say.

"Me?" Ivy splutters. "Couldn't be!"

"Then who?" Frank sings. "Eliza stole the cookie from the cook-cookie jar!"

"Not now, Frank," I hush him.

"What's your evidence?" Ivy says.

"First," Eliza says, "you and Guinevere had a big fight. Second, you keep pointing fingers at everyone else."

To my surprise and horror, Ivy's eyes suddenly twinkle with tears. "Y-you think I'd hurt my mother?"

Smythe pulls a handkerchief out of his pocket and hands it to Ivy. She snozzes into it.

"Possibly. You and Guinevere haven't seen each other in five years, and now you're cozying up to her. You have to admit, that does look—" I elbow Eliza, and she cuts off. Ivy breathes out of her nostrils like a bull about to charge.

"I want to find Mom," Ivy says, "but I can't work with you—not if you're building a case against me. I'm sorry to have to do this, but you're fired."

Fired? I *can't* be fired! My mom's life is ruined if I'm fired!

"I'm sorry," I say repeatedly. Eliza and Frank keep apologizing with me, but it's too late. Ivy won't hear another word from us. Every time we open our mouths, she plugs her ears and says, "Is that the wind talking?"

When we try to plead with her some more, she howls, "La la la! I can't hear you!"

And when we try to plead with her even more than more, she hollers, "Wow, the silence is deafening today!"

After an hour of apologizing, she still won't listen, so we have no choice but to go home. And just like that—with one accusation—I've ruined my mom's career for good.

CASE CLOSED.

I STUDY THE riddle again.

In my garden:
All but two of my flowers are roses.
All but two of my flowers are tulips.
All but two of my flowers are lilies.
How many flowers do I have in my garden?

My brain is spinning. I turn to Eliza. "I don't get it," I say.

"This *is* a really tough one. Let me think. . . ." She curls her hair around her finger. "I think the best way to figure it out is to draw it." She bends down and begins to draw different-looking flowers in the dirt. "Trial and error is sometimes a really great strategy with puzzles. So let's draw this garden with two of each kind of flower and see what happens.

"Concentrate, Eliza. You can do this," she mutters to herself. "Now . . . 'All but two of my flowers are roses.' So every single flower—except two—are roses."

"That's not true in this garden," I say. "We'd have to get rid of one lily and one tulip. Then all the flowers would be roses . . . except for two."

Eliza crosses out one lily and one tulip.

"Good thinking, Carlos," she says. "Now for the second line. 'All but two of my flowers are tulips.'"

I think again. For that line to be true, every single flower except two would have to be a tulip. It's *almost* true. It would be true if there were only one lily and one rose, instead of one lily and two roses.

"We have to get rid of a rose, Eliza."

Eliza nods and crosses out a rose.

"You read my mind, Carlos! Now we know the first line is true. And the second line is true. Now the last line: 'All but two of my flowers are lilies.'"

My head hurts from all this thinking, but I take a deep breath. I know that every single flower in the garden has to be a lily except two. And that *does* work. And suddenly, the answer is crystal clear. All the lines work if there are only three flowers in the garden! One rose, one tulip, and one lily. Three is the answer to the puzzle!

ADD ONE HUNDRED TO THE ANSWER OF THE RIDDLE AND TURN TO THAT PAGE.

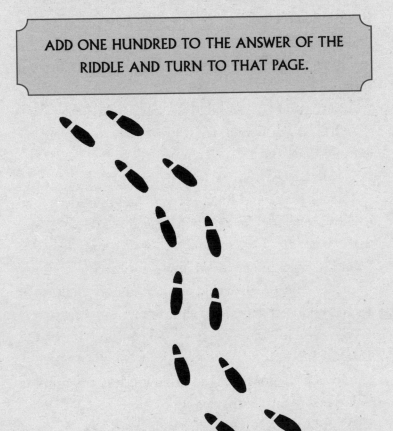

"COME ON!" I say. "Through the pink door!"

"Wait!" Eliza says. "I haven't finished solving the puzzle yet."

I sigh. Eliza could take *hours* on a puzzle, because she likes to attack it from all angles and think about it in different ways before she's confident in her answer. But we don't have time to spare. We have to stop Otto and save Mom's agency!

I open the pink door, and a soft light shines into our room.

"Pretttttyyyyy!" Frank says. "Let's follow that!"

"Eliza, if I'm wrong, we'll just turn around and try another door. But I'm not wrong."

"Well . . . okay," Eliza says.

I usher Frank and Eliza through the pink door, and I follow. The trail leads down a narrow staircase, and at the bottom, I have to hunch to walk along the path. Soon I'm crouching over so low, I'm practically on my stomach. And I realize that the cool dirt of the tunnel is starting to get gooey and slimy.

"I'm stuck!" Frank cries. "In a TUNNEL OF BOOGERS!"

Ewwwww! Boogers? I look down, but the gunk is neon pink. Wait . . . that's not boogers!

"IT'S BOOOOOGERS!" Frank screeches.

"No, it's not!"

"It's SNOT!" Frank cries. "THAT'S EVEN WORSE!"

"That's the same thing!" screams Eliza.

"It's *not* snot," I say.

"IT'S SNOT SNOT!" Frank cries, and I realize this could go on forever.

The hot pink gunk starts drying on our hands, and I realize we're totally cemented to the tunnel. Like statues, unable to move or crawl.

Frank bends down and licks the snot . . . I mean, the gunk. "Tastes like unicorn!"

"How would you know?" I snort.

"I'm going to eat my way out!" Frank says.

"Don't," Eliza gags, but Frank doesn't listen. (Really, does he *ever* listen?)

Frank is an eating machine, a human garbage disposal. He licks and licks until we're finally free. But even without a watch, I know we're hours too late to stop Otto.

"*Buuuuuuuurp!*" Frank belches.

At least Frank got a good meal out of all this. That's more than I'll get ever again after Mom is through with me. . . .

CASE CLOSED.

WE DECIDE TO confront Maddock, now that we know he had cheated the LeCavaliers out of money in the past.

We catch Maddock's scent right away. We sniff all the way down the hall, following our noses like bloodhounds until we smell him out.

When I start to get a cologne headache, I know we're close. We round the corner and come to a set of glass doors. Beyond the doors and inside the room, there's Maddock, sitting on the couch, leaning over papers that are sprawled out on a marble table. Behind him stands a stone statue of some naked guy and a grand piano.

We open the glass doors, and Maddock looks up from his workspace. For a moment, he seems surprised, but a second later he crinkles his nose.

"You found me," he says.

"We followed our noses!" Frank says. "You smell like a skunk!"

"Well, as you can see, I have *work* to do for Guinevere LeCavalier—"

"This will be quick, I swear," I say.

"Then cut to the chase already," Maddock says.

Eliza looks at me, waiting for me to ask the first question. I think she's afraid of offending her interviewee again—after what happened yesterday with Smythe—but I know there's no stalling or easing our way in with Maddock.

I take a deep breath as I glare at Maddock. Here goes

nothing. "We think you're trying to take Mrs. LeCavalier's money."

Eliza looks shocked.

But Maddock laughs. He caps his pen and leans back against the white sofa.

"Well, *of course* I'm trying to milk Mrs. LeCavalier for her money! The old cow is filled to the neck with more money than she can ever possibly spend. If I ever find out who is threatening the old bat, I'll kiss them! She's never needed my services more often than now, and I'm charging her up the wazoo for my legal advice!"

Maddock makes my skin crawl. He straightens his tie, runs a hand through his slick hair, then turns back to his papers. "And on that note, I have work to be doing."

But . . . we haven't gotten any information out of him yet! I've barely begun asking him questions.

"Come on. You must know something else!" I say.

"I don't."

"You're lying, then!" Eliza says.

"LIAR LIAR PANTS ON FIRE!" Frank chants. "CHEATER CHEATER PUMPKIN EATER!"

"We're going to prove it was you," Eliza says to Maddock. And I try to resist groaning. She shouldn't say that to a suspect! Now Maddock's going to be extra careful with everything he does because he knows we're watching.

Maddock sniffs. "Aren't you supposed to see who the evidence points to *before* you accuse someone? It seems like you're accusing me first, and *then* plan to position the evidence to support your hypothesis."

"HIPPOPOTAMUS!" Frank shouts, and I shush him.

Eliza glares at Maddock. And sure, he *does* seem guilty with that gross smirk and his annoying attitude. But we shouldn't get too hasty with the blame game. Mom always says a good detective is patient.

"We have information we can hold over his head," Eliza whispers in my ear. "We need to get an adult involved."

"What? No!"

She hides her mouth behind her hands, and I'm trying to ignore the creepy way Maddock is smiling at us. "If we tell Guinevere about Maddock's suspicious behavior, he's going to have to come clean about overcharging her. And imagine what else we might find out!"

"No way! We can't do that!"

"Trust me, Carlos."

"No, trust *me*, Eliza!"

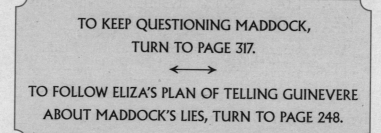

TO KEEP QUESTIONING MADDOCK,
TURN TO PAGE 317.

←——→

TO FOLLOW ELIZA'S PLAN OF TELLING GUINEVERE
ABOUT MADDOCK'S LIES, TURN TO PAGE 248.

THIS HINK PINK puzzle is *easy*. I enter *Art Bad Blue Hare Read* into the keyboard beneath the doorknob, and the floor starts to rumble. Then it slides out beneath our feet—a trapdoor!

"AHHHHHHHHHHHH!" we shriek as we fall.

BOING!

We land on a trampoline in a dark, dark room. I feel my way off to the edge of the trampoline and try not to panic.

"Where are we?" Eliza says.

"We could be in a treasure cave!" Frank says. "Or a secret villain's lair! Or a dragon's mouth! Or inside a toilet!"

"It seems like we're in some sort of closet . . . or room," I say.

Suddenly, bright lights flick on from the walls—they're so bright it's *blinding*. And then a voice recording starts to play, echoing around the room with a scratchy, throaty voice. I wonder if we're listening to Mr. LeCavalier.

> "You've solved the puzzle very wrong,
> And now you'll pay the price.
> You'll be stuck down here for two days.
> Next time, you should think twice."

* * *

"Two days!" I sputter. "But we can't afford to wait that long! The criminal will get away by then!"

"I don't see what choice we have," Eliza says.

And she's right. We're trapped.

CASE CLOSED.

"IT'S MADE OF spaghetti!" shouts Frank. "No, cheese! No, cat hair! No, wait, Play-Doh!"

Eliza smiles. "No, Frank, a greenhouse is made of *glass*. The whole point of the riddle is that it's supposed to trick you into answering that a green house is made of green bricks. But really, a greenhouse is a glass building that houses plants. Get it?"

"Why can't it be made of earwax?" Frank says. "That's much better!"

"No, it can't be made of earwax! That doesn't even make sense!"

"Welllllllllll . . . what about bananas? Or rectangles? Or snickerdoodles?"

"Now you're just shouting random words," I tell him.

"No, Frank! You're missing the whole point of the riddle! The answer's glass! I'm sure of it!"

Frank crosses his arms. He doesn't like being told no. Even when he's wrong.

"So if the answer is glass," I say, "where does the clue lead?"

"Have you checked all the glass sculptures in this house?" Eliza asks.

Guinevere LeCavalier sighs. "Of course I have. You're welcome to look around, but I promise you I've found nothing over the years. My daughter, Ivy, and I tore this place apart, looking through every piece of glass we own, and we found *nothing*. A long time ago . . . when she used to live with me." Guinevere LeCavalier frowns. She sips her tea. "You know, tomorrow will be the first time I've seen her in five years . . . since my husband's funeral."

Eliza and I stay silent, hanging on Guinevere's every word. But Frank picks his nose and flicks a booger.

Guinevere LeCavalier doesn't seem to notice. She slumps in her chair, like all the jewels she's wearing weigh her down. I guess it must be heavy to wear millions of dollars in gemstones on your shoulders.

"Who can believe it's been so long since I last saw Ivy? Time is a fiend, children. It moves faster and faster the older you get."

I have no idea what she's talking about.

Eliza leans forward awkwardly and pats Guinevere's hand.

"But alas!" Guinevere LeCavalier says, snapping back to attention. "You aren't here to listen to me ramble! You're here to catch a potential killer. So what more do you need to know?"

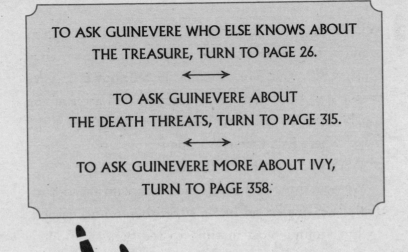

TO ASK GUINEVERE WHO ELSE KNOWS ABOUT
THE TREASURE, TURN TO PAGE 26.

←—→

TO ASK GUINEVERE ABOUT
THE DEATH THREATS, TURN TO PAGE 315.

←—→

TO ASK GUINEVERE MORE ABOUT IVY,
TURN TO PAGE 358.

87

WE RUN THROUGH the maze, using our map as a guide. But we can't seem to connect to Exit One. Most of the walls are ridiculously tall, but at last we pass a spot that seems to have crumbled a bit at the top, because we can climb over into another part of the maze, where Exit One is waiting for us.

"YAYYYYYY!" Frank cheers.

We walk through the exit, and it's dark up ahead. Suddenly there's a sound like a sword being unsheathed. I whip around—just in time to see bars slide down from the ceiling behind us, like a prison cell.

"INTRUDER ALERT! INTRUDER ALERT!" blares an alarm.

"What's going on?" Eliza screams, holding her ears.

We're trapped! I feel around the cell until I find a note, which I can barely see in the dim light.

My daughter, Ivy, is too smart to take the wrong exit. Therefore, you must be a thief after my treasure. And this jail cell is where you will remain forever.

CASE CLOSED.

"WHO ELSE MIGHT have a problem with Mrs. LeCavalier?" I ask.

"You should ask Smythe," Patty says with a snort.

"Smythe!" I echo. "Why would you say that?"

"Just . . . go talk to him about it."

"Noooooooooo!" Frank groans, from his spot on the floor. "Do we *have to*?"

Eliza glares at him.

"Let's just say I know firsthand that Smythe has a very good reason to be angry with Guinevere. But you'll have to ask him."

"Can't you just tell us?"

Patty shakes her head no. "I can't. It's not my juicy secret to tell." She giggles, and I can tell she really *loves* dangling information above our heads.

"Or," Patty continues, "perhaps Guinevere's daughter, Ivy, is the one sending the threats. They've had problems for years."

Guinevere had told us that Patty convinced Ivy and her husband to run away together, but sometimes in the detective biz, it's good to play dumb. "What kind of problems?" I say, blinking innocently.

Patty stares me for an uncomfortably long time. "Guinevere drove her daughter away. They fought constantly because Guinevere didn't like Ivy's boyfriend. Well, her *husband* now."

Eliza frowns. "Guinevere said *you* convinced Ivy to run away."

I smack my head. I wish I could tell her we were supposed to be playing dumb! But then . . . Eliza's so smart that I bet she has no idea how to play dumb.

"Oh, Guinevere says that, does she?" Patty cries. "Well, that's a bald-faced lie! Ivy came to me in tears. She had just told her mother that she wanted to marry Walter, the love of her life. And do you know what Guinevere LeCavalier told her daughter?"

Eliza and I shake our heads. Frank picks his nose.

"Guinevere told Ivy that she'd never see a penny of her own inheritance and she'd be kicked out of the house. Ivy told me all about it, the poor dear. But I swear—she decided on her own that she wanted to run away with Walter."

"So," Eliza says breathlessly, and I realize she's figuring something out. "You're saying Ivy got cheated out of her inheritance money? And got kicked out of the house?"

"A LEAD!" I say, jumping up so fast that the dogs panic and dash out of the room. I sit back down again. I have to remain professional. Even though this is ONE. AWESOME. CLUE. "Too bad Ivy doesn't fly in until tomorrow," I add.

"That's all I know," Patty says. "I swear it, by the

snout of all my puppy-wuppies." She grabs my hands. Her palms are moist and cold. "I've done nothing wrong. I'm allowed to despise my sworn enemy, but I would never do anything illegal."

I remove my hands from her clammy grasp. "There, there," I say to Patty. I think for a moment, then continue, "It sounds like Guinevere bullied you. We understand why you hate her."

It's exactly what Patty wants to hear. She puffs up. "Why, yes. I knew you'd understand."

I assure her a few more times that she's a much better person than Guinevere, and each time I say it, she gets happier and happier. By the time she guides us to the door, she's practically glowing.

Once we're back on Patty's front lawn, I realize we had spent more time in there than I thought. Or maybe we didn't get an early enough start. It's late, and I'm going to have to go home soon and check on Mom.

"Do you believe her?" Eliza asks me.

I try to replay the conversation in my head. Patty seemed honest and open with us . . . except for one thing. "She's obviously hiding something about Smythe," I finally say, "but I am not sure she's guilty."

"Well," Eliza says, turning to stare back at Patty's house. "We could snoop around when she's not home.

Maybe we'll find something in her house."

"Or we could go talk to Smythe directly," I suggest.

TO TALK TO SMYTHE, TURN TO PAGE 64.

←——→

TO GO SNOOP THROUGH PATTY'S HOUSE,
TURN TO PAGE 259.

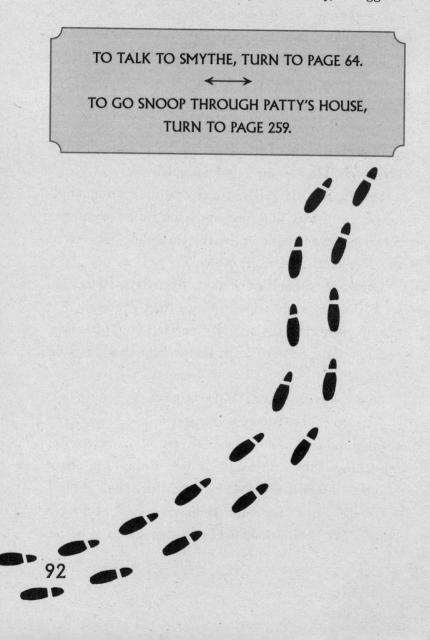

92

"WE SHOULD HEAD left, Eliza."

I eagerly pull her to the left path. We wander for what feels like days. Or weeks, even. Walking, walking, trudging, trudging. This treasure must be buried really deep beneath the house. When we get thirsty, we lick the wet walls of the cave. When we get hungry, we nibble on stray worms and roaches. But we keep on going.

Finally the ground begins to slope up, and there's a ladder to climb.

"This must be it!"

We climb up the ladder, open the hatch, and—

"What the . . . *what?*"

We're at the base of a mountain. But how we got there—or where we are exactly—I have no clue. Because there aren't any mountains close to town. We could be anywhere. And who knows how long it'll take us to get back?

I've been asking myself how far I'm willing to go to solve this case . . . but I think I went a million steps too far.

CASE CLOSED.

WE HEAD TO the basement.

It's dusty down here. There are hundreds of bottles of wine, and even a few round barrels. It's like a pirate's dream lair. The lighting is dim—I think some of the bulbs have blown out. It doesn't seem like anyone has been down here for a while.

We run around the perimeter of the room, searching for some entrance to a secret treasure tunnel. I put my hands on the cold cellar walls, looking for a draft or a breeze, but . . . nothing.

"Eliza?"

"I can't find anything! Looks like this is a dead end."

"What about Frank?" Frank says.

"Uh . . . what about him?" I reply.

"Frank found something," he says. "Frank is the best best BESTEST detective in the world, and you're jealous."

"And Frank likes to talk about himself in the third person, apparently."

"Frank does not know what that means," Frank says. "But Frank does not care, because Frank is awesome."

Eliza walks over to him. "What did you find, bud?"

"Funny bottles!" Frank says, pointing to a bunch of neon-colored bottles on the bottom of a shelf, so low that you'd have to lie on your stomach to see them. Frank yanks on one of them, and one of the walls across the room rotates until it's completely sideways.

"You did it!" Eliza says.

"I LOVE TO CRAWL," Frank says.

I walk over to the open passageway and peer in. There's a definite slope in the floor—we'll be walking down, even *deeper* underground. It's dark and cold in the tunnel, and I hear growling noises ahead.

I swallow my fear and trudge forward.

"Come on!" I whisper, grabbing Eliza's and Frank's hands. "We have to catch Otto! Everything depends on us!"

We walk inside. At first, the dim lights from the basement illuminate the tunnel, but as soon as we get ten feet inside, the wall swivels shut behind us, and we're stuck in the dark.

There's something snarling at the end of this tunnel, and it gets louder as we blindly—and carefully—walk forward.

Be brave! I whisper to myself. Then I resolve to think about something safe . . . something that won't eat me. Like a puppy or a kitten . . . but I guess a giant puppy or a killer kitten *could* eat me. So, how about a baseball? Yes, a baseball wouldn't eat me—

"What's that?" Eliza says, pointing up ahead.

A single spotlight shines down on a gray stone table.

And on the table, there's a chart marked one through one hundred.

1	2	3	4	5	6	7	8	9	10
11	12	13	14	15	16	17	18	19	20
21	22	23	24	25	26	27	28	29	30
31	32	33	34	35	36	37	38	39	40
41	42	43	44	45	46	47	48	49	50
51	52	53	54	55	56	57	58	59	60
61	62	63	64	65	66	67	68	69	70
71	72	73	74	75	76	77	78	79	80
81	82	83	84	85	86	87	88	89	90
91	92	93	94	95	96	97	98	99	100

Color: 1, 4, 7, 8, 9, 10, 11, 14, 17, 20, 21, 24, 27, 30, 31, 34, 37, 40, 41, 42, 43, 44, 45, 47, 48, 49, 50, 54, 60, 64, 70, 74, 80, 84, 90, 94, 100.

A single pencil lies next to the chart.

As I pick up the pencil, I realize that the loud snapping noises seem to be coming from right below us. I gulp.

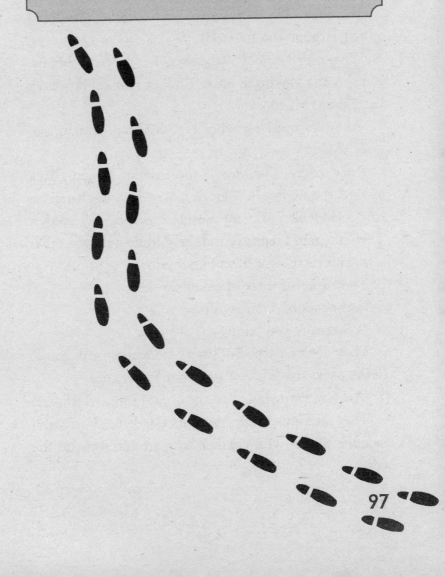

IF YOU KNOW THE SOLUTION OF THE PUZZLES,
ADD ONE HUNDRED AND TURN TO THAT PAGE.

←——→

TO ASK ELIZA FOR A HINT,
TURN TO PAGE 255.

97

TIME TO HAVE an honest chat with our two biggest suspects. "The jig is up!" I say. "We know about your affair!"

Eliza and Frank pop out of their laundry baskets in surprise.

Maddock's black eyes grow wide, while Patty looks shiftily around the stairwell.

"Y-you all know?" Patty says, her voice wobbling. But she isn't looking at me or Eliza or Frank. She's looking right at Maddock.

"Are you thinking what I'm thinking, shmoopsie-poo?" Maddock says softly.

Patty nods. *"Get them!"* she shrieks, lunging back toward the bedroom. Before I even have a chance to run, Maddock yanks me upside down by my ankles. Then he grabs Frank around the middle with the other arm, and Patty's got Eliza in her grip.

They drag all three of us outside.

"Let gooooo," Frank whines.

"Where are you taking us?" I shout.

They don't answer, but soon I see where we're going: in the backyard, where Patty's pet Yorkies are.

"Are you throwing us to the dogs?" Eliza whimpers.

They shove us inside Waggie's dog kennel—a small wooden shelter with chicken wire around some of the edges.

"Bad kids!" Patty scolds through the fencing. "Think about what you've done!"

I feel all around the ground, the chicken wire, and the walls, but we're locked in, and there's no way out.

We're in the doghouse . . . in more ways than one.

CASE CLOSED.

SUDDENLY, THE ANSWER of the upside-down books is staring me straight in the face. "One hundred!"

As soon as I shout it out loud, a rumbling noise erupts from the library, and one of the bookshelves swings open, like an enormous twenty-foot door.

"HOORAY!" Frank shouts. "A SECRET ROOM!"

That's promising, I think. The only reason people have secret password-protected rooms is to hide stuff, right? Maybe we'll find something important behind the bookshelf.

As if she's reading my mind, Eliza says, "There must be something big back here!"

Together, we slip into the room. Behind the door is a small, cramped space with a desk, a drippy candle, and a lighter. Eliza reaches for the candle and lights it. She pulls the bookshelf in behind her, so that anyone who walks by the study can't tell that we've opened up this secret room. But she doesn't want to close it completely, just in case, so she leaves it open a crack. A sliver of light from the other study room—the fake decoy room—sneaks into this secret real study room.

But . . . this secret study is so small that it's really more like a large closet. Eliza sits on top of the creaky desk, I lean against the peeling red wallpaper, and Frank plops on the carpet.

"I have a good feeling about this," Eliza says. She gives me a knowing smile. "We've got this. For your mom."

"For Las Pistas," I add.

"For me!" Frank says, pulling on a drawer. When it slides out, there's a stack of letters.

"Blahhhh, *more paper?*" Frank cries. "Boring!"

Eliza pulls the letters out of the drawer, and underneath is a little black notebook.

"Look!" I say. "A notebook!"

Frank's eyes light up, and he tries to wrench it from my hands, but I hold on tight.

"No," I say to him, even though he rarely understands the word.

"What should we look at first?" Eliza asks.

TO LOOK AT THE LETTERS,
TURN TO PAGE 285.

←→

TO LOOK AT THE NOTEBOOK,
TURN TO PAGE 164.

WE START BANGING on the door. Then we all shout at the top of our lungs.

"HELLO! ANYONE THERE?"

"WE'RE IN HERE!"

"LET ME CRAWL!"

Bang, bang, bang, bang, bang.

We smack the door for what feels like hours. We throw shoes against the door. We throw ourselves against the door. We knock with our fists. My hands are raw and achy.

"Eliza," I finally say. "I don't think anyone can hear us."

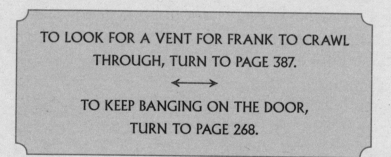

TO LOOK FOR A VENT FOR FRANK TO CRAWL THROUGH, TURN TO PAGE 387.

←→

TO KEEP BANGING ON THE DOOR, TURN TO PAGE 268.

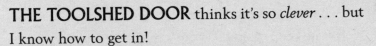

THE TOOLSHED DOOR thinks it's so *clever* . . . but I know how to get in!

"Three," I say aloud. "There are three flowers in the garden."

As soon as I say it, I hear a *click* from the lock, and the door swings open with a *creeeaakkk.*

Smythe has to duck to fit in, and all of us squish inside the cramped space.

"Is there a light?" Eliza asks.

"Got it," Smythe grunts, and he pulls down on a string dangling from a single bulb.

In the flickering light, the first things I notice are the pictures. There are hundreds and hundreds of pictures of Guinevere LeCavalier tacked up all over the walls! There are photos of her with her eyes scratched out. Photos of her with darts in her face. Photos of her from the time she was very young to the present day. Photos of her from newspaper clippings. There's even a portrait painting of her that looks like it was snatched from the house. And tucked in the corner are a few pictures of Ivy and Mr. LeCavalier, with devil horns on their foreheads and marker mustaches.

I shudder. This is *too creepy.*

"Yikes," Eliza breathes, and Ivy lets out a curse word.

Frank ducks down, I'm assuming to get away from those pictures of Guinevere. But then he starts crawling around the floor.

"There's no room to crawl!" I tell him.

But he keeps going. "What's this?" he says. "A worm! What's this? A rope! What's this? A secret door! What's this? A dead flower!"

"Wait, Frank!" Eliza says. "Go back to the secret door! Is that for real? Or are you playing make-believe?"

"Oh, I make believe it's real, all right," he says.

All of us rush forward to see what Frank's looking at. Beneath a tiny skylight window, there's something that looks like a wooden trapdoor built into the ground.

"Open it!" I say.

Frank flips open the top, and there's a ladder, and a dark, dark hole that leads down.

I gulp.

"Dad had an entrance to his treasure tunnels from the toolshed *all along?*" Ivy says.

"We have to split up," Eliza says, and I know she's about to be very logical. "Ivy and Smythe, you two should wait at the house. When the police get here, send them down after us. Also, be alert. Guinevere and Otto could come out another exit and end up somewhere else in the house."

They both nod.

"Be safe," Ivy says, ruffling my hair.

"Don't die," Smythe grunts. I think that's the nicest thing he's ever said to us.

When they're gone, Eliza searches in the drawers,

riffling through all of Mr. LeCavalier's gardening stuff.

"What are you looking for?"

"A flashlight," she answers, slamming the last drawer shut. "But there aren't any. Next time we take on a case, remind me to buy a tool belt."

If there's a next time, I think miserably. I can almost feel this case slipping out of our grasp. One wrong move, and it's over for Mom.

"I'll have to get used to living by flashlight, if we can't afford to pay our electric bill," I grumble under my breath.

"What did you say?" Eliza says sharply.

"Nothing," I say. I can't help it. Everything stinks.

"You said you'd have to live by flashlight if you can't pay your bills," Eliza says. "What does that mean? What's going on?"

"Eliza, it's nothing."

"It's something," she says. "This isn't the first time you've been upset this week."

"We don't have time for this—"

"Then you better tell me quick," she says. "Spit it out. What's been bothering you?"

I want to tell her—but I don't at the same time. I've been keeping this from her for so long I don't even know where to start.

"Carlos," she says.

"It's my mom!" I blurt out. "She's broke. *We're* broke."

Eliza sighs. "*That's* what's been on your mind this

whole time?" She puts an arm around my shoulder. "You're not alone. We don't have a lot of money, either."

"Yes, you do! Your dad has a steady job."

"A steady job that doesn't pay well. At least when your mom gets paid, it's a lot of money all at once."

"Yeah, but then nothing for months after that. At least your dad gets paid every week!"

"Carlos, it's not a competition—"

"YES IT IS!" Frank says. "AND I WIN!"

"I'm just saying we're in this together," Eliza says. "And we're here for you and your mom. That's why we took this case in the first place, right? To earn the paycheck in her place?"

I nod.

"Well, the best way to do that is to save Guinevere," she says. "We have to keep going."

I could kick myself. I should have told her from the start—she's made me feel so much better. She is the *best* friend in the world. I hug her. Then all three of us stare into the pit we're about to climb down. "I'll go first," I say, sounding a lot braver than I feel.

I put my foot on the top of the ladder, slowly and carefully heading into the darkness.

I have to feel my way down the ladder, being careful to make sure my foot hits every rung. After all, I have no idea how far down this hole goes. For all I know, if I fall off the ladder, I could drop a thousand feet.

I reach down with my foot. Touch the rung. Then grab the next lowest rung with my hands. I reach down again with my foot—only this time, there's nothing there.

"Wait! Freeze!" I say, and Eliza and Frank dead-stop above me.

"What's wrong?" Eliza says.

"There are no more rungs for my feet!"

"Do you feel the ground?" she asks.

"No!"

"Whatever you do, don't let go!"

"What if I farted?" says Frank.

"What?" Eliza and I both say.

"What if I farted?" Frank giggles. "Eliza, your face is near my butt. I could fart on you."

"DON'T. YOU. DARE."

Suddenly, between my hands, there's a word that lights up. It's glowing green.

"Slink," I say. "There's a word lit up between my hands, and it's *slink*!"

Then there seems to be a bunch of words lighting up. Below *slink* is *stink*, and below *stink* is *sting*. And to the left-hand side of me, there are weird phrases.

As I read them out loud to Eliza, she gasps. "I know what this is! It's a word ladder. I've done puzzles like this on paper before, but never with an *actual* ladder!"

"How does it work?"

"As you climb down the ladder, you can only change *one* letter of the word before it. Use the clues on the side of the ladder to help you figure out what the next word should be."

STARTING WORD: SLINK.

1. A terrible smell.
2. A bee _____.
3. When you injure a shoulder, you wrap your arm in a _____.
4. Informal (and not proper) vocabulary.
5. Not straight up and down, but on an angle.
6. Many of these grow in my garden.
7. You fly in this object.
8. A long, flat piece of wood.
9. Fill in the _____.
10. To quickly shut your eyes and open them again.
11. Unable to see.
12. Tasteless and boring.
13. A _____-new item.

FINAL WORD: change one letter to complete the ladder.

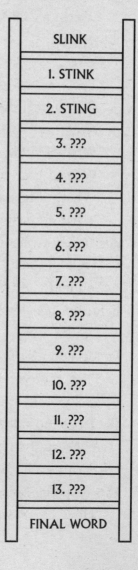

SLINK

1. STINK

2. STING

3. ???

4. ???

5. ???

6. ???

7. ???

8. ???

9. ???

10. ???

11. ???

12. ???

13. ???

FINAL WORD

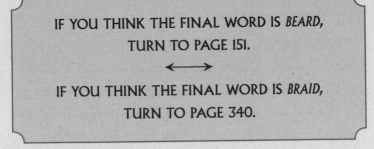

IF YOU THINK THE FINAL WORD IS *BEARD*,
TURN TO PAGE 151.

←→

IF YOU THINK THE FINAL WORD IS *BRAID*,
TURN TO PAGE 340.

THE DOOR OPENS.

"I KNOW WE NEED THE MONEY. Yes, I'm planning to go into the treasure tunnels just as soon as I get a ch—" Ivy pauses at the sight of us in her room. There's me and Eliza, holding some papers from her suitcase, and Frank, wearing her fancy hats and trotting around in her high heels.

"Walter, I have to go," Ivy says, and she hangs up the phone.

She blocks the door, looking mad, feverish, murderous.

TURN TO PAGE 234.

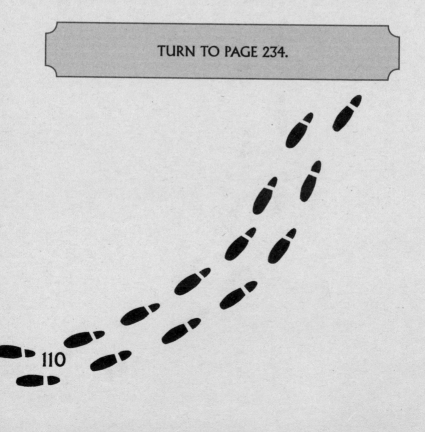

110

"WE THINK YOU did it," I say, pointing at Smythe.

"Me?" Smythe snorts. "You've got to be joking!"

"We know you wanted to go work for Patty Schnozzleton." I steal a quick glance at Guinevere. She looks betrayed. "And you feel unappreciated by Mrs. LeCavalier."

I pause for a breath, and Eliza jumps in. "Anyone walking by the mailbox could have set up the first threat. But painting the library and unscrewing the chandelier require access to this house. And you have easy access."

"AND YOU'RE MEAN!" Frank adds.

Smythe is so angry he looks like his head's about to pop off. "Yes, but just because I *could have* doesn't mean I *did*." His voice is shaking. He takes a deep breath and calms himself. "It's true, I've been frustrated with my job lately. But I would never threaten Mrs. LeCavalier. I was there for her wedding. I was there when Ivy was born. I was her shoulder to cry on when Mr. LeCavalier passed. I've been loyal to this household for thirty years."

He looks at Guinevere pleadingly, his eyes wide. He's a good liar, I think. Because for a second, I believe him.

But it's not up to me anymore. It's up to Guinevere, and I have no idea what she's going to do. She clutches one of her gemstone necklaces and looks around the foyer. First at the mess. Then at her daughter, then at Maddock, then at us. It's like she doesn't know what to do. Her mouth pinches tightly and her nostrils flare.

Suddenly Guinevere shrieks, "Call the police! ARREST THAT MAN!"

We all quickly surround him.

"It's not me!" Smythe says, sweat running down his face. "It's not!" He licks his lips, looking around for an exit. His eyes are shifty and darting.

Guinevere glares at him. "*Smythe!* Dial the police!" she commands, snapping her fingers. "Oh, wait, I mean . . . SOMEONE ELSE! Dial the police!"

Maddock flips open his cell phone and dials 911, and the police show up about five minutes later.

"YOU'LL BE SORRYYYYYY!" Smythe calls as three officers force him into the back of a police car. Then they drive him away.

I feel like cheering! We got our bad guy—the case is solved!

After the officers leave, Guinevere comes up to us, teary-eyed and snotty. "My dearest detectives! Thank you so much for all your help! I never would have suspected Smythe! I owe you everything!"

I grin.

Eliza beams.

Frank tries to lick his own nose.

Guinevere gives us big sloppy forehead kisses. Then she hands us a check and has a policeman drive us home.

When I walk into my house, I wonder how I'm going to tell Mom about stealing her case, but luckily, she's sleeping. The weight of the past few days and all the pressure I've been feeling to save my mom's agency sinks in, and I crawl right into bed. I can deal with Mom in the morning. . . .

BRRRRRRRNNNNNNNGGGGGGG!
BRRRRRRNNNGGGG! The sound of our telephone.

I pop out of bed and look at my clock: 3:48 a.m.

Who in the world would call our house at almost four in the morning?

I walk to our kitchen and pick up the phone.

"Hello?" I yawn.

"Detective Serrano! This is Guinevere LeCavalier!"

Guinevere LeCavalier? What—why? "What can I do for you?"

"You can give me my money back."

At that, I fully wake up. *"What?"*

"Someone destroyed my house with a wrecking ball to expose secret underground tunnels. Ivy and I only just escaped, but I'm sure my fortune is on its way to being stolen—if it hasn't been already," she says. "And guess what? It wasn't Smythe. Because he is safely locked away in jail. So who did this, detectives?"

I—I don't know. And I tell her that, much to her dismay and angry screams.

I hang up the phone, a sinking feeling in my stomach. So it wasn't Smythe after all. We sent an innocent man to jail, and we gave the real culprit a chance to steal the treasure. . . .

It's all my fault.

The next day, Mrs. LeCavalier goes to the press, making sure everyone knows what a dreadful job my mom did. After that, my mom's agency goes bankrupt, and Mom loses her private eye license. So not only does Mom's entire career go *kaboom*, but with all the horrible things being said about her, she can't get a job anywhere. To escape the heat, Mom moves us to Antarctica (the coldest place she could think of).

You know how, in a mystery, they say the trail goes cold?

Well, this trail went *ice-cold*.

CASE CLOSED.

I HAVE TO stop Eliza—and take matters into my own hands. After all, this is *my* mom's agency on the line.

"ELIZA, STOP!" I shout.

"Just let me handle this, Carlos, and I'll get you the money you need."

"I don't need the money," I tell her. "I need to solve this case! We're trying to save my mom's agency, remember? Not just pay our bills! Which means we need to close this case. We can't do that if you cut a deal with the criminal."

Otto's eyes widen, and he tightens his grip on the treasure.

Frank's eyes ping-pong back and forth between Eliza and me.

Eliza glares at me. "Carlos, be quiet! I have this under control."

"I WILL NOT BE QUIET! You're going to ruin Mom's agency. I can't let you do that!"

"I would never! Trust me—"

"Oh ho!" Otto shouts, hugging his treasure chest. "You were going to trick me, weren't you, girl? But your plan has been foiled!" He dashes off in the other direction.

We run behind him, but he ends up climbing up a ledge that we're all too short to reach.

And then he escapes. With the treasure. For good.

"Carlos, you dummy!" Eliza cries. "You ruined my whole plan!"

Eliza is so mad at me for not trusting her that she gives me the silent treatment—and gets everyone in my school to give me the cold shoulder. The only one in town who will talk to me is Mom, but she's so mad at me for ruining her case and destroying her agency that she only tells me I am grounded. Then she gives me the silent treatment too.

The only one who will talk to me is . . . me.

"How ya doing, Carlos?"

"I'm great, Carlos! How are *you*, Carlos?"

"Oh, Carlos! What spectacular company you are!"

"Do you think all this talking to yourself will make you go crazy, Carlos?"

"Why, Carlos—why would you ever say a thing like that?"

"HAHA, CARLOS. YOU JOKESTER. HA HA HA! HA!"

CASE CLOSED.

THIS BOX PUZZLE is difficult! "I don't see any more boxes. Do you, Eliza?"

"Yes," Eliza says, pointing out the remaining two boxes. "See that? Those are the last two."

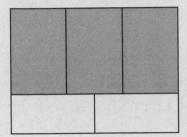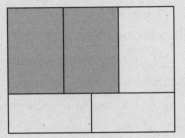

"So that makes . . . five plus three plus two . . . ," I count.

"Ten rectangles total," Eliza says.

"TEN!" Frank shrieks.

ADD FIFTY TO THE SOLUTION OF THIS PUZZLE AND TURN TO THAT PAGE.

TIME TO PLAY the blame game. I look at Eliza for support, and she nods.

"We suspect that Patty and Maddock are behind all this."

"GUILTY!" Frank hollers.

"Us?" Patty gasps.

Maddock is silent.

But they move so close to each other that they're practically like conjoined twins. Patty laces her fingers through Maddock's, and I try not to vomit up my breakfast.

Ivy squints at me. "What proof do you have?"

"Patty has been mad at your mom for years—she admitted to us that she wants revenge on Guinevere. And Maddock knows about the treasure *and* has access to the house."

"We suspect," Eliza continues, "that they've been working together to threaten your mom."

"Plus they're all kissy-kissy!" Frank adds with some smoochy sounds.

"And the most important thing," I say confidently, "is that they both were talking about a secret plan for today. And how Guinevere was going to be so surprised—"

"Not Guinevere!" Patty says. "We were talking about my friend Betty! We're throwing her a surprise party this afternoon!"

"Wait, what?" I say. A surprise party? That's *it*?

"I may play a few pranks every now and again, but I don't want to *kill* her!"

Eliza smacks her head. "Of course! Why was I so stupid?" Suddenly her smile grows wide. "I've just figured it out. I know exactly who's behind all these death threats."

Ivy, Smythe, and Patty look interested and eager, but Maddock strokes his goatee like he couldn't care either way.

"It's THEM, isn't it?" Frank says, pointing at Patty and Maddock.

"No," Eliza says.

"It's THEM, then!" Frank says, pointing at Ivy and Smythe.

Eliza chuckles. "Actually, it's not them either."

"Then whoooooooooooo?" Frank says. And then he starts who-whoing like an owl.

"Yeah, who?" I say with a sharp glare at Frank.

Eliza sits down on the bottom step of Patty's stairs. The wood creaks beneath her, and one of Patty's dogs runs up and tries to lick Eliza's face. She points at Ivy. "You said the culprit has taken Guinevere into the tunnels to help find the treasure, right?"

Ivy nods.

"This means that Guinevere is *with* the culprit at the moment. In order to be guilty, you'd have to currently be on a treasure hunt with Guinevere LeCavalier."

"Okay?" I say.

"But," she continues, leaning against the bannister, "there *is* someone we know who isn't here. Someone who was here yesterday and the day before . . . but who isn't anymore. Any guesses who?"

"THE COOKIE MONSTER!" Frank shouts.

But it's not the cookie monster. I don't know how or when or why, but there's only one suspect who is missing today.

"Otto," I breathe.

Patty harrumphs. "We would like an apology."

"Or we'll sue." Maddock smirks.

"Sorry," I say.

"I'm not!" Frank says, and Eliza nudges him.

Eliza twirls her hair thoughtfully. "Now that we know what we're up against—or *who* we're up against— the only thing left is to follow Otto. But where is Otto?"

Smythe grunts. "Try the toolshed."

"How dare you suggest the toolshed!" Ivy gasps, looking like she could smack Smythe.

"What's wrong with the toolshed?" I say.

Smythe blushes sheepishly. "Mr. LeCavalier loved to garden, you see. He split much of his free time between his study and his toolshed. But he was a very private man. He never let anyone inside the toolshed. Even after his death, we have been forbidden to enter—out of respect to his memory." He turns to Ivy, an apologetic wince on his face. His droopy eyes sparkle with tears. "The only reason I suggest it is because I've seen Otto hanging around the toolshed a few times."

Come to think of it, I've seen Otto near the toolshed too. I think about the shed, with its green-spackled paint. Wait a minute . . .

"Green house!" I say. "The toolshed is *green*!"

Eliza smacks her hand on her head. "Yes, of course!" She closes her eyes and recites, from memory, the clue to the treasure hunt we received from Guinevere that very first morning.

"The red house is made of red bricks.
The blue house is made of blue bricks.
The white house is made of white bricks.
The gray house is made of gray bricks.
What is the green house made of?"

"It's not glass," Eliza says. "The clue is pointing us to an actual *green* house on the LeCavalier property!"

"We have to check it out!" I insist.

My stomach turns as I think about everything we

have to lose: Guinevere's life, a treasure, my mom's company, and my mom's trust (though I *may* have already lost that one).

But most important is my mom's happiness. I took this case for her—so that she wouldn't have to give up the thing she loves most in the world. I can't fail.

GO TO THE TOOLSHED ON PAGE 310.

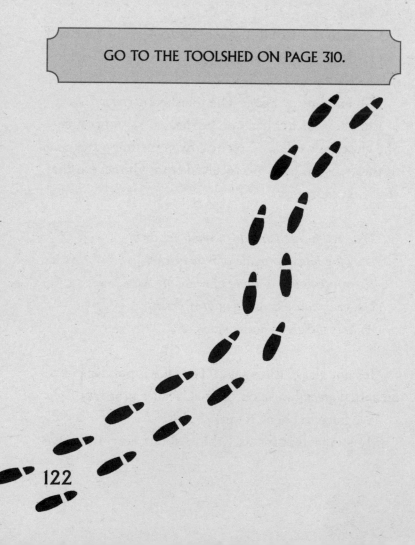

I DON'T WANT to have to accuse anyone. After all, it's too early to tell who's behind this. It could be anyone.

I can almost hear Mom's voice in my head, saying, "Keep your cards close to the chest."

"We're not sure yet," I finally say.

"Well, *get* sure. The clock is ticking! And my mom doesn't have much time left!"

"So, what do you want us to do?"

"Come up with a plan!" Ivy shouts. "Catch the culprit!"

I look over at Patty's house. Maybe there's some way we can follow them or catch them. I turn to Eliza for help, but she has sunk down into a chair, her eyes closed. Her most intense thinking face. Frank, meanwhile, has sidled up to a window.

"Eliza?" says Frank.

"Yes?" she replies through gritted teeth.

"Eliza?"

"Yes?"

"ELIZA?"

"*What*, Frank? Spit it out!"

"Can I play outside?"

Eliza groans. "I'm trying to think, Frank! Can't you please be quiet?"

"I just wanna go outside. So I can make a whistle out

of the long grass! Or a daisy chain."

"What long grass?" I say. "Otto is constantly mowing the lawn."

"There shouldn't be any long grass," Eliza says.

"Well, there *is*," Frank insists.

Eliza jumps up and runs to the window. Then she turns around with a grin. "Frank is a genius!"

"I know! Duhhhhhh."

And for once, I think that *both* Thompsons are totally crazy. "What in the world are you talking about?"

"The lawn is half mowed, Carlos. Like someone stopped right in the middle of the job."

Ivy raises an eyebrow. Smythe frowns.

"And I didn't notice it before, but the bushes are trimmed unevenly. And your weed infestation is, well, still infested."

"So?" Ivy says.

"When did Guinevere hire Otto?"

"A month or two ago," Smythe says. "Why?"

"Because I don't think your landscaper is a landscaper."

Could she be right? Could Otto somehow be tangled up in these death threats? After all, he *is* always asking us about the case.

"The icing on the cake," Eliza says, "is that we know for a *fact* that Patty and Maddock are in Patty's house

124

together. And you guys are here. But Otto is conveniently missing, and so is your mom. I have a hunch that they're together."

"But where?" I say, looking out the window. I peer around the yard, and I almost kind of think Otto is going to pop up like he always does. But he doesn't. The whole yard is silent and still . . . from the grass to the blue sky to the green shed on the edge of the LeCavalier property—

"Wait a second!" I say, with a closer look at the green shed. A small green house. The *greenhouse.*

"GREEN HOUSE!" I shout. "That first clue, remember?" I retrieve the very first clue to the treasure that I got from Guinevere LeCavalier:

The red house is made of red bricks.
The blue house is made of blue bricks.
The white house is made of white bricks.
The gray house is made of gray bricks.
What is the green house made of?

Eliza gasps and jumps up, and that's how I know it just clicked for her too. "Carlos!" she says in awe, her voice a whisper.

"What?" Frank says, tugging on my arm. "What does it mean?"

125

"We thought that clue pointed us to something *glass*, because a greenhouse is made of glass. We didn't even consider that there's a tiny green house on Guinevere's lawn! The clue points us right to it!"

"Then it's settled," Eliza says. "We should go check out the toolshed."

GO TO THE TOOLSHED ON PAGE 310.

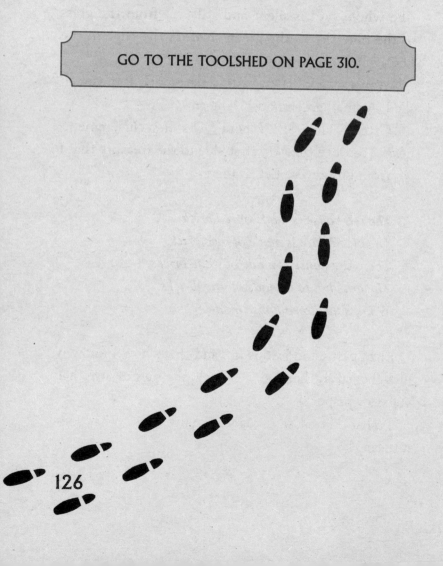

126

I FINALLY CONVINCE Eliza that we should head straight to Patty's house.

Just kidding, I actually *beg* her to go to Patty's house first.

"Pleeeeeeeeaseeeee!" I say, grabbing her left arm.

"Pleeeeeeeeeaseeeee!" Frank says, grabbing her right arm.

Eventually she sighs heavily and groans, "All right! All right!"

Just like yesterday, we creep up to Patty's Yorkie-shaped hedges, slink along the yellow stucco, and sneak into her open garage. It is overflowing with junk. There is so much needless stuff in Patty's garage that she can't even fit her car in there.

We navigate through her mess, creak open her side door, and tiptoe into her house through the laundry room. I peek my head out and look down the hall—it looks like it leads to a kitchen.

The only trouble is, we've never been in here before, and the layout is different from Guinevere's house. I don't want to get caught because we don't know where to go.

I'm about to whisper to Eliza and Frank to follow me to the kitchen when I hear Patty coming closer, her footsteps getting louder with each step.

Oh no! We have to hide!

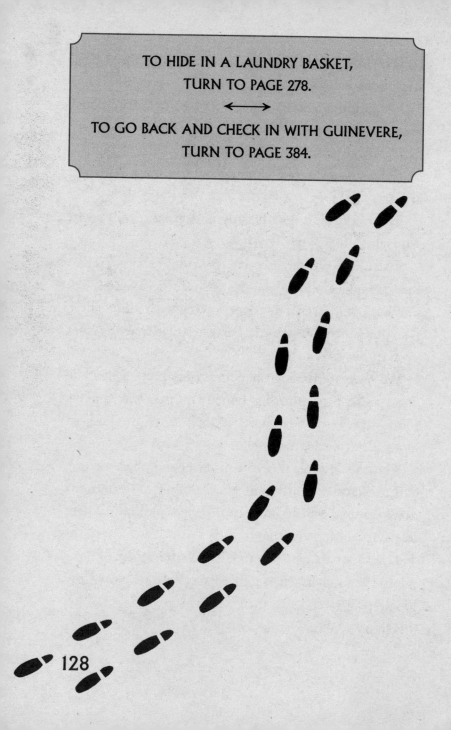

TO HIDE IN A LAUNDRY BASKET,
TURN TO PAGE 278.

←→

TO GO BACK AND CHECK IN WITH GUINEVERE,
TURN TO PAGE 384.

128

WE HAVE TO take action, and we have to be sneaky.

"Frank," I say, putting my hands on his shoulders, "it's all up to you, buddy!" I point at the vent. "Are you ready to crawl?"

"YEAH!" Frank shouts, and I put my hand over his mouth. "Mmmm!" he hums.

"But Carlos!" Eliza says. "Isn't this dangerous?"

I don't know, but what else are we going to do. "He's our only hope."

I let go of Frank's mouth, and he says, "I *want* to crawl! I love crawling!"

"We know," Eliza and I say.

"If I see a dust bunny, can I eat it?" Frank says.

"No," Eliza says.

"Yes," I say.

"Be safe, Frank," Eliza says. "If you see Otto, run and hide! If you see anyone else, get their help immediately! Come back for Carlos and me. Here, take the emergency money from Mom."

Frank nods. "Got it!"

Then Frank and I hop onto Mr. LeCavalier's creaky desk, and I lift him up as high as I can. Frank opens the vent and sticks his upper body into it. With one last push from me, Frank wiggles himself all the way in.

And then he's gone!

Eliza and I are silent as we wait, and it feels like hours.

With each minute that passes, the more I have the sinking realization that he must have run into Otto—or some other sort of trouble.

And right when I'm *sure* Frank was caught by Otto, the door to the bookshelf opens, and Frank is standing there with powder all over his face and a doughnut in hand.

"Frank," I say. "Did you get help? Where's Otto? Where did you go?"

"To Go Nuts for Doughnuts," Frank says. "I used the emergency money for DOUGHNUT FOOD."

"Doughnuts aren't an emergency!" Eliza scolds.

"Yes they are. It's *always* an emergency when I'm not eating a doughnut! Duhhhh."

"But what happened to Otto? Did you let him escape?"

Frank shrugs and takes another bite of doughnut. "Ooooooops!" he says, spitting chewed-up pieces everywhere. "I forgot. Sorry."

CASE CLOSED.

"LET'S SEARCH THE toolshed!" I say.

We don't need Smythe to take us there—we know exactly where it is. We head to the rickety shed in the backyard, with its peeling green paint and its rotting wood. The shed looks more fragile than a Popsicle-stick house, but I bet Mr. LeCavalier hid *something* useful in here. It's so creepy that it seems like the perfect place to find some clues.

With one hand on the door, I pause for a second. I thought I saw a shadow under the door. Could it be a person? Or an animal that's using the shed for shelter?

"Hello? Is anyone in here?"

I open the door slowly.

THUNK.

Darkness.

The next thing I know, I wake up in a hospital room, while Eliza fills me in on what I missed: I got hit in the face with a shovel. Eliza and Frank ran for help for me, but by the time they got back, the person who had whacked me in the face was *gone*. They didn't see who it was. Worst of all, Guinevere LeCavalier's treasure was stolen. The culprit left one final note in the mailbox, bragging about getting away with the treasure chest.

This failure feels like a smack in the face.

CASE CLOSED.

WHEN I GET home from my first day of detective work, I collapse on the couch. My feet are *aching* and my socks are worn through—there are two new holes at the bottom. Which stinks because I don't have that many pairs. Somehow socks always mysteriously disappear whenever Mom and I go to the laundromat.

I sit on the couch, rubbing my feet for a while, and when they're finally starting to feel better, I hobble over to my mom's room.

She's fast asleep, so I leave some cold medicine, a spoon, and a tall glass of water by her bedside table. Then I go to my room and flop onto my bed. I *should* brush my teeth, but I'm just so tired from the long day and my painful walk home—and so I curl up in my covers and fall asleep in record time.

THE NEXT MORNING, I wake up in a puddle of sweat. And not just from the lack of air-conditioning.

One day gone, and we're no closer to solving the case. I'm nervous. What if we don't figure it out? What if I ruin my mom's agency?

No. I can't think about that. Failure is *not* an option.

I shuffle to the bathroom and take the coldest shower of my life. After I get dressed, I check on Mom again. I bring her a new box of tissues, soup I warmed up in the microwave, and a washcloth drenched in cold water to bring down her fever. That's always what she does for me.

"Hummy, I still feel abful." She sneezes loudly, then coughs up a storm.

"You look a little better today, Mom," I say. But that's a lie. She looks green and clammy. But maybe if she starts thinking healthy thoughts, she'll get over the flu faster.

"Don't cob in, Carwos! I don't wah you to get sick!"

"Mom, I'll be fine," I say. I put the cold washcloth on her forehead, and she groans with relief. Then I drag her fan over from the other side of the room so that it's blowing right on her face. I'd nominate myself for son of the year if I wasn't sneaking around behind her back.

My stomach twists a little.

"Just rest up, Mom," I say. "Don't worry. Everything's going to be okay."

"Did you call Cowe?"

"Who?"

"My pardner!"

"Oh—oh, yeah. I called Cole," I say. And then I realize she must be really, *really* sick, because Mom can always spot a lie three sentences before I tell it. "You can just relax, Mom. Rest."

She chokes again on a round of hacking coughs. "Ugh. Carwos, go outside and pway wif Ewiza, okay? Stay out of twouble!"

My heart skips a beat. I hate lying to Mom, but she'll thank me when Eliza, Frank, and I save the agency. She *needs* this case. She needs us! She just doesn't know it yet.

"Feel better," I say, and I close the door.

I call Eliza, and within ten minutes, she and Frank arrive at my house. Eliza shows me her backpack full of stuff—she's much more prepared today. She has a notebook, a pen, snacks, and water bottles for all of us.

"Ready for duty," she whispers, just in case. I doubt Mom overhears—her whole ears-nose-throat system is very messed up right now—but like all parents, she has super-amplified hearing.

From my house, we walk to Guinevere's home. We spend the time discussing what we know so far:

1. Ivy, Maddock, and Smythe definitely know about the treasure.
2. Maddock and Smythe have access to the house and could easily deliver the threats.
3. Smythe is crazy sensitive to questions, and Maddock doesn't want to talk to us at all.
4. Ivy is supposed to arrive this morning.
5. Otto claims to know nothing but seems to have been pushing us to go home.
6. Some lady in the P. Schnozzleton house was watching us from across the street.

Lead suspect? WHO KNOWS?

We still have plenty of questions that need to be answered. Who is P. Schnozzleton, and why is someone from that house spying out the window? What might Otto be hiding? Why is Smythe so angry? Where is the treasure? And most importantly: *who* needs the treasure, and *why* would someone want to threaten Guinevere LeCavalier?

We had a good start yesterday, but we need to do better today. For Mom.

When we arrive at the house, Smythe answers the door and glares at us.

"Whooooo is it?" Guinevere calls from somewhere inside the house. She comes rushing to the door. "Ah! Detectives! Come in, come in!"

She ushers us inside. We march in—but not before Frank sticks out his tongue at Smythe.

"Can I ask you a question?" I ask as soon as we're away from the front door.

Guinevere pauses by the stairwell and turns to face us. The reflection from her diamond necklaces is so blinding that I wish I had sunglasses with me. "A follow-up question? But of course! Ask away!"

"How did you come to hire Otto?" I ask.

"I found his flyer in my mailbox, and he charged twice as much as the other landscapers in town. That's how I *knew* he was quality. Just like how my lawyer, Maddock, charges twice as much as other lawyers. The more something costs, the more it's worth. Never pay half price for something that's worth twice as much, is what I always say!"

Does she even realize how lucky she is, not to worry about money? Guinevere is practically throwing it away. Hopefully she can throw some of it at my mom and me.

"And how did Smythe come to work for you?" asks Eliza.

"Smythe . . . ah, yes. He was my great-aunt's cousin's son's neighbor's nephew. He started his employment here when he was just a boy."

I look around to make sure Smythe isn't nearby, but

I don't see him anywhere. "And was he . . . happy?" I ask. "Back then?"

Guinevere laughs, and the whole hall echoes with it. "Yes, of course! He loved my husband, Winston. And he positively *adores* Ivy."

"And when did he, uh, stop being so happy?"

Guinevere frowns. "I don't know . . . but now that Ivy's back, I hope to see him as happy as a clam that just ate a mountain of jelly beans!"

"Is she here? Already?"

"My daughter's in the living room. Perhaps you'd like to question her?"

"Absolutely!" Eliza says.

"No," says Frank, and Eliza hushes him.

Guinevere leads us through an archway made of marble and opens a set of double doors, leading to a room with lots of green velvet couches, gold walls, embroidered tapestries, three bookshelves, and a fireplace (which isn't on, obviously, since it's the middle of a blazing-hot summer).

A woman looks up from the couch, and . . . Oh. My. Goodness. She looks exactly like Guinevere LeCavalier, only thirty years younger.

"TWINSIES!" Frank yells. "You're like twins . . . except *you're* old." He points to Guinevere LeCavalier.

I wince. Frank, what are you doing? Never insult the client!

I watch Guinevere's face carefully. She looks shocked at first, her mouth making a perfect O. But then she recovers with a tiny laugh. "My Ivy *does* look exactly like me, doesn't she?"

Ivy scowls, folding her arms across her chest. "I think I'm more like my *father*—inside *and* out," she mumbles.

"Ah, the woes of motherhood!" Guinevere says, her voice overly cheery. She sheepishly plays with the jewelry around her neck before looking at Eliza and me. "You try to teach your children proper manners and—*ahem* . . ." She clears her throat and glares at Ivy. "*Appropriateness in front of guests*, but they never listen!"

"Speaking of children, is it just you and Ivy?" Eliza asks. "You and Mr. LeCavalier didn't have any other kids, did you?"

"No, *we* didn't. But my husband . . . well, my husband *did* have another child from a previous marriage. I've never met the boy. He wrote a few letters to the house, back when he was a teenager. He wanted to talk to his father, but I stopped that nonsense right away—that boy wasn't part of *this* family. It was ages ago, though. When my husband separated from his first wife."

I look at Ivy, and she's watching her mom, wide-eyed and stunned. Then I glance at Eliza, and *she* is staring at Guinevere like she's a cockroach. I agree.

How could this woman, with the nice round face and the jelly-bean tea, force Mr. LeCavalier to stop talking to his own son? That's terrible! That's inhuman!

"That's . . . that's awful," I finally say.

"Isn't it just?" Guinevere LeCavalier says, and I think she missed my point.

Suddenly Frank gets up on the arm of the sofa, his dirty sneakers treading all over Guinevere's nice couch. "I HAVE A QUESTION!" Frank shouts. "What was his name? The son!"

My jaw drops. That actually wasn't a terrible question!

"Preston," Guinevere says coldly. "Now, is there anything else you need from me before you interview my daughter?"

Eliza looks at me urgently, her gray eyes flashing, and somehow I can just tell that she wants me to ask more about Preston LeCavalier. But my gut is telling me that pushing Guinevere on this topic is a bad idea. Guinevere doesn't seem to want to talk about him, and I don't want to make her mad.

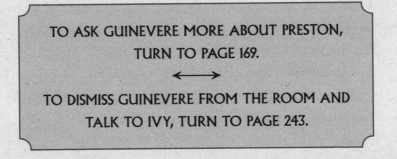

TO ASK GUINEVERE MORE ABOUT PRESTON, TURN TO PAGE 169.

←——→

TO DISMISS GUINEVERE FROM THE ROOM AND TALK TO IVY, TURN TO PAGE 243.

"HOW DO YOU know about the treasure?" I say, putting my ear against the crack at the bottom of the door.

"How could I *not*? My father used to talk about it all the time."

"Your father?" Eliza repeats.

Otto sighs. "My real name is Preston LeCavalier. I'm Mr. LeCavalier's son from his first marriage."

He pauses to let that sink in . . . and it's sinking in like a bulldozer to the face. In our very first conversation with Guinevere, she'd mentioned that Mr. LeCavalier's first family had sent her threats before. If only she—or we—had realized that history was repeating itself now!

Otto clears his throat. "My father used to mention the hidden treasure all the time to me . . . before he tossed my mother and me out of the house like a pair of moldy socks."

"Black socks, they never get dirty! The more that you wear them, the blacker they get! Sometimes I think I should wash them, but something inside me keeps saying not yet, not yet, not yet, not yet!" Frank sings.

Eliza elbows him. "Shhhhhh!"

"I never knew how to get beneath the house," Otto continues, "but thanks to you kids, I think I've figured it out."

140

"Us? What did we do?"

"You kept everyone thoroughly distracted. Now that everyone's outside watching Patty get arrested, I have the whole house to myself. I'd love to stay and chat, but . . . money calls."

And then he walks away, leaving us alone in the dark, dark closet.

TURN TO PAGE 196.

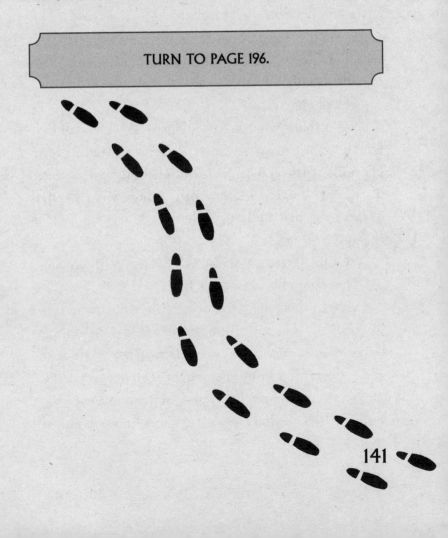

"THE DEATH THREAT last night," I ask Smythe. "What did it say?"

"I don't know," Smythe says.

"Can we look at it?" Eliza adds.

"No, you cannot."

"What!" I shout. "Come on, you said you'd help us."

Smythe walks over to the desk in the middle of the room and sits down in the chair.

"You can't see it because Mrs. LeCavalier took it with her. There was a letter on her pillow—with a box of chocolates."

"Box of chocolates?"

"Well, that's what we thought until we opened it." For the first time ever, Smythe looks a little nervous. He pulls at the collar of his butler uniform and clears his throat. "Instead of chocolates, there were all sorts of dead roaches. Belly up. Their little legs up high in the air."

"COOL!" Frank says. "BUGS ARE AWESOME."

"That's a nightmare!" says Eliza.

"Mrs. LeCavalier screamed her head off, and I had to clean up the bugs. But she never showed me the letter. She was holding it very tight to her chest as she and Ivy left for a hotel. I've never seen her so rattled." Smythe's mouth puckers, and his droopy eyes look serious. "If you don't hurry up and find the culprit,

142

we might all be in trouble. So what are you waiting for?"

TO ASK SMYTHE WHERE TO INVESTIGATE NEXT, TURN TO PAGE 337.

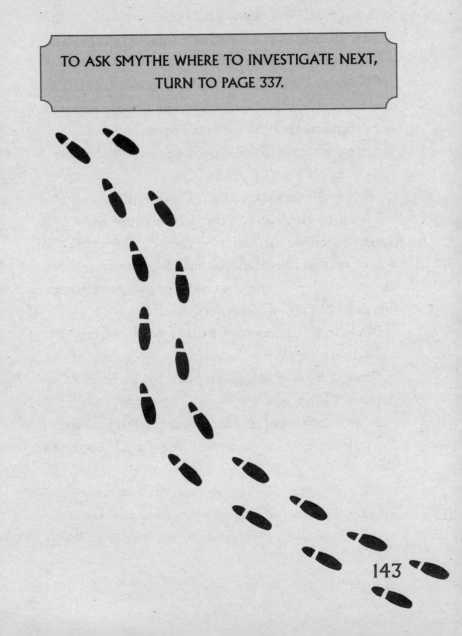

IF WE WANT to be treated like professionals, we must act like professionals—and that means reasoning with Smythe. With our words. Like grown-ups. Sigh.

Smythe frowns at us. "What's it going to take to get you kids off this property?"

"We can't leave. We *have* to keep investigating! This case depends on it!" I insist, keeping my eye on Frank as he starts picking the leaves off a nearby bush.

Eliza nods next to me. "We'll never solve the case if you cut us off from our clues."

"Be good little kids, and go play on a playground."

I want to growl at Smythe. Just because we're kids doesn't mean we can't *also* be good detectives. I'm so sick of people like Maddock and Smythe treating us like we're babies. There's no *way* I'm going to abandon this case! Not when Mom needs me!

But before I can open my mouth to yell at him, Eliza grabs my arm and steps forward.

"Isn't it a little suspicious that you're here all by yourself?" Eliza says.

Smythe looks confused for a moment. But his expression quickly morphs into a menacing stare. "Suspicious how?"

Eliza grins, and I know she has him. "Let me see . . ." She hums. "First, you planted a threat somewhere in the house. Then when Guinevere found it, you probably

144

convinced her to go to a hotel. For her own safety, of course. Now that the house is completely empty, you can search for the treasure all by yourself! You don't have to worry about either of the LeCavaliers figuring it out—and you don't have to let the detectives in."

My mouth drops open. I didn't even think of that, but Eliza's right! This *could* have been Smythe's secret evil plan all along!

"Don't be ridiculous," Smythe says. "I care about the LeCavaliers. I'm a loyal employee—"

"Elizaaaaaaa! This flower tastes weird!" Frank whines, and I inhale sharply because with all the fighting with Smythe, I forgot to watch Frank, and he started eating things!

Smythe grins wickedly. "Ahhh, yes, a poisonous oleander plant. I told Mr. LeCavalier not to plant those, but thank goodness he ignored my advice. You better get him to a doctor before he gets sick. Those plants are known to cause vomiting, nausea, dizziness, and fainting."

As if on cue, Frank throws up all over the grass.

"FRANK!" Eliza says. "What in the world were you *thinking*, eating a strange flower?"

"It looked like cotton candy!" he groans. "But it tasted like POOP."

Eliza looks at me, concerned. Her eyes are pooling with tears.

As much as I want to save my mom's agency, staying alive and unpoisoned is more important. We *need* to get Frank to a doctor. I call 911.

After Frank spends a few nerve-racking hours vomiting into a hospital trash can, the doctors say he's going to be fine. Phew! But when I call Guinevere LeCavalier to see if we can resume the case, she fires us for abandoning her in her time of need. Boo!

CASE CLOSED.

WE HAVE TO tell Guinevere what we know about Ivy. It's only right.

We run downstairs and find Guinevere lying on a couch in the family room, with Smythe massaging her feet. Gross!

"Mrs. LeCavalier!" Eliza pants.

"It's Ivy," I jump in.

"What about my Ivy?"

"We think she's the one who's been sending the threats. She wants the treasure because she needs the mon—" I stop at the look on Guinevere's face. She looks stunned, and not in a good way.

"I . . . what? You come into my house and you—you say *this*? How dare you accuse Ivy of this horrible crime! I think you should leave now! And you are never, NEVER invited back in this house again. I'll be calling the agency to tell them how dissatisfied I am with your service." She claps her hands. "*Smythe!* Get Las Pistas Detective Agency on the line!"

Smythe grins like he's being asked to eat a tray of cookies or something.

He brings a telephone on a silver platter into the room.

"Hello? Detective Serrano? I have three representatives from your agency, all of whom are *highly* unprofessional."

Fifteen minutes later, I wince as Mom storms up to us, leaving a trail of snotty tissues in her wake. Otto trails behind her, picking the litter off his precious landscaped lawn.

"Carwos!" Mom shouts. "You are gwounded *fowever*!"

Mom is so mad that she signs me up for highway trash cleanup for the rest of the summer. And because of me, Mom's agency goes bankrupt due to bad press, and she has to get a job as an elephant pooper-scooper at the zoo.

I really messed up bad.

CASE CLOSED.

ONCE I FINISH coloring the squares, I hold up the paper. "Forty-nine? What's forty-nine?"

When I say forty-nine out loud, the ground under me starts to shake and rumble and crumble and—"AHHHHHHHHHHHHHHHHHHHHHHHHHH!!!!!!!"

We all scream as we fall, fall, F

A

L

L

!

BOING! We land in a net that hovers above a pit of three snapping alligators. One to eat each of us. And boy, do they look hungry!

Eliza is ghostly white. Frank, on the other hand, keeps wiggling his fingers through the net, baiting the alligators to take a nibble.

"Frank!" I shout. "Don't!"

Suddenly, with a creak, the net lowers an inch toward the alligator pit. I look around frantically. There! Behind Eliza, I see six alligator-shaped candle sconces, illuminating a message that's scratched deeply into the stone wall.

CHOMP CHOMP, SNAP SNAP! ALLIGATORS BITE! SOLVE THIS PUZZLE QUICKLY, AND BE SURE TO GET IT RIGHT.

A | B | C   J   N . | O. | P   W
D | E | F   K ✕ M   Q. | R. | S.   X. ✕ .Z
G | H | I   L   T | U. | V   Ẏ

IF YOU KNOW THE SOLUTION OF THIS PUZZLE,
ADD THREE HUNDRED AND TURN TO THAT PAGE.

←→

TO ASK ELIZA FOR A HINT,
TURN TO PAGE 186.

150

"THE ANSWER IS *beard*!" I say aloud. "It's *beard*!"

Suddenly something mushy and sticky starts leaking out of the rungs of the ladder. . . .

"Ugh!" Eliza says. "It's superglue!"

"I'M STUCK!" Frank cries.

I try to wrench my hands away from the ladder, but I can't move them either.

We stay cemented to the ladder for hours and hours—until finally the police find us. It takes them five hours to chip the glue off our hands and feet.

No wonder they have warning labels about superglue.

Only this was super super super SUPERglue.

If only I could use it to glue my mom's eyes shut, so she doesn't see what a horrible mess I've made of her career.

CASE CLOSED.

I HAVE TO set the tapestry on fire. The fire will distract Otto, and that's when we'll make our break.

I take the lantern in my hands and smash it against the tapestry on the wall. The glass breaks, and within seconds, the cloth is ablaze.

Otto looks at the burning tapestry, and his grip goes slack on Guinevere. And that's when Eliza, Frank, and I run forward to rescue her.

Only . . . the fire roars and rages. It grows and grows and grows like a hideous monster. It blocks our exit, and the only way to escape it is to go deeper into the tunnels.

And so we run farther into the caverns, leaving Otto in the chamber behind us.

But little did we know that it's an actual labyrinth down here, and we get lost wandering the tunnels. So lost, in fact, that we can't figure out how to get out, and no one—not Ivy or Smythe or the police or Mom— ever figures out how to find us.

Eliza, Frank, Guinevere, and I survive by eating the bugs crawling along the cave walls, telling stories of the good old days before we decided to take this case.

CASE CLOSED.

WE DECIDE TO see if the red paint we found at Patty's matches the paint from the second death threat. If it matches, it makes Patty look *really* guilty. Which means we're that much closer to saving my mom's job!

The can is a little heavy, so I help Eliza carry it across the lawn. I pray that Patty doesn't drive up as we're stealing this paint can from her house. And luckily, she doesn't.

When we reach Guinevere LeCavalier's lawn, we pause for a moment to rest. I am panting. It's so hot that it feels like being inside an oven.

"Hey, kids," says a familiar voice from the garden. It's Otto, Mrs. LeCavalier's landscaper. "Where are you coming from . . ." His eyes narrow on the paint can as he approaches us. "What's that?"

"Paint," Frank says. "Duh."

He smiles. "Where did you find that? And where are you going with it? Is it a clue? Want to run any theories by me?"

So many questions! Is that suspicious?

"Mind your own BEESWAX!" Frank yells, stomping on Otto's toe.

"Owwwwwwwww!"

"Frank!" Eliza shouts. "That was very rude! Apologize! Now!"

"I'm sorry you're a NOSY NELLY," Frank says.

"Frank!"

"I'm sorry you're a SNOOPING SNOOPY," Frank says.

"Frank!"

I shake my head. "You're making it *worse*, Frank!"

"I'm sorry I'm NOT SORRY."

"Kids," Otto says. "Don't you think you should get an adult's opinion on your case?"

"We don't need adult supervision," Eliza says. "We are *very* capable of handling this case by ourselves."

"HARUMPH!" Frank finishes.

When we arrive at the crime scene, it is just as bad as I remembered. There are books *everywhere*. Pages torn out and ripped all over the floor. There's a toppled wooden bookshelf, and broken splinters are poking out dangerously. And on the far wall, a message is dripping in bloodred paint:

You are running out of time.
Find that treasure, or meet your doom.
HA HA HA HA HA HA HA HA HA HA HA HA

I gulp.

"Carlos, help me open this paint can!"

I bend down beside Eliza, and together we pry off

the top. Then I dip my finger into the paint can and begin to write on the wall underneath the message, so we can compare the colors.

When I step away, we all look at my message: *IT MATCHES.*

"No doubt about it," Eliza says. "It's the exact same paint. But wh—"

CRASH!

"AHHHHHHHHHHHHHHHHHHHHHH!" comes the sound of a bloodcurdling shriek from the other room.

RUN TO THE SCREAM!
TURN TO PAGE 362.

"I'LL TAKE THE office and bedroom!" I say, running through the hall of the creepy Patty portraits. I start opening random doors. I discover a room with nothing but a pool table in the middle, then a room with a hundred dog beds on the floor, then—Patty's office!

The room is tidy, tidy, tidy. She must be one of those people who talks about proper places for everything and everything in proper places . . . or something like that.

I open her filing cabinet, and there are folders for everything. Some even date back forty years! The files all have boring names, like taxes and Fancy Club and receipts. Nothing that says Guinevere LeCavalier.

I open the middle drawer and riffle around inside.

"Hey, wait!" I say, closing the drawer. Then I open it again. Then I close it. Then open.

Hmmm . . .

It's weird. From the outside, the drawer seems deep. But when I pull the drawer open, it's shallow inside.

I knock on the bottom of the drawer, and it sounds hollow to me. I think the drawer might have a false bottom. My heart skips a beat as I pull everything— tape, stapler, stamps, paper clips, pens—out of the drawer.

Now that the drawer is empty, it's easier to see the words carved into the bottom.

156

As I was going to visit St. Ives,
I passed by seven different wives.
Each wife had seven sacks,
Each sack had seven cats,
Each cat had seven kittens.
Kittens, cats, sacks, wives,
How many were going to visit St. Ives?

Beneath the words, I notice there are buttons like a calculator to punch in a number. So . . . I guess I'm supposed to figure out how many people are going to St. Ives, wherever *that* is.

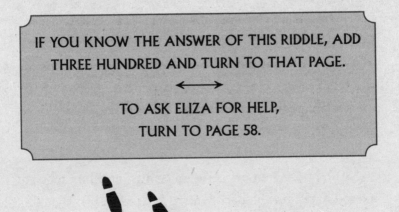

IF YOU KNOW THE ANSWER OF THIS RIDDLE, ADD THREE HUNDRED AND TURN TO THAT PAGE.

←——→

TO ASK ELIZA FOR HELP, TURN TO PAGE 58.

I DECIDE TO attack Otto. I have to try.

I scour the ground for something I can use. There are a few medium-sized rocks that could work. I pretend like I'm bending over to tie my shoelace, but what I'm *really* doing is palming a smooth rock.

Otto doesn't even notice. He's too busy fussing with the latch on the treasure chest. At last it clicks open and—for a moment—Otto's head disappears behind the top lid.

And *that's* the moment I need.

I run forward and clunk Otto's head with a cave rock.

"Flibbertigibbet," Otto babbles. Then he collapses on the ground.

"WE DID IT!" Frank squeals. "HOORAY FOR US!"

We leave Otto passed out and retrace our steps all the way to Ivy's closet, where—to our surprise—there are six police officers trying to cram inside. Only they are too big and won't fit.

"We have Otto," I say. "You have to follow us!"

"Stand back," an officer commands, and he takes an ax and hacks up the back wall of Ivy's closet so that the adults can fit into the passageway.

With the police officers, we retrace our steps and reach the cave. The empty treasure chest is still open, but Otto is *gone.*

"Oh no!" I say, my stomach swooping. "But he was

right here. . . . I hit him with a rock. . . . He was out cold!"

Guinevere bites her nails. "How will I be able to sleep? What about my safety?"

Eliza and I look at each other. "What can we do?" I say.

Guinevere grins widely. "Well, I'm glad you asked!" She drags us upstairs, hands us three dog costumes, and pats us on the head.

"You three are now my watchdogs. I need you to circle the perimeter and watch for Otto. And, of course, bark if something's wrong."

"Okayyyyy," I say, stepping into the dog costume. "For how long?"

"For as long as it takes to catch Otto, of course!"

I start to protest. "But what about—"

"Shhhh shhhh shhhhh!" Guinevere says, patting me on the head. "Good dogs don't speak. Now have a biscuit!" And she shoves a dog treat in my mouth.

It's chalky and dry, and it makes me cough.

"Good doggie!" Guinevere says. "Now go outside and guard me!"

"ARF!" Frank says.

And that was the summer Frank, Eliza, and I became human dogs.

CASE CLOSED.

"THE BLUE DOOR!" I say. "It has to be!"

"Hold on . . . ," Eliza says.

But I tap my foot. We don't have time for Eliza's waffling. She's good at puzzles and everything, but sometimes she takes *foreverrrrrr* to solve things because she likes to check her work. It's why she's always the last one done on tests, even though she's the smartest person in our class.

So I open the blue door, push Eliza and Frank inside, and hop in after them.

But there is no ground.

"AHHHHHHHHHHH!" I shout as we fall forward.

WHUMP.

We land in the alligator pit we just escaped from.

Three alligators slink toward us, and I can practically see them licking their chops, their black eyes hungry. And dinner has just been served.

Uh-oh.

CASE CLOSED.

I ENTER THE password *light ball slice* into the box, and an alarm starts blaring.

"INTRUDER! INTRUDER! INTRUDER!"

It's coming from the box, but it is so loud that I cover my ears . . . so loud it makes me dizzy . . . so loud I have a headache . . . so loud I can't move! I crawl up into a little ball and hold my ears tight; it's the only thing I can do.

"Owwwwwww," Frank wails. "My ears!"

"INTRUDER! INTRUDER! INTRUDER!"

It could be ten minutes or ten hours—but sometime later, the police (wearing noise-canceling headphones) knock down the door and take us to the police station for breaking into Patty's house. Let's just say my mom is *not* happy to get my phone call from jail.

The caption on my mug shot? *Carlos Serrano: Criminal, Failed Detective, and Son of a Banana Factory Inspector.*

You heard me right: after I ruined Mom's life, she had to take the first job that came along, and now she inspects the fruit at a banana-ripening factory. The only mystery that comes Mom's way: why is this banana less ripe than the others? Real inspiring stuff, I know.

CASE CLOSED.

"WE'RE GOING TO look in the desk drawers. I have a good feeling about that."

"HOW DARE YOU!" Frank shouts, swashbuckling his invisible sword. "DO AS YOUR CAPTAIN SAYS, OR I'LL . . . I'LL . . . FEED YOU TO THE SHARKS!"

"Shhhhhh, Frank! Calm down!" Eliza says, patting his shoulder.

He responds by trying to bite Eliza's hand.

"Frank!" she cries.

They start bickering, like always—but I can't pay attention to them. I have to find something important in Mr. LeCavalier's desk.

I pull open the top drawer, but it's only office supplies. I pull open the middle drawer, and same thing. Then I open the bottom drawer, and it's full of papers with gibberish on them. They're all full of random numbers and shapes, written in black ink. It looks like incomplete homework.

"Eliza, come help me read this."

She studies a stack of papers with me and sighs. "Carlos, this is junk. Just doodles and math problems . . . it's all useless."

"AHA!" Frank jumps in, and he rips the papers out of our hands and crumples them.

"Frank!" I shout.

He grins wickedly as he picks up a paper off the

floor and tears it into three pieces.

"Frank!" Eliza scolds.

Frank starts pulling more papers out of the desk drawer and shredding them.

Rrrrip! Rrrrip! Rrrrip!

"This is fun," Frank says. "I like destroying things!"

"Stop!" I holler.

"Frank, *no*!" Eliza yells.

"Aha!" Smythe roars from the doorway. Uh-oh. "I knew it, I knew it, I knew it!" Smythe leaps into the room and points at the ripped-up papers all over the floor, his face as red as a cooked beet.

"This isn't what it looks like," I say quickly, even though it's *exactly* what it looks like, down to the last piece of paper mid-rip in Frank's hands.

"I knew I couldn't trust you in my employer's house," Smythe says. He bends over and starts collecting the little bits of paper, cradling them all to his chest. "You've ruined Mr. LeCavalier's files, you little monsters!" He sneers at us. "You've broken your promise, but I'll keep mine. . . . Out, out, *out*!!!"

Smythe chases us out of the house and slams the door in our faces. We knock for hours and hours and hours, but he never lets us back in.

CASE CLOSED.

I PICK UP the notebook. It's so old and crusty that I have to pry it open. And it has a strange smell. Usually I like the smell of new books *and* old books, but this one smells like it's been dipped in vinegar.

"Ewwwwwww. IT SMELLS LIKE FOOT!" Frank shouts.

The handwriting is faded, and I can barely make it out in the candlelight. I pass the book to Eliza to read aloud.

> Dear Diary,
> My ~~family~~ is falling apart. Guinevere gave
> Ivy an ultimatum today

"What's an old tomato?" Frank asks.

"*Ultimatum*," Eliza explains. "It's a demand. A final offer. Like 'If you don't do this, then this terrible thing will happen.'"

"Kind of like a threat!" I realize. Then I cover my mouth because I don't want to admit that I didn't know what an ultimatum was either.

Eliza nods and continues reading.

> Either she breaks up with Walter Kramer
> and receives our inheritance money, or she
> stays with him . . . in which case we would

write her out of our wills. Neither option seems ideal, for I love my daughter, and I wish her to have my fortune. I keep trying to talk to my dear Guinevere, but she won't listen. She is afraid the boy might be marrying Ivy for her money. Of course, just one look at them, and you can see they're moony for each other.

Must continue to work on Guinevere. I fear what will

Eliza looks up. "The rest of it's all faded. I can't see it."

"Make up the rest," Frank says. "It was a good story so far."

"We know the rest of the story," Eliza says. "Obviously, Ivy and her mom got in a fight about all this. Then Ivy ran off and married Walter Kramer, and the LeCavaliers wrote her out of the will. Years later, she's having money problems."

"Well, at least we know what the fight's about now," I say. "She has motive—to find the treasure *and* to threaten her mom. Payback, right?"

"Piggyback?" Frank says, perking up.

"No, no, *payback*. It means revenge!"

Eliza flips through more pages in frustration. "I just

wish we could read the rest of the diary. Mr. LeCavalier must have spilled something on it—the pages are all waterlogged and faded."

"We still have the letters," I tell her.

TO READ THE LETTERS, TURN TO PAGE 285.

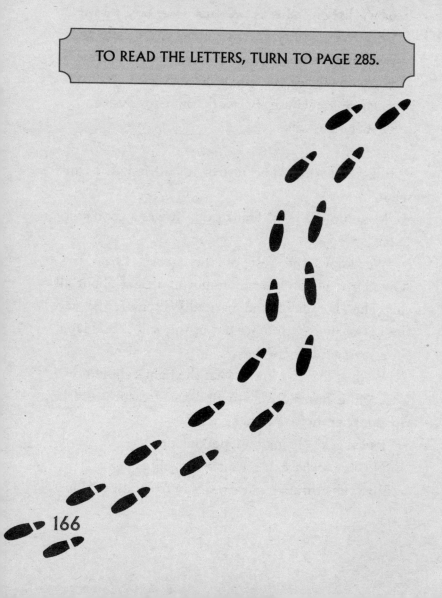

166

WE CAN'T TELL Otto details about the case, but maybe he knows something about Ivy. It doesn't hurt to ask.

I shield my eyes as I look at Otto—the setting sun is right behind his head. Now's the time I wish I hadn't accidentally stepped on my five-dollar flea-market sunglasses.

I clear my throat. "What do you know about Ivy?"

"So she seems suspicious, huh?"

Eliza opens her mouth to answer, but I jump in first. "That information is classified."

"CLASSIFIED!" Frank echoes from right behind Otto.

Otto jumps up and holds his heart, looking as though he might pass out.

"You can't just go sneaking up behind people and scaring them!" Eliza lectures.

"Why nottttttt?" Frank whines.

I roll my eyes and turn back to Otto. "So what do you know about Ivy?"

"Not much," Otto says, "since she lives in Wichita. But I've seen her around today, and she doesn't seem happy to be home. The thing is . . ." Otto drops his voice and leans in. "I don't want to speak ill of my employer's family. Or betray their trust. I'm a little nervous to tell you. . . ."

"You can trust us," I say, and Eliza nods in agreement. Her eyes are eager and wild, though, like she knows he's about to tell us something juicy, and she can't *wait* to hear.

"Okay, but you have to promise you won't tell anyone you heard it from me."

Suddenly Frank inserts himself into the middle of our group huddle. "Secrets are no fun unless they're shared with FRANK!" Eliza puts a hand over his mouth to quiet him down, but Frank squirms out of her grip.

"No . . . I'm sorry, kids. I just can't say."

I stare into Otto's ice-blue eyes, searching for a clue. But the only thing I walk away with is an instinct that it's time to go home. I have to check in with Mom before she catches on to what we're doing.

We will pick this up tomorrow.

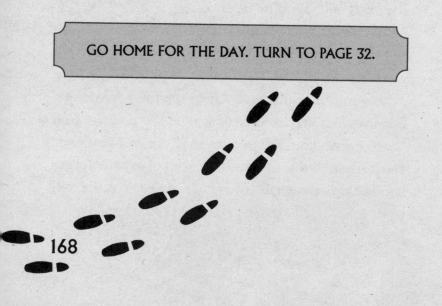

GO HOME FOR THE DAY. TURN TO PAGE 32.

AFTER THINKING FOR a moment, I decide to listen to Eliza's weird eye cues. "Could we hear more about Preston?"

Guinevere wrinkles her nose. *"Why?"*

"It can't hurt!" I say. "Everything is important."

"All bits of information can lead to clues," Eliza says.

Frank makes a giant raspberry with his mouth. "All clues lead to BORING!" he whines.

Guinevere raises her eyebrows. Her mouth scrunches tighter, like she just ate something sour. "How dare you bring up Mr. LeCavalier's most *indecent history*? You are disrespecting him! Disrespecting me!"

"I didn't mean . . ."

Eliza stands up. "Stop being so oversensitive." I kick Eliza, but she continues. "It would help us if we knew more about Mr. LeCavalier's first family—"

Guinevere points at Eliza wildly. "There! You said it! *First* family! With that judgmental tone!"

Eliza furrows her brow. "What are you talking about? I'm just trying to collect important information here. I'm not judgmental. *You're* the one being overly defensive."

I groan and sink down into the couch. "I'm sorry!" I shout, trying to correct Eliza's error, but it's too late. Ivy cringes like she's waiting for her mother to explode, but instead Guinevere sniffs.

"I'm done with your distastefulness." Her voice is as sharp as an icicle. *"Smythe!"*

Smythe hustles into the room.

"Please escort these rotten detectives off my property. And inform them that their services are no longer needed."

Smythe turns to us, but before he can say anything, I talk directly to Guinevere. "Please! We're just trying to be thorough!" I think of my mom in panic. Her agency—and happiness—is on the line! "Please, please, pleeeeeease!"

"Smythe! Inform the detectives that we are done here."

"YOU FART FACE," Frank says, pointing at Guinevere.

"Smythe! Please tell the detectives that a *proper lady* never does anything so indecent as passing gas."

Smythe turns to us and opens his mouth.

"LIAR!" Frank shouts, and Smythe deflates, clearly disappointed we're not giving him a chance to do his job. "GIRLS DO FART! I'VE SMELLED ELIZA'S!"

"Frank!" Eliza says, mortified. She hides behind a couch pillow.

"Are you calling me a liar?" Guinevere says, her face twisted into a scandalized expression, her eyes glinting with fury. Ivy trembles beside her mother.

170

"No! I *already* called you a fart face!"

Guinevere turns as purple as an eggplant. "*Smythe!* The door!"

Smythe grabs us in his arms as easily as if we were three melons. Then he drags us down Guinevere's fancy hallways and shoves us out the door.

"And don't come back!"

No no NO!

In baseball, I'm so used to the whole three-strikes-and-you're-out rule, but with Guinevere LeCavalier, it was one strike and the whole game is over. I know Eliza wanted me to push our witness, but maybe I should have trusted my gut after all.

Just thinking about losing this case makes me want to cry. I've ruined Mom's career, her passion, her chance at happiness.

How am I possibly going to explain this to her?

CASE CLOSED.

"IT'S MADE OF ham!" shouts Frank. "No, spider webs! No, wait, baby teeth!"

Eliza frowns. "Hmmm . . . what does it mean?"

"Well," Guinevere LeCavalier says, sipping a cup of her disgusting jelly-bean tea. "This is the *only* thing my daughter, Ivy, and I were able to figure out . . . before she left me to go marry *that man*. I haven't seen her in five years! I'll never see her again!" Guinevere howls.

"Isn't she coming to visit tomorrow?" Smythe says from the corner of the room, and I jump. I forgot that he's popping in and out of the room—he's so quiet, like a giant spider you never hear coming.

Guinevere dabs her face with a napkin. "Oh, yes, I forgot. *Anyway*," she says, picking up the parchment with the clue on it. "The answer is *glass*. A greenhouse is made of glass."

"Oh! Of course!" Eliza cries. "It's a trick! It's trying to get you to answer that it's made of green bricks, but really, the riddle is referring to a *greenhouse*, which is a building made of glass!"

"I still think it's made of artichokes," Frank says.

I roll my eyes. Frank *definitely* didn't inherit the puzzle-solving gene.

"Okay, glass," I say. "But what's that supposed to tell you?"

Guinevere shrugs. "I can't help you there. I have no

idea what I'm supposed to do next. Feel free to check all the glass and kitchenware in the house. I've torn this place apart, and I've found nothing."

"Is that what happened to the library?" I ask.

Guinevere snorts mid-sip, and tea spurts out her nose. "None of that was me!" she says, dabbing her nose with a handkerchief. "The torn books and toppled shelves were all the handiwork of our perpetrator."

Frank belches.

"*Excuse* him," Eliza says sharply, and Frank sticks his tongue out at her.

"The library was the second threat on my life."

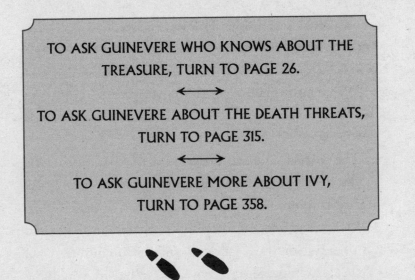

TO ASK GUINEVERE WHO KNOWS ABOUT THE
TREASURE, TURN TO PAGE 26.
←——→
TO ASK GUINEVERE ABOUT THE DEATH THREATS,
TURN TO PAGE 315.
←——→
TO ASK GUINEVERE MORE ABOUT IVY,
TURN TO PAGE 358.

WE RUN AFTER the noise, bounding down the hallway like three dogs off their leashes. We round the corner and see the source of the crash—a knocked-over table with hundreds of dead flowers all over the floor. There's also a stuffed bear in the center. Only . . . I should say, it's an *un*stuffed bear. The bear has a knife in its stomach, and stuffing is coming out of it. And it seems to be holding an envelope.

But most surprising of all—in the middle of the whole mess is a woman I don't recognize. She has thin lips, puffy hair, and makeup that gives her raccoon eyes.

She looks at me in panic. "I—I didn't do this! It wasn't me!"

"A LIKELY STORY," Frank yells, walking up to her and pointing his finger so close to her nose that he's practically picking it.

"What are you doing at this crime scene?" I say, edging closer to the stuffed bear. My shoes crunch on the dead flowers.

The second I swoop down to pick up the envelope in the bear's arms, the woman tries to run, but Frank grabs her around the middle. "Got her! Got her!"

Moments later, footsteps come pounding, and Guinevere, Smythe, Maddock, and Ivy run into our hall.

"Patty Schnozzleton?" Ivy says. "What are you doing here?"

P. Schnozzleton! The lady who's obsessed with

getting revenge on Guinevere LeCavalier! The lady who was creepily watching us from her window! This is *her*? At the scene of the third death threat . . .

"ARREST HER!" Guinevere LeCavalier howls. "Call the police! Call the FBI! Someone lock up this maniac!"

"I didn't do this!" Patty says insistently. "I just heard a noise and came running."

Eliza folds her arms. "You heard this *all the way from your own house*? I find that unlikely."

Patty blanches.

"Aha!" Guinevere says. "*Smythe!* Get the police!"

"Hold on," Eliza says. "Let's open the letter."

I open the letter and read it aloud:

> To Guinevere,
> Roses are red.
> Violets are blue.
> These flowers are dead.
> And soon you'll be too.
> Love,
> Twenty-Four Hours Left

I gulp.

"Y-you!" Guinevere says, pointing at Patty. "YOU MENACE TO SOCIETY!"

Guinevere keeps shrieking, and I wring my hands.

175

The letter is *frightening*. I don't even want to think about what might happen in twenty-four hours. . . .

Patty Schnozzleton *does* seem awfully guilty. She was at the scene of the crime immediately after it happened. But we *can't* just call the police on Patty before we even listen to her side of the story. After all, if Patty didn't do it, maybe she saw something. There's a lot at stake here, now that we only have one day left. Mrs. LeCavalier and my mom could both be in deep trouble if we don't solve the case—and fast!

We need to give Patty a chance to explain. But Guinevere LeCavalier won't like that.

"You evil woman!" Guinevere shrieks.

"You old hag!" Patty screams back.

"I'm going to get you for this!"

"Well, I can't say that I'm going to get you, because I don't want to incriminate myself, so I am definitely *not* going to get you back!"

"Sarcasm!" Guinevere hollers. "That's sarcasm!"

"Hey!" I say. "Quiet!"

But they keep screaming over me.

"Quiet!" Eliza and I shout. "Quiet!" Smythe, Maddock, and Ivy chime in.

Suddenly Frank puts a hand on my arm. "Let *me* handle this," he says. Then he takes a deep breath and hollers, "QUIIIIIEEEEEEETTTTTT!!!!!!!!"

176

Guinevere and Patty shut right up.

"Thank you, Frank," I say. "Mrs. LeCavalier, with your permission, I'd like to interview Ms. Schnozzleton before we call the police. After all, no one *saw* her set up this threat. She might be telling the truth."

"I am! I am!" Patty nods.

"Can't you just continue your investigation with Patty behind bars?" Guinevere complains.

Eliza shakes her head no.

"Fine," Guinevere LeCavalier says, "but I want to witness the interrogation."

This time *I* shake my head no. "We can't allow that. Detective-suspect confidentiality."

"In the meantime," Eliza says, "you're clearly not safe here. I think you should pack your bags and go to a hotel—"

"Leave? Are you sure?"

"Better safe than sorry," Eliza says, which gives me prickles on my arms. Suddenly I feel the urge to investigate fast! Like there's a fire within me. I have to *move* on this case!

Guinevere frowns, and she looks like she's going to refuse, but finally she nods. "Okay, I'll relocate to a hotel. But you detectives call me the *moment* you have this all figured out. I'm counting on you to solve this within twenty-four hours." She puts her hand on her forehead dramatically. "I can't live like this anymore. All this worrying has been putting a damper on my daily afternoon massages at the spa. I've suffered so much."

We walk outside with Patty, and on the lawn, Otto looks at us and gives us a small wave from the toolshed. He starts to walk over to us, but I gesture no. This is *not* a good time.

"You kids saved me back there. Thank you," Patty says.

She starts to walk down Guinevere's driveway, but we run in front of her and block her way. "We were serious about questioning you," Eliza says.

"Who are you kids? Her relatives?" Her eyes narrow.

"We're detectives," I say.

"Detectives! W-what in the world is going on in that house?"

"Guinevere LeCavalier has been getting a series of death threats," I explain.

Patty's eyes bulge out, and she starts to choke on her own spit. "Death . . . death *what*? Are you serious?"

"You just saw one," I say. "What do *you* think?"

"Hehehehehe!" Patty chortles. "Serves her right, the wicked witch! But it has nothing to do with me! I was just here to play a harmless prank on her, not *kill* her!"

"YEAH, RIGHT!" Frank shouts.

"It's true . . . I just want to make her mad. It's like poking a bear with a stick. It's fun."

"Poke poke poke!" Frank says, taking his finger and poking Patty in the side.

She frowns at him. "Stop that, now."

"Poke!" Frank says one last time.

"What prank were you trying to pull, Patty?" I ask.

She lowers her voice and looks around. Her eyes are wild, and when she smiles, there's lipstick on her teeth. "I was about to replace all the milk in her milk cartons with cottage cheese. Hehehehehe!" She giggles. "But then I heard a loud noise and ran to it—and you three arrived seconds later."

"Have you pulled any pranks on her before?" Eliza asks. "Maybe one involving a library and a note in red paint?"

Patty scrunches her eyebrows. "No. The only other prank I played on her was at the last charity ball, when I replaced her fork and knife with a spork! Hehehehehe! She looked like a *fool*, trying to eat with that!"

"Spork!" Frank giggles. "I like that word! Sporkie spork spork!"

Is the definition of prank different for old people? Because that sounds like the most unfun prank ever.

"But *why* were you pranking Guinevere in the first place?" Eliza asks.

179

"Because she ruined my life!" Patty cries, throwing her arms in the air. "A long, long time ago, we were *supposed* to plan a benefit ball together—to raise money for the repopulation of dodo birds. But I ended up doing all the work while Mrs. LeCava-Lazybones sat in a lawn chair, Smythe popping grapes into her mouth."

"I'm hungry!" Frank says. "I want grapes!" Eliza digs into her backpack and hands him a bag of raisins. "Eliza, those aren't grapes! Those are raisins!"

"Shhhhh! No, no, no, Frank, these are *magic grapes*," she says. "These are grapes that have been kissed by the sun."

Frank stares at the bag of raisins for a moment. . . .

"OKAY!" he announces, taking the raisins. I breathe a sigh of relief.

"Anyway," I say with an apologetic look at Patty Schnozzleton. "Please continue."

Patty sniffs. *"After* the ball, I got recognized for my work, and Guinevere got none of the credit. She was jealous and started spreading rumors about me. Very! Untrue! Rumors! And she turned all our friends against me, and ever since then, I've been cut off from everyone! Alone!" Patty bangs her fist on her chest like a passionate gorilla.

And speaking of monkeys, she seems *completely* bananas.

"Let me get this straight," Eliza says. "You want to

embarrass Guinevere, not hurt her. So you watch her house to see if there's an opening for one of your pranks."

Patty nods.

"Well, in all that spying, have you seen anything that can be useful to us?" I ask. "Anything suspicious?"

Patty scrunches her face up tight. She's thinking real hard. "Come to think of it," she says, lowering her voice, "Otto, her landscaper, was acting strange."

Eliza and I both make sure Otto isn't anywhere near us.

"Strange how?" Eliza prods.

"I don't know how to describe it. But it seems like he's always looking around. He likes to make sure no one's nearby. Maybe you should ask him."

"We will," I assure her. With this new lead, I'm wondering if we should search the garage. We know Otto keeps tools in the garage—if he's guilty, I wonder what else we might find in there. Or maybe we should finish interviewing Patty before we run off. . . .

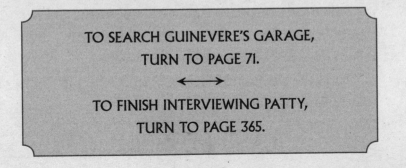

TO SEARCH GUINEVERE'S GARAGE,
TURN TO PAGE 71.

←——→

TO FINISH INTERVIEWING PATTY,
TURN TO PAGE 365.

WE WANDER AROUND the maze, but every way is a dead end, and we can't find Exit Two. We walk back and forth a gazillion times, but we're like lab rats that just can't find the cheese.

After hours of walking around, we are hungry and thirsty and my feet are aching. I lean against the wall, panting. Eliza is quietly watching me. She knows what I'm thinking . . . that we have to give up. It's been hours since Otto locked us in that closet . . . and he had such a head start on us that there's no way we'll *ever* catch up.

"I hate to say this," Eliza says, putting her hand on my arm, "but I think we made a wrong turn. We may have to call it quits—or we'll starve down here."

"I want to go hoooooome," Frank whines.

"We blew it," I say, on the verge of tears.

As you can guess: once we flop the case, Mom's career explodes . . . and not in a good way. Just to pay the bills, Mom has to take a job as an envelope licker at—weirdly enough—a company that sends out bills to other people. Poor Mom licks so many envelopes that her mouth is permanently puckered into a sour position, and her mouth is so dry from all the licking that she can't even talk to me when she gets home from work.

Or maybe she just doesn't *want* to talk to me. (Not that I blame her for that.)

CASE CLOSED.

WE SEARCH THE halls for Smythe. He's not in the destroyed library with the threat on the wall, or the living room, or the study, or the kitchen, or the dining room, or the theater room, or the ballroom, or the foyer.

Where could he be?

"I have an idea," Eliza says with a wicked grin. "Let's search his room. We might be able to find out a lot more peeking through his stuff than we'd be able to find out by talking to him. He isn't exactly the most agreeable person."

"Or," I suggest, "we could search Ivy's room. After all, she pointed a lot of fingers at everyone else. Very suspicious, right?"

TO SEARCH SMYTHE'S ROOM,
GO TO PAGE 355.

←→

TO SEARCH IVY'S ROOM,
GO TO PAGE 19.

"CAN YOU TELL us more about the treasure?"

She laughs softly. "My father *loved* talking about that treasure! He was an engineer whose first love was mathematics, and he always told me about the puzzles he set up for me. Told anyone who would listen."

"What do you think the treasure is?" Eliza says.

"Who knows? I don't know anything about it!" she says quickly.

Too quickly.

"Where do you think the treasure is?" Eliza asks.

Ivy folds her arms. "I don't know that either. In fact, you can save yourselves a whole lot of time by just assuming I know as much about the treasure as you do."

"But you have to know something!" I say.

"YEAH!" Frank says. "Do you even know your *name*?"

"Ivy," she says, looking unamused with Frank. "Listen, I haven't thought of my dad's treasure in years. And I haven't even tried to find it since long before I ran awa—" She cuts off, looking sheepish and mad at herself.

"Ran away?" I prod.

"Er . . . my mom and I had a fight."

I perk up. Could this be relevant to our case?

"Don't look so eager," Ivy says, pressing her lips

together tightly. "My mom fights with *everyone*. There isn't a person alive who wouldn't want to threaten her."

TO ASK IVY WHO SHE THINKS IS THREATENING HER MOM, TURN TO PAGE 208.

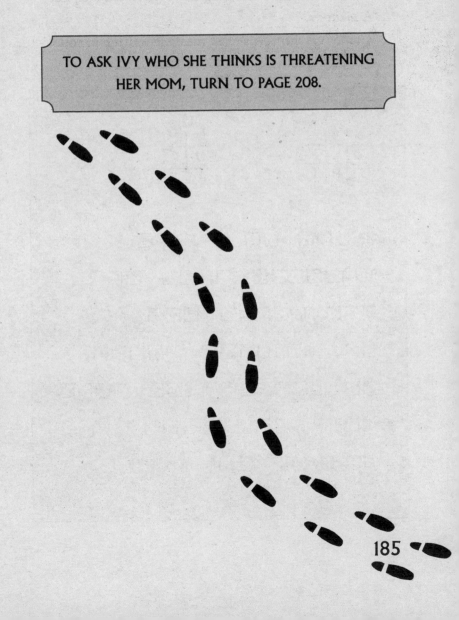

"**WHAT IN THE** world *is* this?" I ask Eliza. "It looks like nonsense to me!"

"It's not nonsense!" Eliza grins. "It's called a cipher."

"A *what*-er?"

"Cipher. SY-FER. A secret message written in code!"

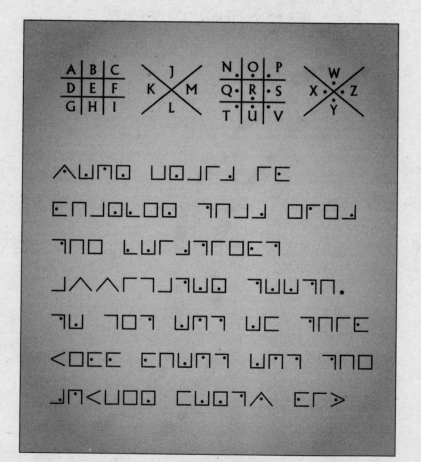

"We can solve this," Eliza mumbles, coaching herself through the puzzle. "We just have to pay attention to the lines around the letters. That's the key to the cipher."

"So the letter *A*," I interrupt. "The lines around it make a backward *L* shape. So I'll mark down *A* whenever the symbol matches that?"

"Exactly," Eliza says with a nod. "Okay, so if I look at the first word in the coded message, it's an upside-down *V* with a dot in it . . . so that first symbol stands for—"

"*Y!*" Frank shouts. "I FOUND IT FIRST! I WIN!"

"Good job, Frank," Eliza says. "Now the second symbol in the first word is an open-box shape with a dot inside it. If we look back at the key, we can see that the symbol stands for . . . an O."

I run my hand through my hair. "I never thought I would say this about a puzzle, but this is actually pretty fun. I think I got the third one. It stands for the letter *U*, right?"

Eliza hums. "And the last symbol—a box with a dot in the center—makes an *R*. So the first word is *YOUR*."

"Let's keep going!" I say eagerly.

WHEN YOU KNOW THE SOLUTION OF THE PUZZLE, ADD THREE HUNDRED AND TURN TO THAT PAGE.

I DON'T WANT Frank or Eliza to get hurt. I mean, I *must* save Mom's agency, but the most important thing is that we are all safe.

I move out of Otto's way.

He sneers and walks past us, then veers toward a dark passageway I didn't even notice.

"Wait!" Eliza says. "I wouldn't go that way if I were you."

Otto glares at her.

"I can tell you're lost," she says quickly, "or you wouldn't be in the back of this dead-end cave. Listen, the only reason we decided to get into the detective business is to save Carlos's mom's agency. They're almost bankrupt."

I flush. That was something private I told her in confidence!

"How about we strike a deal? We'll help you get out of here if you give us half the money. That will help Carlos's mom pay her bills. What do you say?"

I almost choke. What is she *doing*? We don't negotiate with criminals!

Otto snorts. "I'm not giving you half of my fortune."

Eliza smiles sweetly. "Then name a fair price."

"Ten percent."

"Forty."

"Fifteen."

"Thirty-five."

"Twenty," Otto says.

"Deal."

And they shake on it. *They actually shake on it.*

Detective agencies can't make deals with criminals for money! And if Otto gets away with this scheme, my mom's agency will never get another client again.

"Follow me," Eliza says, leading Otto back the way we just came.

I could try to stop her. Or . . . maybe I should trust her. The wrong choice could ruin my mom's case—and her life.

TO STOP ELIZA, TURN TO PAGE 115.

←—→

TO FOLLOW ELIZA, TURN TO PAGE 326.

WE RUN OUTSIDE, where Guinevere, Ivy, and Smythe are sitting in lawn chairs, snickering about Patty's arrest.

"Ooooo hooooo!" hoots Guinevere. "Did you see Patty's face?"

"Classic, ma'am," says Smythe gruffly. As though he is forced to agree with his employer.

I run up to Guinevere. "Where is Patty?"

"Weren't you watching? She just got carted off by the police! All thanks to you!"

Eliza and I exchange a glance.

"We were wrong," Eliza says. "It wasn't her after all. It was Otto!"

"Otto?" Guinevere scratches her head. "Now, now, detectives, I know you're probably feeling guilty at the sight of Patty's uncouth wailing, but you did a good job—"

"NO!" Frank says, and he stamps his foot. "LISTEN."

And so we explain about getting locked in the closet, what Otto had told us, and how we escaped. "We need to go after him," I finish. "Now!"

"We came to ask—do either of you know how to get to the treasure? Just a clue. Anything helps," Eliza says.

"I told you everything I know," Guinevere says.

"I know nothing," Smythe grunts.

Ivy blanches. She looks like she's about to cough up a

drumstick. "Okay, fine!" she says. "I can get you in . . . but I won't be able to go with you."

Eliza turns to Guinevere with a very serious frown. "Can you and Smythe call the police while Ivy helps us out?"

Guinevere nods fearfully. Her eyes are as big and watery as the glittering diamonds on her fingers.

"This way!" Ivy says, and we follow as she leads us to her room. "Dad always said that there's no better hiding spot than the back of your closet. It never really meant anything to me growing up, but when I was a teenager, I found a small door in the back, behind all the clothes. I think it's a way in. I wanted to go myself, but by the time I found it, I was too big to fit."

We crawl to the door, open it, and peer inside. There's a slide that twists all the way down like a bendy straw. But I can't see where the slide ends.

Here goes nothing . . . well, not nothing, since my mom's whole life, her happiness, and her career are on the line. So I guess I should say: here goes *everything*.

Before I chicken out, I jump in.

"AHHHHHHHHHHHHHHH!" I shout.

"AHHHHHHHHHHHHHHH!" Eliza yells.

"MOMMYYYYYYYYYYYY!" Frank cries.

Faster and faster and faster and *BOOM*.

We land in a ball pit. Me first. Then Eliza smacks into me. Then Frank topples onto both of us.

"Yay!" he says. "Let's do it again!"

"Let's not," Eliza says, swimming over to the edge of the ball pit. The pit is surrounded by solid-earth walls on three sides, so there's only one way out.

I follow Eliza. We spill onto a dirt path that twists around like an S, leading right up to a thick wooden door. There's no way around the door—and no way back unless we want to climb up the slide. To keep going, we have to go through.

As I move closer to the door I notice doodles carved into the door.

TUNE
TUNE
TUNE
TUNE

TO THE

I stare at the pictures for a moment, then I open the door, just to see what's inside.

Inside, there's a dimly lit hallway that branches off into two trails. The paths are both cobblestone and identical—just veering off in opposite directions. We can take the left path or the right path.

I close the door and look at the clues again.

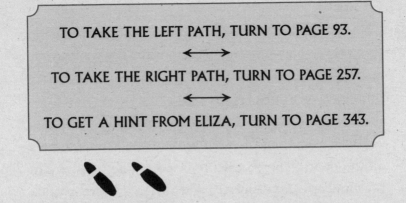

TO TAKE THE LEFT PATH, TURN TO PAGE 93.

TO TAKE THE RIGHT PATH, TURN TO PAGE 257.

TO GET A HINT FROM ELIZA, TURN TO PAGE 343.

193

THE SUN'S STARTING to set, and I know we should probably go home for the night, but I really want to spy on Smythe more, and I need my shoes. A few more minutes won't hurt, right?

"Come on," I hiss. "Let's go around back."

Eliza, Frank, and I crawl around the house and try all the doors. There's the big wooden one with a rainbow unicorn carved into it. Then there's a screen door. Beneath some bushes, there's a cellar door. Last we try a sliding door.

Unfortunately, they're all locked.

Maybe we can get in through a window. The first-floor windows are too high for any of us to reach on our own.

"Frank," I whisper. "I'm going to give you a boost. You have to open the window and pull yourself in. Then you can open a back door for us."

"Okay!" Frank says.

I grab him around the waist and pick him up. He squirms like a wormy fidget bug, and he's slipping from my grip—

"Look out!" Eliza cries.

Frank tumbles on top of me.

"Are you hurt?" Eliza whispers, checking her brother for scrapes.

"I'm SUPER FRANK!" he says, jumping to his feet.

194

I lift him again, and he's still as wiggly as a twisty straw, but he eventually grabs the windowsill.

"Now you have to push up on my butt! *Butt.*" He snickers.

I push up on his butt . . . then his legs . . . then his shoes until he's half inside.

"EEEEEEEEEEEEEEEEEEEEKKKKK!!!!!" comes a shriek from inside. "BURGLARS!!!! MURDERERS!!!!! SNEAKS IN THE NIGHT!!!!!!!! CALL THE POLICE, SMYTHE!!!"

Then comes an enormous *thump.*

Which—as we find out later when the ambulance arrives—is the sound of Guinevere LeCavalier having a heart attack and dropping dead on the dining-room floor.

CASE CLOSED.

THE SECOND I'M positive Otto is gone, I slump against the closet door and groan. "I ruined everything. Mom is going to kill me. We can't aff—" I choke back the words. I still haven't told Eliza about our money problems. I know I have to tell her the truth, but I can't.

"It's okay, Carlos. We'll figure it out."

"Figure it out how?" I yell. "We're locked in a tiny closet in an enormous mansion, and nobody knows to look for us. Otto could escape, and time is running out." I think of Mom, and I start to get choked up.

"Carlos?" Frank says, poking me in the side. "Are you crying?"

"Want to tell me what's going on?" Eliza finally says. "Why did we take this case? Why are we really here?"

Every time I think about telling her, the words fizzle out in my throat.

"We're in a lot of danger, Carlos," she says. "I have to know it's for a good reason."

"Mom," I say. "She isn't . . . we aren't . . ." Eliza grabs my hand, and it steadies me. I take a deep breath. "Mom's last case went belly-up. And she hasn't been able to get work for a while. Six months. If Mom loses this case, her career is over. We'll lose everything: her job, the house, the car. I'm trying to save her . . . and myself, too."

"Why didn't you tell me earlier?"

"I don't know," I say, except I do know. I could only admit this in the dark. Just imagining her face, full of

196

pity, makes me flush with shame. "I guess," I finally say, "I didn't want you to look down on me."

"Look down on you?" Eliza says. "I could never!" She pauses before saying firmly, "Real friends don't care about that stuff."

For the first time in weeks, I feel like I can breathe again. I had no idea how hard it was to keep a secret like that—and how much worry I was carrying on my shoulders.

"And this is not the end," she says. "I've thought of two possible ways out of this closet. We can bang on the door and hope someone comes to rescue us. Or we can look for a vent."

"A vent?"

"Frank can crawl through it, get to another room, then unlock this door from the outside."

Frank begins to cheer. "HOORAY! I LOVE CRAWLING!"

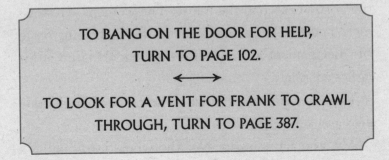

TO BANG ON THE DOOR FOR HELP,
TURN TO PAGE 102.

←——→

TO LOOK FOR A VENT FOR FRANK TO CRAWL
THROUGH, TURN TO PAGE 387.

I ADD UP the numbers in the octagon, with Eliza checking my work, of course, and I get ninety-eight. And so I punch in the number on the box's buttons, and it opens up with a click.

Inside is not at all what I expected. I thought there'd be treasure, like gold or silver or diamonds. But there are just old photographs that are faded and brownish. There's a picture of Mr. and Mrs. LeCavalier holding a baby. There's one of their wedding. A whole bunch of Ivy at different ages.

And at the very bottom of the box, there's a picture that's turned around. Facedown. On the back it says: *Winston, Alaina, and Preston (age 10).*

"Preston!" I say excitedly. We can finally put a face to the name.

I turn the picture around. It's weird to look at a picture of Preston when he was my age, knowing that he's now in his thirties or forties. In the picture, Mr. LeCavalier is in the middle—I recognize him immediately from all the portraits around the house. The woman—Preston's mom and Mr. LeCavalier's first wife—is holding on to Mr. LeCavalier's arm, and Preston is looking up at his father adoringly.

I squint at Preston. He has blond hair and bright blue eyes and a dimpled chin. . . .

My stomach plunges. No, the whole *world* plunges

198

out from under me. I accidentally drop the picture.

My heart is thrumming. It's all making sense—it's all coming together. There's only one suspect I know with blond hair, bright blue eyes, and a butt chin.

"It's Otto!"

"What?" Eliza says. She and Frank both dive for the picture at the same time and knock heads. "Oooooowwww!" they groan.

"Preston . . . is Otto! Otto is Preston! They're the same person. *The same person.*"

"NO WAY!" marvels Frank. "Wait, what does that mean?"

Eliza picks up the picture and stares at it for a second. Then she looks up at me, her eyes twinkling. "He *would* have known about the treasure if he was Mr. LeCavalier's son!" she says. "And he would have hated Guinevere LeCavalier for breaking up his family—"

"He has access to the house," I say. "He has free rein of the garage to store his tools!"

"He always is asking us about the case," Eliza recalls. "Always wanting to know how much we know."

"What a *meanie*!" says Frank.

"We have to get out of this room," I say, suddenly feeling more claustrophobic and panicked than ever. "As long as we're locked in here, no one else knows! We have to stop him!"

Suddenly there's a rattling noise and the sound of rushing air. And a voice—Otto's voice—coming through the vent, saying, "You shouldn't have taken this case. Good-bye, little detectives."

The sound of Otto's voice coming through the vent gives me shivers.

"Otto!" I shout. "Preston!"

"Get us out of here!" Eliza cries.

"OLLY OLLY OXEN FREE!" Frank hollers. "NO, WAIT! OTTO OTTO OXEN FREE!"

But it's no use. Otto doesn't say anything, and I have a bad feeling that he's no longer on the other side of the air vent.

But, well, if he knows *we* know he's guilty, then I'm really afraid of what he'll do. Because there's no way he'll just let us tell Guinevere.

I have to stay calm . . . like Mom would be. Stay calm . . . think this through . . . don't panic. But I can't get my body to listen to me. I am getting really hot and sweaty. My shirt is soaked through, and I feel almost lightheaded.

Eliza sits down on the desk, and she's panting something fierce. Frank has shed both his shirt and shorts—he's down to just his boxers.

"Why?" I wheeze, pointing at Frank.

"I'm sweatyyyyyy," he whines. "And hot."

Eliza picks up a letter and fans herself. "I'm exhausted. Quick nap," she says with a yawn.

I yawn too.

My eyes start to shut. . . .

"WAIT!" I shout. "This room! It's getting hotter and hotter by the second! Otto's turned the heat on!"

"He's smoking us out . . . literally!" Eliza gasps.

"I'm thirsty," Frank complains.

"That's the point, Frank!" Eliza says. "Otto wants us to get dehydrated so we pass out. Then he can . . . er . . . get rid of us."

I gulp, and I don't want to know what "get rid of us" even means.

"We have to get out of here!" I say. My shirt is sticking to my back.

We begin searching again—this time, for another exit, or something to help us get out of the room. For a second, I think about having Frank crawl through the air vent to get help, but then I remember that the hot air is coming *from* the vent. There's no way I can send Frank in there.

The panic is rising in my throat. This room is so small—we're going to burn up in no time! We have to get out of here.

I climb onto the desk and reach up to the ceiling, feeling around for anything that will help. Nothing—just

201

old peeling wallpaper. I can barely breathe, and I sway on the spot. I'm going to faint.

I reach out to the wall for support, and my palms smack against a piece of the wall that feels different than the rest. "Help!" I shout to Eliza. My tongue feels weird . . . like it's a useless worm lolling in my mouth.

Eliza climbs onto the desk with me. Only, when I look at her, it's not Eliza—it's Frank!

"Frank to the rescue!" he croaks.

I try to lift him up, but he's so sweaty that he's slippery.

"Pyramid!" Eliza pants. "Carlos! Get down!"

I know exactly what she means. I get down on the desk on my hands and knees, and Frank uses my back like a stepladder. He starts knocking on the wall, banging on it like crazy. And I'm one second away from yelling at him to get serious, when he hits a hollow part and—*POP!* It opens like a mailbox flap.

Frank hops off me, and I stand up to look at Frank's handiwork. Inside this piece of wall is a thermostat . . . an old-fashioned one, with buttons instead of a screen.

I start pressing the down button, but nothing happens. Then I press a whole bunch of random buttons, but nothing happens when I do that either.

I start to sweat even more.

"What's wrong?" Eliza calls from the floor.

"The buttons on the thermostat aren't working!" I gasp. "But they're flashing when I press them, so I know it's on."

"Otto probably tampered with the wiring!" Eliza says. "Open up the back of the thermostat!"

I do what she says, and there's a whole bunch of tangled wires.

"Eliza! Help!" I say. "There are three wires, but they're all tangled!"

"Just keep calm," she says. "Unplug the wire that hooks up to the air vent. But be careful not to unplug the wrong wire—we don't know *what* those other wires might be connected to. One wrong move, and . . ."

"KABOOM!" says Frank.

I gulp.

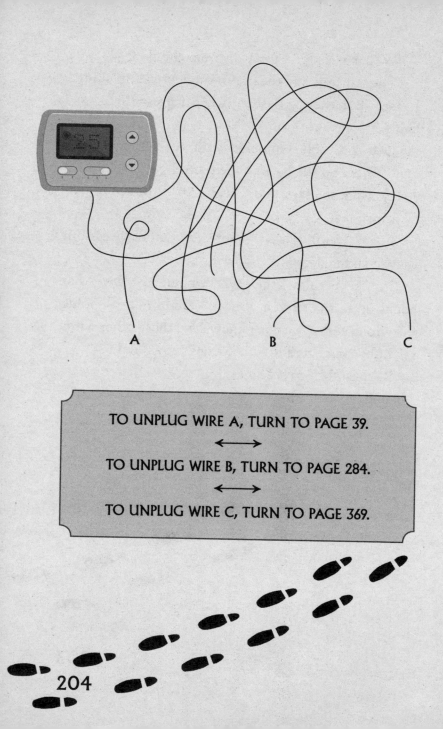

TO UNPLUG WIRE A, TURN TO PAGE 39.

←→

TO UNPLUG WIRE B, TURN TO PAGE 284.

←→

TO UNPLUG WIRE C, TURN TO PAGE 369.

WE MUST FACE Smythe sooner or later. I pick sooner.

The whole room shakes as Smythe comes lumbering toward us.

"You kids!" pants Smythe as he steps into the room. "Are in . . . so much . . . trouble . . ."

Frank moves so close to me, he's practically a leech on my side. And Eliza cowers.

Smythe's jowls wobble as he stomps even closer to us; beads of sweat drip down his face.

"Please!" I say. "We just want to solve the case! Don't you want that too?"

"Obviously he wants that," Eliza says, folding her arms. "Because otherwise he'd be the perpetrator."

"The POOPINATOR?" says Frank.

"No, the *perpetrator*! It means the culprit!"

"The armpit?"

"The criminal, Frank!" Eliza sighs. "It means criminal. If he doesn't want to help us, then he's against us. And if he's against us, then he's probably the one behind the threats."

"Maybe I don't want to help you because I don't believe you *can* help," Smythe says. "I don't know why Guinevere brought kids in to deal with an adult matter."

"Because people underestimate kids," I say, my voice steely. "And you wouldn't believe some of the information we've found out."

"Like?" Smythe says.

"Like we can't tell you."

"NAH-NAH-NAH-NAH BOO-BOO!" Frank adds. Smythe rolls his eyes.

"How about you try helping us?" I say. "Because we're solving this case with or without your help."

Smythe glares at me, and his eyes get all thin and slitlike. The longer Smythe stares at me, the twistier my stomach gets. But I just frown back at him. It's like a staring contest. Don't blink! Don't blink! Don't blink!

Smythe blinks. "Fine," he says. "Ask me a question, and I'll answer this time. For real."

There's a lot I could ask Smythe about—like why he's been so angry and sulky with Guinevere LeCavalier—but if he's finally being cooperative, I don't want to offend him. I know from experience that he can be . . . touchy. And something I *am* very curious about is the death threat that appeared last night—the one that drove Guinevere and Ivy from the house.

But on the other hand, if the threats are getting scary enough to force Guinevere to leave, then maybe I should skip questioning Smythe and go straight to investigating. After all, we may not have much time left to figure out who's behind all this! Seems like the criminal is moving in!

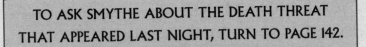

TO ASK SMYTHE ABOUT THE DEATH THREAT
THAT APPEARED LAST NIGHT, TURN TO PAGE 142.

←——————→

TO ASK SMYTHE WHERE TO LOOK TO
INVESTIGATE NEXT, TURN TO PAGE 337.

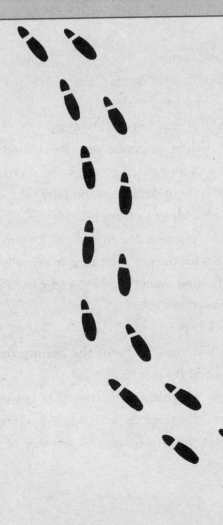

"YOUR MOM MAKES a lot of enemies," I begin. "So who do *you* think is threatening her?"

Ivy shrugs. "It could be anybody."

"Well, if you had to make a guess," Eliza prompts.

"I suppose our butler, Smythe, has been acting rather suspiciously. He could easily be terrorizing my mother from the inside."

I nod. That makes sense.

"But Maddock is a proven liar. Six years ago, my mom was getting sued for slander—"

"WHAT'S LANDERS?" Frank shouts.

"It's . . . er . . . when someone says something bad and untrue about someone else," Ivy says. "Mom spread a rumor about Patty Schnozzleton, the lady who lives across the street and Mom's ex-friend. Mom said that every day Patty ate puppies for breakfast, kittens for lunch, and hamsters for dinner. The rumor actually got around with many high-society types, and poor Patty was the butt of everyone's joke."

"*Butt.*" Frank snickers.

"Someone was watching us from the Schnozzleton house yesterday," I tell Ivy.

"If someone was watching you from that house, it was Patty," Ivy says. "She lives alone. And she's obsessed with getting revenge on my mom. Yet *another* of my mom's enemies."

Frank slinks off the couch, crawls across the floor, and stops when he gets to the fireplace. Then he starts building a pyramid—one log on top of the other.

"Wait!" Eliza says. "I'm confused. What does any of this information about Patty have to do with Maddock? You said *Maddock* was the liar."

"Right. Patty was trying to sue my mother over those nasty rumors, and Maddock submitted falsified billing records."

I scratch my head. "Er, can you explain that . . . for Frank?" I don't want to admit that I have no idea what she's talking about.

Frank blinks at Ivy, and she talks slowly at him. "Maddock told my parents he worked more hours on their case than he did. Which means Maddock got paid for hours he didn't work. He lied to steal money from them."

"What?" I say. In my head, warning signals are flaring! Maddock is a crook! A thief! A criminal! If he could cheat Guinevere out of money, surely he could threaten her too, right?

Eliza can't hide her shock either—her eyebrows are so far up her forehead, they're practically part of her hair. "What did your parents do when they found out?"

"They didn't even fire him," Ivy says with a bitter

laugh. "I wonder if Maddock is weaseling more money out of my mom now, by setting up these threats and hunting after our family treasure. Wouldn't be the *first* time he's intruded in my family's affairs."

"What does that mean?" I ask.

"Only that he was very opinionated when my mom and I were having a . . . disagreement. And his two cents did *not* belong in our business. It was a matter that was between family—and should have *stayed* in my family," she says.

"So, just to make sure I understand this right," Eliza says, "you think Maddock is suspicious because he lied and stole money from your family in the past. Patty might have done it because she's obsessed with getting revenge on your mom. And Smythe seems to be miserable for some unknown reason—and he has access to the house. Do I have that right?"

Ivy nods vigorously.

Eliza looks at me like she's waiting for me to finish the conversation, so we can get back to investigating someone else. But I'm actually wondering about this mysterious fight between Ivy and her mom. Could Ivy be pointing the finger at these other people because they're guilty? Or because *she's* guilty?

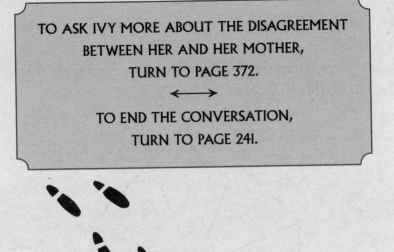

TO ASK IVY MORE ABOUT THE DISAGREEMENT
BETWEEN HER AND HER MOTHER,
TURN TO PAGE 372.

←→

TO END THE CONVERSATION,
TURN TO PAGE 241.

211

"OH NO!" I groan. "I don't understand math with letters!"

Eliza brings the flashlight closer to the puzzle. "We can do this. Together."

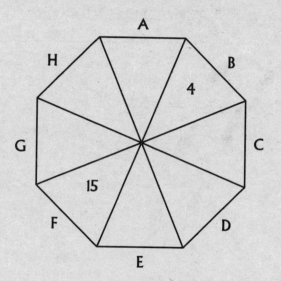

A plus A equals B.
F divided by 3 is C.
C times A is D.
D times A is G.
H minus G equals D.
B plus B plus B equals E.

"All right, Eliza," she mutters to herself, talking out her puzzle again. "Put your thinking cap on. B is four. And F is fifteen."

"Yeah," I say, "but that's *all* we know. How are we supposed to figure out the others?"

Eliza points to the reminders. "Our clues are right here. And the first one is that A plus A equals B. So double A, and we get B. Since we already know that B is four, what can we double to make four?"

"Even *I* know that!" Frank boasts. "It's SEVENTEEN GAZILLION!"

I snicker. "It's two," I say.

Eliza fills in the number two.

"And if F divided by three is C," she mumbles. "Then C is—"

"Five!" I say.

Eliza nods and writes a five in the C wedge. "C times A is D. Which means two times five is—"

"ONE THOUSAND!" Frank shouts.

"Ten," I say over him.

Eliza smiles. "Carlos, you're crushing this one! You don't even need me."

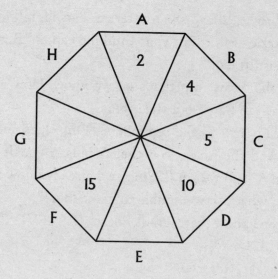

REMINDER

A plus A equals B.
F divided by 3 is C.
C times A is D.
D times A is G.
H minus G equals D.
B plus B plus B equals E.

ADD UP A, B, C, D, E, F, G, AND H. ADD ONE
HUNDRED AND TURN TO THAT PAGE.

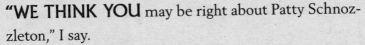

"WE THINK YOU may be right about Patty Schnozzleton," I say.

Eliza nods. "We found red paint in her house. The same red paint that was used for the death threat in the library."

"Not to mention," I add, "Patty admitted she wants revenge on you."

Guinevere grins, nice and wide. *"Smythe!"* she says gleefully. "Call the police! After all these years, I finally got her! *I finally got her!"*

As Smythe runs into the kitchen to call the police, Eliza and I high-five.

"Let's go watch the police pull up to her house," I say.

Guinevere says she, Ivy, Smythe, and Maddock will meet us outside in a moment. But Eliza and I don't wait. We sit on the porch, but Frank is especially antsy, so he rolls around in the driveway, wrestling with an imaginary monster.

Our view is blocked as Otto drives by on his lawn mower, which seems ridiculous because the grass is already short. "Hi there, kids," Otto says, stopping the mower's engine. "What are you looking at?"

"We're waiting for the police."

Otto stiffens. "Oh . . . I didn't realize you'd solved the case. . . ."

"It was Patty Schnozzleton," I say.

Otto combs a hand through his smooth blond hair.

"Patty! Well! Who would've thought? Well, I'll see you later!"

Eliza squints. I know that face—she sees something important.

"His lawn mower," she says quietly.

I look at the mower. It's all perfectly green . . . except for a little splash of red by the ignition. It looks like a red handprint that dried on the vehicle. But why would Otto's hand have been red? Unless . . .

Eliza gasps. "*You* painted the second death threat! Then you touched your lawn mower, and the paint dried. We've caught you red-handed!"

Otto shakes his head. "I—I don't know what you're talking about!"

"Why didn't I see it before?" Eliza says, getting to her feet. "You probably landscape everyone's lawn in this neighborhood, so you have easy access to everyone's property. You kept the paint at Patty's house so you wouldn't get caught with it—or so you could frame her. And you snuck into Guinevere's house to leave her death threats."

"That's why you're always asking us about the case!" I say. "You want to make sure we hadn't caught on to *you* yet!"

"You're crazy," he says with a laugh. "You kids are *crazy*."

"All the evidence points to you," Eliza says. "The

only thing I can't understand is . . . how do you even know about the treasure in the first place?"

The police pull up and stop in front of Patty's house. I *have* to tell Guinevere they're about to arrest the wrong person. I run into the house, and Eliza follows.

"Mrs. LeCavalier!" I shriek.

"Mrs. LeCavalier!" Eliza hollers.

"Oh no you don't!" says Otto from the front entrance.

Eliza and I run around the shattered chandelier glass, and Otto chases us. I'm screaming and screaming and screaming. My lungs are sore. I turn around—Otto is getting closer.

"MRS. LECAVALIER!"

"Oh no!" Eliza cries, pointing out the window. Guinevere is sitting on the lawn with Ivy, Smythe, Maddock, and a bucket of popcorn. She's pointing at Patty and laughing as poor Patty is being dragged out of her house in handcuffs.

Mrs. LeCavalier, Ivy, Smythe, and Maddock must have gone out the side door.

THUMP.

A heavy footstep at the end of our hallway.

I run. Eliza runs. We run, run, run.

We are in a house alone with the culprit.

And he is *fast*. His footsteps sound closer and closer and—

WHACK.

My head explodes with a sharp pain.

My vision goes fuzzy.

Then dark.

"Carlos, wake up!" whispers Eliza, her voice trembling. She pets my hair like I'm a cat.

I groan.

"Oh, thank goodness!" she says, hugging me. "You're okay!"

"Frank?" I croak.

"Here!" Frank says, like I'm taking attendance or something.

"He got Frank too. Even though Frank didn't know anything."

"He got me with candy," Frank says. "Or he PROM-ISED me candy. But so far, I see no candy, Mr. Meanie."

I open my eyes. Wherever we are, it's dark. I can barely see anything. I reach around the ground, just to try to get my bearings, and the only thing I can feel are lots of shoes.

"Where are we?" I ask.

"A closet in Guinevere's house."

"Can we scream for help?"

"Frank and I tried that," Eliza says. "No response."

I try to sit up, but I still feel dizzy. "Can we call for Otto? Maybe he can hear us."

218

A voice, cold and cutting, comes from the other side of the door. "I can hear you."

"Are you going to keep us here forever?"

Otto laughs. I don't know why I didn't notice it before, but he has a really nasty laugh. "I'm sure someone will find you in a year. After you starve to death."

Eliza grips my hand.

"But what if I have to pee?" Frank demands.

I want to laugh and cry . . . and give Frank a hug. Clearly he has no idea how much trouble we're in.

"Will you answer our questions?" I ask.

A pause. "I don't see how it will hurt," Otto says. "Just a few. Then I have to go collect my treasure."

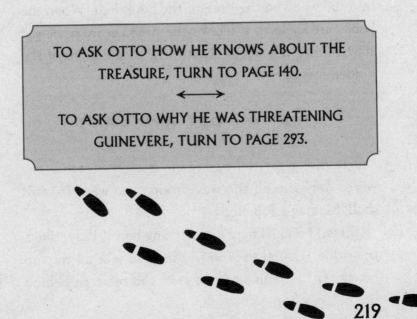

TO ASK OTTO HOW HE KNOWS ABOUT THE
TREASURE, TURN TO PAGE 140.

←——→

TO ASK OTTO WHY HE WAS THREATENING
GUINEVERE, TURN TO PAGE 293.

I GO FIRST on the bookshelf ladder, and Frank follows me.

"UP, UP, UP!" he barks. "WALK THE PLANK, YOU . . . YOU JELLYFISH FACE!" Then he laughs hysterically.

"Do you see anything up there, Carlos?" Eliza calls from the bottom rung.

Not yet.

In the movies, sometimes if you tug on a book, it opens up a secret passageway. So I start pulling all the books off the shelf and throwing them down on the floor.

And that's when I see something: marks carved into the wood on the back of the bookshelf. When the books are shelved, it blocks the message from view. I start pulling out books frantically, to see more of the hidden message.

STUDY IS LOST AND CAN'T

I think—since the bookshelf is circular—that the words might go all the way around the whole room's shelf. Making a full circle.

"Eliza! Frank! There's something here!" I say. "Push the ladder around the room! I have to take all the top books off the shelf so I can read the message behind them!"

Eliza and Frank slowly move the ladder—with me holding on for dear life—around the room, and I fling the books off the top shelves to reveal the words carved into the back of the circular bookshelf. When I'm done, there's a poem that loops around the whole room.

AROUND AND AROUND AND UPSIDE DOWN, MY STUDY IS LOST AND CAN'T BE FOUND. BUT WITH A LOOK AT MISPLACED BOOKS, UNSCRAMBLE THE FIRST AND HEAD INBOUND.

When I finish reading, I scratch my head. What does that even mean?

"Eliza?" I say.

She scrunches her eyebrows and bites her lip—her thinking face.

"Upside down? Misplaced books? Oh!" she gasps. "The books I was rearranging! They were upside down for a reason!"

My stomach drops. "Oh no! Did you ruin our chances at solving this puzzle?"

"Don't worry—I remember which ones were upside down."

She runs to the bookshelf and unorganizes the bookshelf again. Meanwhile, I crawl down the ladder so that I can get a good look at the books, too.

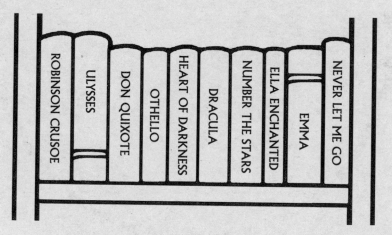

Frank moves to pull one of the books off the shelf, but Eliza catches his hand.

"Look with your eyes, Frank!"

"Awww," Frank complains. "I like looking with my hands."

Eliza nods toward the books, then turns to me with a dazzling grin. "I think I get it."

"You do?" I say. "Because I'm totally lost." I'm more lost now than I am in math class—and that's saying something.

"'With a look at misplaced books, unscramble the first,'" she recites.

"Uh-huh . . . ," I say. Honestly, all I hear is *blah blah blahbity blah*.

Eliza hums. "The first . . ."

"The first *what*?"

"Yeah!" Frank echoes. "The FIRST WHAT?"

"It has to be the first letter of each book title," Eliza says. "The first word wouldn't make any sense, so it must be the first letter of each book that was upside down. *That's* the answer to this puzzle!"

I pull out a piece of paper and get to work.

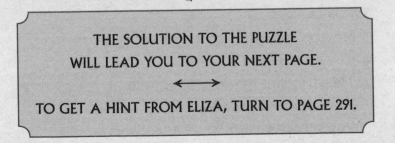

THE SOLUTION TO THE PUZZLE
WILL LEAD YOU TO YOUR NEXT PAGE.

←——→

TO GET A HINT FROM ELIZA, TURN TO PAGE 291.

AFTER THINKING IT over, I realize that Eliza might be right about investigating the past.

We arrive at Guinevere's house very early, only this time it's eerily quiet. Patty Schnozzleton isn't staring at us from her window, and Otto is nowhere to be found on the lawn. And when we ring the doorbell, it takes Smythe ten minutes to get us.

"Mmmmf," he grunts. We strut forward, but Smythe blocks us from entering the house with his legs like tree trunks. "You can't come inside right now," he says. "The missus and miss are not home."

I check my watch—it's *crazy* early! Like, butt crack of dawn early! That's really weird. "If they're not home, where are they?"

Smythe squints. "They checked into a hotel late last night, after a death threat appeared."

My heart starts pounding.

"A-another one?" Eliza squeaks.

"I can't let you in here."

"CAN'T?" Frank says, putting his hands on his hips. "OR WON'T?"

Smythe considers for a moment. "You're right. I *won't* let you in here."

Then he slams the door in our faces.

"Now what?" Eliza says.

"A good detective never gives up!" I say.

"TO THE BATMOBILE!" cries Frank, and he runs down the steps. I grab him around his middle and lift him up, but he keeps pedaling his legs, even though he isn't moving.

"No Batmobile, buddy," I say.

As far as I can see it, we only have one option if we're going to continue the case.

We have to break in.

Breaking and entering is a crime . . . which goes against Las Pistas Detective Agency's code of honor, but drastic times call for drastic measures. We can't let Mom down. A third death threat, and I am getting desperate to end this mystery.

We circle around to the backyard. Way far back, near a line of trees, there's a toolshed and a small garden of vegetables and flowers. Lining the house are tall hedges in the shapes of teacups, big enough for me to sit in. Guinevere really likes her leafy water.

"Quick! Behind the hedges!" Eliza says.

She and I run behind the hedges, but Frank crawls on his stomach, slithering along like a snake. At first it's kind of funny, but after two minutes, it's annoying. After five minutes, I'm fuming.

"Come! On!" I whisper-yell at him.

"I'm an international super-secret agent ninja spy

detective zombie wizard," he says. "That's what I want to be when I grow up!"

"We don't have time for this! We have to solve this case *now*! The clock is ticking!"

Eliza studies me. "Carlos. We're on the case. It's going to be oka—"

"It's not!" I say, feeling myself flush from the pressure. I think about Mom, her agency, our broken-down house, our non–air conditioner, and I want to *burst*. But it's all a secret, and it's eating up my stomach. "It's not okay, Eliza. This is all just a big game to Frank! And a puzzle to you! But it's *real* to me!"

I run forward, grab Frank by the ankles, and start dragging him to the house.

"Come on, Frank!"

"Noooooooooooooooooooo! Get off me!"

"You're hurting him, Carlos! Let go!"

Frank claws at the grass, curling his fingers around clumps, but I keep tugging him forward.

Then he starts to cry and kick his legs. A full-on meltdown.

"Carlos, what is *wrong* with you?" Eliza says, running to her brother's side. I drop Frank's ankles, horrified, and she sweeps him up in her arms.

I can't even look at him. "I am so sorry, buddy. I didn't mean to hurt you. I just . . . I'm letting the pressure get to me."

226

"What pressure?" Eliza says.

I look down. "I'm just nervous . . . about my mom." I've kept this secret from her for so long, I just can't tell her. "But that's no excuse to be mean to Frank. Can you forgive me, Frank?"

"If you buy me a cookie," Frank says.

"Of course."

"Ten cookies."

"Sure."

"A hundred cookies!"

"Okay."

"A HUNDRED MILLION COOKIES!"

Eliza frowns. "What do you mean you're nervous about your mom? What does that have to do with us right now?"

I press my lips together tightly.

"Carlos . . ."

"We're having money problems," I say as quietly as I can. "The last case Mom had was six months ago, and it was a complete failure. It ruined her business. This case is *it*. The last straw—it determines whether Mom remains a detective or we go bankrupt. We might have to move in with my abuela." My whole throat feels wobbly, and I can't say anything.

"I didn't know about your mom's last case," Eliza says. "Why didn't you tell me?"

I can't look at her. I shrug as I stare down at my shoes.

227

"Carlos, we're best friends. I'm supposed to be here for you, but it's hard to do that if you don't tell me what's going on," Eliza says gently. "Best friends never keep secrets from each other, okay?"

"Promise," I say, swallowing the lump in my throat.

"And don't worry. We *will* solve this case for your mom."

I nod. We have to keep going for Mom. *Think of Mom!*

"Hey! I thought I told you kids to get lost!" Smythe shouts, swinging open the back door. "What are you still doing here?" He glares down at us. He is one scary dude.

I have seconds to figure out a plan, but I have two pretty good ideas. . . .

TO TRY TO RUN BETWEEN SMYTHE'S LEGS, TURN TO PAGE 21.

←——→

TO TRY TO REASON WITH SMYTHE, TURN TO PAGE 144.

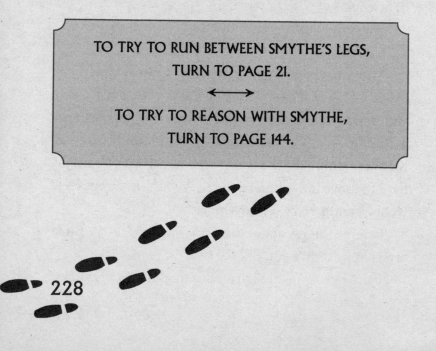

"COME ON!" I say to Eliza and Frank. "The only way we're going to get out of here is if we find a key for the door."

I start opening drawers and crawl under the desk, but I don't see any key. Eliza and Frank are rustling around behind me, and for three people who are supposed to be quiet, we sure are making a lot of noise.

"You kids okay?" says a muffled voice from the air vent.

"Please!" I shout. "Help! Come help us! We're locked in a secret room behind Mr. LeCavalier's study!"

"I know that," says the voice. And with a sudden jolt in my stomach, I realize who it is: Otto. Again! "I don't know how you shut off the air," he says, "but you can't stop *this*!"

Sssssssssssssssssssssssssss!

Through the vent, garden snakes and worms of all kinds come pouring in, flooding the room! Soon they're up to my ankles . . . then my thigh . . . then my waist. They're just getting funneled in! Like Otto has a dump truck of snakes and worms!

The pile keeps on growing. It's as high as my chest! As high as my neck! As high as my mou—*mmmmmm!*

CASE CLOSED.

MAYBE I NEED Eliza's help after all.

I hand her the phone, and she starts filling in more of the numbers, muttering to herself as she works.

"That's good!" I say, taking the phone back from her. "I can handle the rest!"

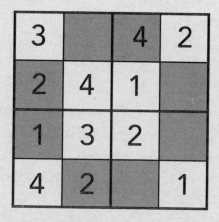

"You got this, Carlos. Just remember that every row and column has to have the numbers one, two, three, *and* four, with no repeats."

"No repeats!" repeats Frank.

WHEN YOU HAVE SOLVED THE PUZZLE,
ADD UP THE NUMBERS IN THE HIGHLIGHTED
BOXES AND MULTIPLY THE SOLUTION BY TWO.
TURN TO THAT PAGE.

I'VE COUNTED THE circles on the tapestry, like, fifteen times, and I'm pretty sure I've got the right answer. I enter thirty-one into a number pad beside the tapestry, and suddenly the wall begins to sink down into the earth with enormously loud rumbles.

Ahead, Otto has his hand on Guinevere's shoulder, and it looks threatening . . . like he's trying to keep his hand as close to her neck as possible. Their bodies are facing another puzzle on the wall ahead, but their faces are turned over their shoulders, so they can both stare at the sinking wall—the only thing that separated them and us.

Otto lifts his lantern. He squints in our direction, and when he recognizes us, his face lights up with a terrible, toothy smile.

"Ah," Otto says. "You've joined us."

I don't know why I ever thought he was friendly. His eyes are icy, and his cheeks are stone, and his teeth are sharp. He looks about as friendly as a knife.

I raise the lantern in my hands to get a better look. It's terribly dark in the next room, but I have to be brave. "Let Mrs. LeCavalier go!"

"Detectives!" Guinevere wails, snotting into her sleeve. "You found me!"

She starts to move, but Otto's arm instantly curls around her neck.

"D-don't," I say tensely. "Let her go."

I take a step forward, but Otto snarls, "Move, and you'll regret it."

My stomach drops, and my heart is beating quick and fast. What do I do? *What do I do?* Frank moves closer to me, and I know he's scared. And Eliza is unusually silent.

"Eliza?" I whisper.

She whimpers. "Whatever you do, don't look at the left wall!"

Which, of course, is the one thing to say to make Frank and me look there.

At first I don't see what she's looking at . . . and then I do: behind Otto and Guinevere, and ten feet up, there's a hole in the cave wall, where rows of bats are sleeping upside down.

"I thought you were afraid of bugs, not bats," I mutter.

"Yes, but I'm not the biggest fan of anything that can give me rabies, either."

Fair point.

"Stop whispering over there!" Otto growls. "Line up, single file. And walk slowly to me. Let's all get in this room, shall we? It'll be . . ." He grins, his teeth like bones. "A *party*."

I need some way to distract Otto. As far as I see it, I have two options: I could ask him a lot of questions, to stall and buy me some more thinking time. Or I could be bold and strong, to intimidate him. Which method is going to get me the results I want?

TO ASK OTTO QUESTIONS ABOUT HIS MOTIVES
AND STALL FOR TIME, TURN TO PAGE 382.

←——→

TO TRY TO INTIMIDATE OTTO,
TURN TO PAGE 298.

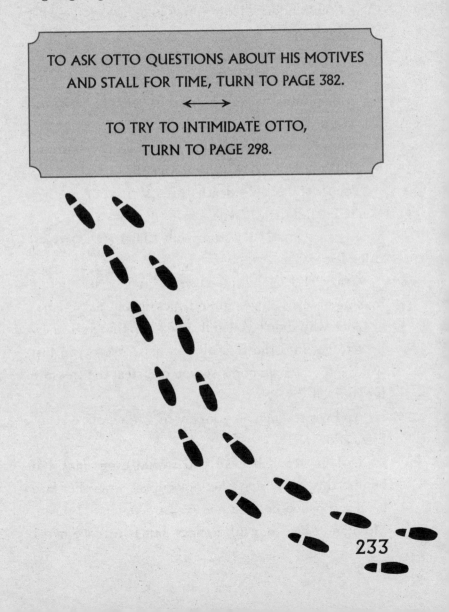

IVY IS A big fat liar, and it's time to face her!

I march up to her, and Eliza and Frank stay behind me.

"What are you kids doing in here?" She turns pinker than a cow's udder. "How—how long have you—what have you heard?"

"You need money, don't you?" I yell.

"Shhhhhhhhhh!" Ivy hushes me.

"You're dying to get your hands on that treasure," Eliza says. "You have a clear motive."

"Motive?" Ivy chokes. She twists her hair around her finger nervously. "Motive for *what*?"

"For these horrible death threats on your mother. You're behind them, aren't you?"

"I—I . . . what?" Ivy stammers. "That is the *craziest* thing I've ever heard!"

"Crazy? I'll show you crazy!" Frank cries, before making his eyes bulge out and sticking out his tongue.

"And why didn't you tell us earlier that you knew how to get into the treasure tunnels? Were you just waiting for us to go home so you can steal the treasure for yourself?"

"And get revenge on your mom while you're at it," Eliza adds.

"I—I just can't believe you would even *think* I'm behind this!" Ivy cries. She looks upset now—her face is all scrunched up, and her eyes are watery. "I mean, Mom and I have our differences, but I still love her! I would never want her dead! I just wish she would see how much I love Walter! Even though he runs a dying restaurant, and I'm just a poor artist, and we don't have two pennies to rub together! Did you know my parents wrote me out of their will? I always thought that Mom would love me and support me no matter what, even if I got into money troubles, which I . . . I . . . I have." She hiccups. Then she sits on her bed and hugs a stuffed seal to her chest.

Then Ivy says a lot more, but I can't understand her, because it sounds like a whole bunch of blubbering and wailing. Like the mating call of a beluga.

"Get out of here!" Ivy finally howls. "Just leave me alone!"

We walk out of the house and sit on the porch steps. Except Frank, who runs around on the lawn, jumping over invisible lava.

"What a liar," I say. "Did you see all those fake tears?"

Eliza rubs her chin. "I don't know what she's trying to prove. I mean, we already know that Ivy really wants the treasure—"

"Now, what's this I hear about Ivy?" Otto says, popping up from the flower bed. He's holding giant flower-clipping scissors.

Eliza and I both jump.

"Sorry! I didn't mean to frighten you," Otto says. "I

couldn't help overhearing."

Frank stops in front of Otto and puts his hands on his hips. "YOU!" he demands. "BE THE VOLCANO."

Otto stares at Frank and scratches his head.

"Noooooooooo," Frank says. "Shout BOOM!"

"Boom . . . ?" Otto says.

Frank falls to the ground and writhes around.

"What were we talking about?" I say, turning back to Otto and Eliza. "I forget."

"You were saying something about Ivy. Is she the one threatening Mrs. LeCavalier?" Otto asks.

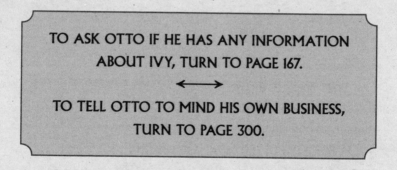

TO ASK OTTO IF HE HAS ANY INFORMATION ABOUT IVY, TURN TO PAGE 167.

←——→

TO TELL OTTO TO MIND HIS OWN BUSINESS, TURN TO PAGE 300.

I REACH INTO Eliza's backpack and grab a handful of raisins. Then I wind up for the long throw, just like in baseball practice. And *boom*! I pitch a handful of raisins straight into the bat cave. Clicking noises start echoing in the alcove, and all at once, the bats swoop out of their resting spot.

They dive at Otto and Guinevere, who shriek and put their hands up to their faces. They're both swiping bats away from their heads.

"FRANK TO THE RESCUE!" Frank shouts, and he dives into the room, grabs Guinevere by the hand, and leads her out. He leaves Otto behind to battle the bats alone.

"Frank!" Eliza scolds. "Bats have diseases! That was a very stupid thing—"

"No time!" I interrupt. The bats are flying our way. "GO!"

I dash in front, trying not to jerk the lantern too much, while at the same time running for dear life. When we reach the word ladder, I'm so relieved to see that the rungs are still there.

I usher Frank up the ladder first, since he's youngest and fastest. Then Guinevere LeCavalier, because she's the client. Then Eliza. Then me. We all climb the ladder frantically, and I even lose my grip a few times, but I quickly grab hold again and keep going up.

When we finally reach the trapdoor and scamper into the toolshed, I breathe a sigh of relief. I hear loud sirens, very close by. We hurry outside and run right into a crowd of police officers.

And at that moment—the moment we realize we're safe—Eliza and I hug each other and laugh.

Turns out, we must go to the hospital. All five of us, even Otto. (Though he's dragged there in handcuffs.)

Just in case one of the bats had rabies, we all need to get vaccinated. And rabies vaccinations are intense. We're going to have to come back *four* different times over the next month to keep getting more shots.

Later, as we're talking to the doctors, Mom, Mrs. Thompson, and Mr. Thompson burst into our hospital room, all three of them wailing.

"What were you kids thinking?" Mrs. Thompson cries.

"I'm so glad you're safe!" Mr. Thompson howls.

"You awe in so much twouble!" Mom blubbers, and then she sneezes again.

"Helloooooooo?" Guinevere says, popping her head into the room. "Did you get your lollipops, detectives?" she asks, and she doesn't even wait for an answer before handing us each one. "I just got my vaccination too."

"Sorry," I say, glancing down at my shoes. "We didn't mean for you to get hurt."

"Are you kidding?" Guinevere says. "I'm perfectly

fine! Why, I'm better than fine! That booster was practically painless. You know what they say about medicine going down!"

"A spoonful of sugar helps?" Eliza suggests.

"A spoonful!" cries Guinevere. "Who said anything about a spoonful? We need a bucketful." She snaps her fingers. "*Smythe!* The jelly beans!"

Smythe trudges into the room, carrying a bucket of jelly beans, just as grumpy as I've ever seen him.

"I need you to pick out the jelliest of jelly beans for me!" Guinevere commands. "And you've removed the blue ones?"

Smythe nods.

"Good! What a terribly *pedestrian* color!"

"Who . . . who is this woman?" Eliza's dad asks.

Ooooops. I forgot that not everyone in the room knows one another. I introduce Guinevere LeCavalier to Eliza and Frank's parents and to my mom, the *true* detective.

"Aha!" Guinevere exclaims. "Just the person I wanted to meet! We must discuss payment. . . ." She trails off for a moment as she digs into her purse. She retrieves four envelopes. "A check for Las Pistas Detective Agency. And three bonus checks for my fraudulent— but excellent—young detectives. I hope you find the payment satisfactory."

Mom, Eliza, and Frank all rip open their envelopes

and stare at the checks with dropped jaws.

I don't even open mine. "For you, Mom," I say.

Mom ruffles my hair. Then she reaches for the check, but I pull it away quickly. "With the one condition that you'll let us help out with a case again!"

Mom smiles. "How cute. Making jokes before the punishment of a lifetime."

Ah, well. That's to be expected.

But don't worry. I fully plan to change her mind.

CASE CLOSED.

I DECIDE NOT to risk upsetting Ivy. If she gets upset, we might get fired!

"Well, thanks, Ivy," I say.

"We'll be in touch," says Eliza.

"NOT!" Frank says, and he marches out of the room.

Eliza and I apologize for him, and then we follow him out.

"That was boring," Frank complains. "I don't like talking to people."

"Sorry, Frank," I say. "But that's what detectives do, sometimes. Lots of times, the suspects hold all the answers."

"It's like a puzzle," Eliza says. "Everyone is holding a little puzzle piece, and you have to collect them all before you can put together the big picture. And Frankie, once we can see the big picture, we'll solve the case!"

"Puzzles are boring! People are boring! Cases are boringgggggg!" Frank says.

"Frank," I say. "I'll give you a piece of candy if you can somersault through this hall without breaking anything."

His eyes grow wide. "OKAY!" he says, and he starts to tumble.

"Good thinking," Eliza says. "That leaves us thirty seconds to talk before he gets bored again. What do you think we should do next?"

"We should probably follow up on Ivy's suggestions, especially now that we know what a dirty, lying thief Maddock is."

"And Patty!" Eliza says. "We know more about her too. Her obsession with revenge sounds like a promising lead."

"And so far, we haven't been able to crack Smythe at all . . . but we need to figure him out—and fast!"

So many leads, so little time! The pressure of solving this case—of bailing Mom out of trouble—is starting to twist in my stomach.

"Well?" Eliza says. "What should we do?"

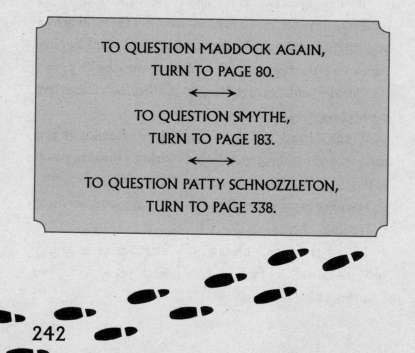

TO QUESTION MADDOCK AGAIN,
TURN TO PAGE 80.

←——→

TO QUESTION SMYTHE,
TURN TO PAGE 183.

←——→

TO QUESTION PATTY SCHNOZZLETON,
TURN TO PAGE 338.

I HAVE TO go with my gut. And my gut says, "Back off and STOP with the Preston talk!"

"We have all we need right now."

"Okay!" Guinevere says, standing up slowly. Her bracelets jangle around on her wrists. "All these death-threat shenanigans are giving me soooo much stress. I'm going to go take a bubble bath to relax myself. *Smythe!*" she shrieks. "Prepare the bubble bath! Lavender-scented bubbles! And rubber ducks!"

Guinevere leaves the room, belting out a song about rubber duckies.

Ivy lifts a cup of tea to her lips. She looks fragile and shaky—like a giraffe in high heels.

Ivy tucks a strand of her brownish-blond hair behind an ear and smiles feebly. I guess she looked a lot like Guinevere LeCavalier at first, but now I think she looks a lot plainer . . . maybe because she's wearing an ordinary T-shirt and white shorts, with no jewelry.

For a second, I try to figure out how old Ivy is. She's younger than my mom, I think. But sometimes it's hard to tell with adults. There's a whole bunch of years, in between teenager and old person, where they all look the same age to me.

"You wanted to ask me a question?" Ivy squeaks.

"Yes," I say. "If you don't mind."

Before I can ask anything, Eliza leans forward and says, "What do you know about your half brother?"

"Preston?" Ivy says, and her voice is as wobbly as a rattling teacup. "I know as much as you know. Mom and Dad never talked about him."

"Did you ever see any of his letters? Or any pictures?" Eliza says.

Ivy shakes her head. "Honestly, he's never been a part of my life. If you want information about him, I think you're barking up the wrong tree here."

"We're not barking!" Frank says. "ARF ARF!" He grins, showing off his baby teeth. "Okay, *now* we're barking."

I roll my eyes.

"Do you think Preston might possibly want your mom's treasure?" Eliza asks.

"It's hard for me to say," Ivy says. "As I've been telling you, I know literally *nothing* about Preston. But even if he did want it—or if *any* of my mom's many enemies wanted it—I think the treasure would be practically impossible to find if you're not Mom or me."

Guinevere's many enemies? Impossible-to-find treasure? I sit up on the couch. I don't even know which thread to follow—they're both full of possibility!

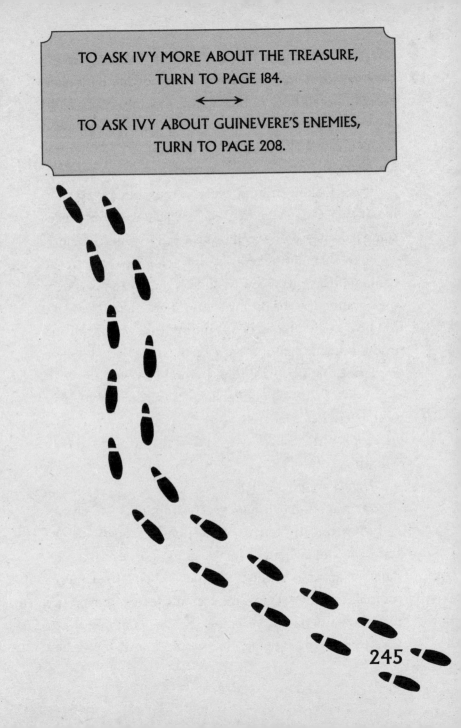

TO ASK IVY MORE ABOUT THE TREASURE,
TURN TO PAGE 184.

←→

TO ASK IVY ABOUT GUINEVERE'S ENEMIES,
TURN TO PAGE 208.

I DECIDE TO go interview Smythe. We run around the house, but Smythe is nowhere to be found. It's okay, though, because we're having fun looking. Frank and I take off our shoes and slide along the polished wood floors in our socks. Frank is pretending he's an Olympic ice skater.

Eliza's looking around every corner, but I can't stop looking *up*. Guinevere LeCavalier has some pretty awesome paintings on her ceiling that I didn't notice before.

There's a painting of a sky with fluffy clouds on the ceiling of the entranceway, there's a painting of a deer being hunted in the dining room, there's a painting of a rainbow made of jelly beans in the walk-in pantry, and in the drawing room, there's a painting of a goddess on a chariot that's being pulled by ponies. Only . . . wait a minute! That's no goddess! It's the face of a younger Guinevere LeCavalier—

"Look out!" Eliza says as I walk facefirst into a column.

"*Owwwww!*" I groan.

"Pay attention to where you're walking!" she says.

I stick out my tongue in response—and dash into the ballroom, where I start leaping and jumping and dancing around because I've never been in a bigger room in my life! Frank mimics my every move, and it's pretty fun having a shadow. Eliza is laughing at our very ungraceful dancing. She would know, too—she's

246

the only one of us who's taken dance classes.

"Whatever you do, Eliza, don't laugh!" I joke, and my voice echoes all around the ballroom. "Hey! That's cool! Helloooo!" I shout.

"Helloooo!" Frank copies.

"Helloooo!" echoes the ballroom.

"Hey, you kids!" bellows a deep, grumbly voice, and we turn to the entrance.

Smythe storms in, his head looking like a balloon about to pop.

"What are you kids doing?" Smythe demands.

Uh-oh. Just as I'm about to apologize, Eliza cuts in. "We knew if we made a loud commotion, you'd find us. You're just the person we want to talk to."

Smythe grunts.

Is Smythe even capable of smiling? I want to ask him about his sour mood . . . or is that too offensive? Maybe I should ask if he's seen anything suspicious around the house.

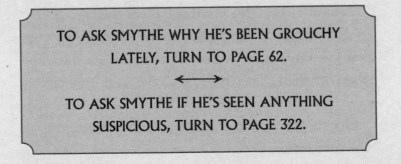

TO ASK SMYTHE WHY HE'S BEEN GROUCHY
LATELY, TURN TO PAGE 62.

←——→

TO ASK SMYTHE IF HE'S SEEN ANYTHING
SUSPICIOUS, TURN TO PAGE 322.

MY HEART TELLS me to trust my own thoughts, but my brain thinks maybe I should follow Eliza's plan. She's so smart—smarter than me—and her plan might save my mom.

I give Eliza a quick nod, and she darts into the hall. Frank and I follow.

"Mrs. LeCavalier!" she calls repeatedly as she leaps through an open area full of couches. "Mrs. LeCav—" *WUMP.*

Eliza runs straight into Guinevere and sends her flying backward. Guinevere lands on a loveseat with a bounce and curses loudly.

"Ooooooooh!" squeals Frank. "You said a *bad word*!"

Guinevere LeCavalier rolls herself off the couch, adjusts her blouse, and glares at the three of us. "What is all this racket?"

I step up. "We came to tell you about Maddock—"

"What *about* Maddock?" says a voice from the doorway. Maddock. He runs a hand through his slick black hair and smirks.

"He—it's him! He's the one!" Eliza says.

Maddock clicks his tongue sadly. "These poor children are *confused*. They've let their imagination run away with them. They have no idea what they're talking about."

Eliza points at Maddock. "He said he was trying to take your money."

248

"I said no such thing," Maddock says.

"Did too!" Eliza says.

"Did not!" says Frank.

"See? Did not!" says Maddock.

"Did too!" cries Frank.

"SILENCE!!!!!!!!!!" Guinevere hollers. The whole room hushes. "Since it's just your word against Maddock's word, there is only one logical way to decide who's telling the truth." She digs deep into her pocket and smiles. "We'll flip a coin."

Eliza's jaw drops. "That's not logical at all!"

But Guinevere isn't listening. "Heads, I believe the detectives. Tails, I go with Maddock. Fate will be our guide."

Without hesitation, she flips the coin in the air. It spins around and around like in slow motion, and I feel like I've just eaten a whole roll of quarters. How could I have left this all up to chance?

Guinevere catches the coin in her hand and opens her palm.

Tails. My stomach sinks. Eliza groans.

"I guess the universe is telling me to believe Maddock," Guinevere says. "Good-bye."

Eliza steps forward "But what about the—"

"You cannot argue with fate," Guinevere insists. "Now scram!"

I scowl. "But—"

"AHHHHHHHHHHHHHHHHHHHHHHHHH!"
Guinevere howls at the top of her lungs. She thrashes her legs and arms like a kid throwing a temper tantrum. She's even putting Frank's fits to shame.

"*AAAHHHHHHHHHHHHHHHHHHHHHHH!*"

Her screaming is so loud that it rattles around in my brain, and we run from her house, hands held over our ears.

As luck would have it, I guess I don't have any when it comes to fate-deciding coin tosses.

CASE CLOSED.

WE WAIT.

And wait.

And wait and wait and wait.

We hold our breath.

Frank squirms.

Eliza freezes.

I listen.

And after what feels like *F-O-R-E-V-E-R*, I hear the door to Ivy's room open and shut again. She's gone!

We open the closet door and spill out.

"That was close!" Eliza says. "Too close!"

"It's her! She's guilty, right?"

"GUILTY GUILTY GUILTY!" Frank sings.

Eliza hums and scrunches her brow. "I don't know. She has motive, but it doesn't necessarily mean she committed the crime." Eliza whistles low. "As far as I see it, we have two options. We could keep this information to ourselves while we investigate further."

"Or?" I say.

"Or we could tell Guinevere LeCavalier right now."

I breathe in deeply. I don't know what to do, but Mom's face pops into my head. For her sake, I hope we make the right decision!

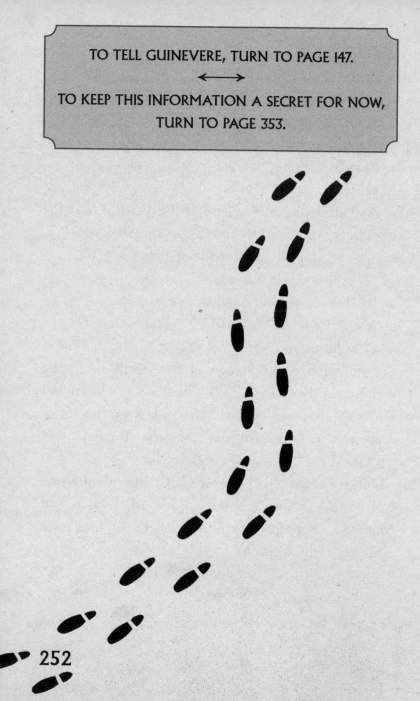

TO TELL GUINEVERE, TURN TO PAGE 147.

←——→

TO KEEP THIS INFORMATION A SECRET FOR NOW,
TURN TO PAGE 353.

"THE GREEN DOOR!" Eliza, Frank, and I say at the same time.

I look at Frank with my jaw dropped. "Did you really just solve a logic puzzle?" Maybe he's more like Eliza than I thought.

Frank grins. "No, green is my favorite color."

I snort.

"Really, though," Eliza says. "The green door works. It makes the first sentence true and all the others false. None of the other doors allow for one true statement and three false ones."

We open the green door and hop through. We follow a rickety wood-plank bridge that sways high above the alligator pit. Really high up.

"Don't look down," I say gently.

"Too late." Eliza gulps.

We walk slowly. I try to forget about the alligators below, ready to take a chomp out of us.

In front of us, the end of the bridge is in sight—

Creeeeaaaaaaaak.

The rope rustles and the wood beneath our feet groans as someone jumps onto the bridge ahead of us. Otto! He's carrying a bulky treasure chest in his arms. My heart sinks—he got to the treasure before us.

"Get out of my way, kids!" Otto growls. Then he runs toward us.

TO JUMP OUT OF THE WAY, TURN TO PAGE 331.

←→

TO BLOCK THE PATH ACROSS THE BRIDGE,
TURN TO PAGE 361.

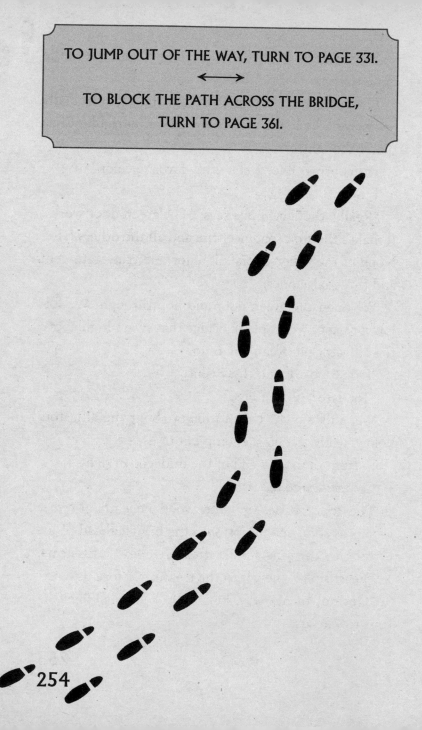

I LOOK AT the chart and scratch my head with the pencil's eraser.

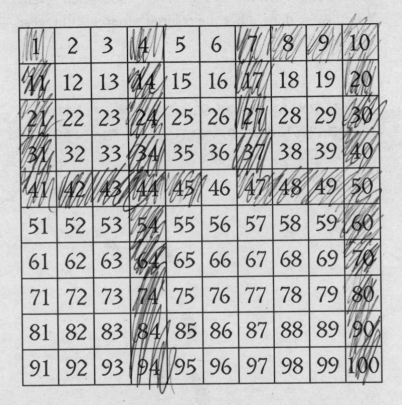

1	2	3	4	5	6	7	8	9	10
11	12	13	14	15	16	17	18	19	20
21	22	23	24	25	26	27	28	29	30
31	32	33	34	35	36	37	38	39	40
41	42	43	44	45	46	47	48	49	50
51	52	53	54	55	56	57	58	59	60
61	62	63	64	65	66	67	68	69	70
71	72	73	74	75	76	77	78	79	80
81	82	83	84	85	86	87	88	89	90
91	92	93	94	95	96	97	98	99	100

Color: 1, 4, 7, 8, 9, 10, 11, 14, 17, 20, 21, 24, 27, 30, 31, 34, 37, 40, 41, 42, 43, 44, 45, 47, 48, 49, 50, 54, 60, 64, 70, 74, 80, 84, 90, 94, 100.

"What do we do with this?" I ask.

Eliza hums and talks through the puzzle out loud.

She's always doing that. "We have to color in the squares they're telling us to color. So we should color the square marked one. Then the square marked four. Then seven. When we're done, I bet the colored squares will reveal a message."

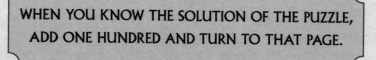

WHEN YOU KNOW THE SOLUTION OF THE PUZZLE,
ADD ONE HUNDRED AND TURN TO THAT PAGE.

"LET'S GO TO the right!" I say.

Eliza smiles. "Well, right is right."

We follow the path to the right, and we run into a dirt room with a cement engraving on the ground. Another puzzle.

The electric candles on the wall flicker dramatically as we all stand over the engraved puzzle and the bronze plaque right next to it.

> **DEAREST IVY,**
> **REMEMBER TO THINK OUTSIDE**
> **THE BOX. NOW, HOW MANY**
> **RECTANGLES DO YOU SEE?**

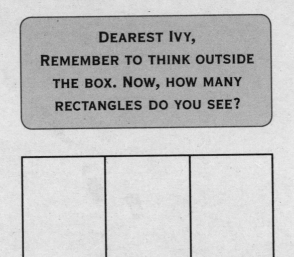

It's weird. There are no doors in the room, and no paths except the one we came from.

"We have to find the solution to advance," Eliza says, answering the question I didn't ask.

We all stare at the rectangles. How many are there? I think.

IF YOU KNOW THE SOLUTION OF THIS PUZZLE, ADD FIFTY AND TURN TO THAT PAGE.

←——————→

TO ASK ELIZA FOR HELP, TURN TO PAGE 329.

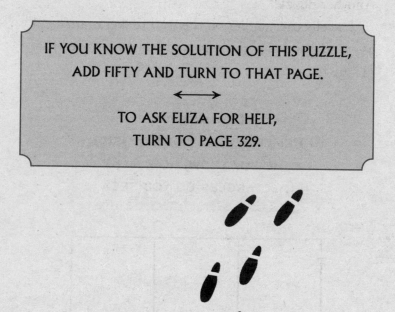

I DECIDE WE should sneak into Patty's place. But we have to wait until she leaves her house, so we sit on the curb and keep watch.

It's disgustingly hot as we keep a lookout. I feel like I'm sitting inside a dog's mouth.

We watch Patty's house for the rest of the afternoon, but she never leaves. We agree to come back and try again first thing tomorrow morning. After all, Patty has to leave her house *sometime*.

When I get home, I bring my mom a tray with cold water, medicine, and soup I warmed up in the microwave.

"Carwos?" she whimpers.

"Here, have some soup, Mom."

Mom looks at the tray, and her eyes well up with tears.

Awww, she's going to thank me!

"ACHOOOOOOO!" She sneezes right into the soup.

"Yuck! Snot soup!" I hand her a tissue.

"Sowwy," she sniffles. "And fank you! But next time, take de soup *outta* de can before you put it in de micwowave. Fire hazawd."

"Okay, Mom."

"You been pwaying wif Eliza and Fwank?"

"Yup." I nod. "And we have plans tomorrow, too."

"And de case? Did you caw Cowe?" She holds her

nose like she's bracing for another sneeze.

"Oh. Yeah," I lie. Usually she can see right through my lies. My gut clenches, and my face is hot with guilt. I hate lying to her. But I just have to remember that I'm helping her. I'm saving her agency and her career and her happiness and her whole life.

That's what my brain says, anyway. If only the guilty feeling in my stomach would listen.

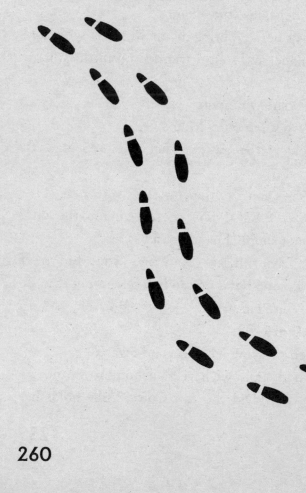

DAY TWO

BRIGHT AND EARLY, I meet Eliza and Frank around the corner. We have to get to the fancy neighborhood on the other side of town, but luckily it's not terribly hot yet. As we walk, I recap what we know, which is:

1. There is bad blood between Guinevere and her daughter, Ivy.
2. Smythe has a reason to be mad at Guinevere, according to Patty.
3. Patty says she didn't send the threats.
4. Guinevere says Patty did.

So pretty much, we've got a nice solid ground of clues to work with . . . but no real direction. It's like one person points to another person, who points to another, who points to another, until we're stuck in this endless suspect circle.

Our goal today is to turn that circle into an arrow. An arrow that points right at our most likely culprit.

At last we walk into River Woods, and all is quiet. When we get to Patty's house, her car is not in the driveway.

Perfect!

But the doors are sure to be locked. So how do we find a way in?

"Hey! Look at me!" Frank calls, his voice muffled.

I whip around. Frank's body is half inside a dog door. The door is way too small for Eliza and me. But Frank—he might just be the perfect size!

"Frank!" I say. "Can you fit?"

"OF COURSE! I'm small." He wiggles inside. Then he opens the door for Eliza and me.

"Frank!" Eliza cries, kissing him on the forehead. "You're a genius."

"No, I'm smart," Frank says.

I close the door behind us and look around. We're in Patty's kitchen.

"There are hundreds of rooms," I say to Eliza. "Where do we start?"

"Well, where would *you* hide something in your house?"

I mean, my house is like an eighth of the size of Patty's. But if I had all the rooms she had, where would I hide something?

"Maybe the basement?" I suggest. "Or the garage."

Eliza hums thoughtfully. "And I'm thinking that her office might have some important information. Frank and I aren't supposed to go in Dad's office because he's afraid we'll mess up his documents."

Frank nods. "NOT. ALLOWED."

Eliza jerks her head toward Frank in a way that tells me that their dad is way more afraid that *Frank*, not Eliza, would mess up his files.

"Her room!" Frank says. "I hide *everything* under my bed. That way, under-the-bed monsters can protect all my stuff."

"Or maybe there's a clue in her nightstand or closet!" Eliza says excitedly.

"NOOOOOoooooooooOOOOOO! UNDER-THE-BED MONSTERS!"

We have too many places to search, and I realize we need to split up. "One of us should search the garage and basement. The other should take the office and bedroom."

"And Frank?" Frank says.

"Frank should play with the dogs," Eliza says.

"WAHOO!"

"So, which rooms do you want, Carlos?"

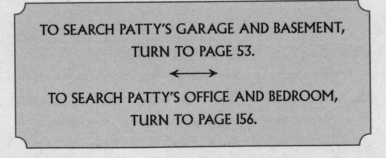

TO SEARCH PATTY'S GARAGE AND BASEMENT, TURN TO PAGE 53.

←——→

TO SEARCH PATTY'S OFFICE AND BEDROOM, TURN TO PAGE 156.

WE *HAVE* TO go confront Smythe.

We sneak out the back door of Patty's house, creep across her property, and cross the street to Guinevere's lawn. The sun is beating down, and I'm sweating, partly from the heat and partly from excitement. For the first time since taking this case, I *finally* feel like we're on to something with this Smythe thing. We might be able to figure out why he's so sulky, and then we'll be that much closer to solving the case for my mom. Good-bye, sweaty sheets, and hellooooo, air-conditioning—

"Hey, kids!" Otto says, popping out from behind a tree like an overeager squirrel.

Eliza and I stop immediately, but Frank runs smack into his legs before bouncing back.

"OUCH!" Frank says, poking his boo-boos.

"How's it going?" Otto asks. "What's happening with the case? Anything exciting?"

I sigh. We do *not* have time for this right now.

"Move aside, Otto!" I say. "We're on an important mission!"

His enormous grin slides off his face into a disappointed frown. He silently steps aside.

Inside Guinevere's house, we find Smythe polishing the silver. But seeing him so busy gives me a better idea. While he's distracted, we could sneak into his room! If we snoop around while he's working, we may

264

be able to find clues uninterrupted.

It takes us ten minutes to find Smythe's room. But eventually we come across a plain wooden door with a tiny nameplate that reads SAMUEL S. SMYTHE.

"That's it!" I whisper.

When I open the door, it creaks, and we tiptoe inside. . . .

Smythe's room is dirty. Disgustingly dirty. There are clothes all over the floor, and all the drawers are open, and papers are everywhere. For someone whose job is to clean up after Guinevere, he sure is messy.

"Check every paper," Eliza says. "We're looking for some sort of written confession from Smythe. Or a letter from Patty that proves they're working together."

I read paper after paper, but none are interesting. Eliza's reading too. Frank is jumping on Smythe's bed because he's still learning to read.

Eliza starts digging through the papers on Smythe's desk. And after a quick moment, she cries, "I found something!"

She hands me a letter:

Dear Father,
I swear I'm going to quit this horrible job. She treats me like garbage, and I haven't gotten a pay raise in ten years. She's been

telling me I'll be promoted soon. It's always "soon" with her, but "soon" never comes! Do you know what happened the last time I asked Guinevere for a pay raise? She said they didn't have the funds right now. What lies! I know for a fact she has a treasure buried somewhere in her

The letter cuts off.

"Why did it stop?" I ask.

"Because he's not finished with it yet. But Carlos! Do you know what this means?"

"Smythe is mad at Guinevere!"

"Yes, he has a reason to send the threats. But also," she says, "he has a motive for wanting the treasure! He hasn't gotten a pay raise! He wants and needs the money—"

CRASH!

"AHHHHHHHHHHHHHHHHHHHHHH!" comes the sound of a spine-prickling shriek from the other room.

RUN TO THE SCREAM! TURN TO PAGE 362.

ELIZA AND FRANK and I link arms. We're an unbreakable chain. We'll never let Otto through, no matter what.

"RED ROVER, RED ROVER, SEND MR. OTTO MEANYPANTS OVER!" Frank sings.

"We're not letting you leave with the treasure chest," I say, more bravely than I feel.

"You can have the chest," Otto says, laughing nervously. He sets the treasure chest on the ground and kneels over it. "I'll just take what's inside."

He looks down at the treasure chest. He's distracted by the treasure and isn't looking at me. I could attack him. But is it too dangerous?

After all, he's much stronger than Eliza, Frank, and me—and I don't want any of us to get hurt.

TO ATTACK OTTO, TURN TO PAGE 158.

←——→

TO STAY PUT, TURN TO PAGE 375.

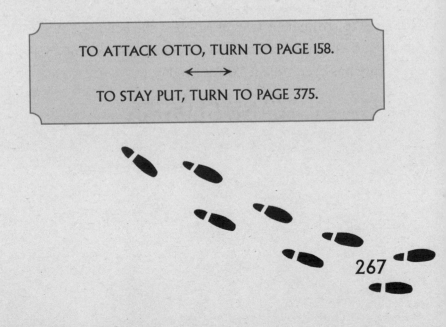

267

KNOCK.

KNOCK.

KNOCK.

KNOCK.

KNOCK.

KNOCK.

KNOCK.

KNOCK. KNOCK.

"Who's there?"

"The detectives!"

"The detectives *who*?"

"YOU hired us!" I shout. "Remember?"

Guinevere opens the door. She's standing there in her nightgown.

"The detectives *who*?" she says again.

"What?"

"You're no detectives of MINE!" she bellows. "While you've been in here playing hide-and-go-seek, my treasure has been stolen! You're fired!"

CASE CLOSED.

"I'M WONDERING WHO might do something like this. Have you ever been threatened before?"

"Once. A long, long time ago. My husband's first wife was very upset, and she used to send threats. And she even got her son—my husband's first child—to send some too. But that was more than twenty years ago."

"Do you have any enemies you've heard from recently?" Eliza asks.

"Tons," Guinevere says, waving her hand.

Tons? How many enemies does Guinevere LeCavalier have?

"Detectives, I don't want to waste your time," Guinevere says. "I know who did it."

"Wait, what?" I stand up and slam my hands on the table. "You know who did it? Why didn't you say anything before?"

"You didn't ask."

Frank whinnies like an angry horse, and Eliza leans forward. "Well?" she demands. "Who is it?"

"It was PATTY SCHNOZZLETON!"

P. Schnozzleton! From the house across the street! I rub my chin. I don't have any practice being a detective, but I'm sure that's what a detective *would* do at a moment like this.

Eliza jumps in, "And what makes you so sure it's Patty Schnozzleton?"

"She's my sworn enemy, my archnemesis—"

There's a tinkering noise behind me, and I whip around. Frank is piling teacups one on top of the other, like a pyramid.

"Frank!" Eliza hisses. "Sit down!"

Frank shakes his head.

"It's okay, Frank. You just keep stacking," I say. "So, about Patty . . ."

"She and I used to be best friends, but then we had a huge fight. She lives in this neighborhood. I know it was her, and I need you to find the proof—"

CRASH!

Broken teacup pieces are all over the floor.

"Oops!" Frank says.

"Frank!" Eliza groans.

"Smythe!" Guinevere calls. "Clean this mess!"

Smythe bursts into the dining room. "Extra work," he grumbles under his breath. He sweeps the broken teacup pieces into a dustpan. "Horrible children," he mutters.

"Hey!" I say.

Smythe glares at me. He looks like he could kill me with an eyelash, so I shut my mouth.

"Smythe!" Guinevere says. "Prepare my footbath! I need you to rub my bunions."

"Ewwwwwwwww," Frank says. "I hate onions!"

"Bunions," Eliza corrects, but from the look on her face, I can tell she doesn't know what they are. I don't either. But if they involve footbaths, I don't *want* to know.

When Smythe marches out of the room, I turn back to Guinevere. "What was your fight with Patty about?"

Guinevere frowns and sips her tea. "Patty and I used to be best friends. We did *everything* together. Including the local Fancy Club. Patty and I worked really hard on the Dodo Bird Unextinction and Repopulation Benefit Ball, and it was a huge success. I did sooooo much work, but Patty told everyone that I didn't help her on the project at all. At the end of the year, she got the Most Influential Millionaire of the Year Award. Just her. Not me. *I* deserved that award!"

"So you stopped being friends? Just like that?" Eliza says. "Over an award?"

"That was just the first straw. Later she turned my daughter, Ivy, against me. When Ivy was marrying that . . . that *man*. Patty was the one who convinced Ivy to run away from home to marry Walter. When Ivy ran away, it broke my poor husband's heart, and he died soon after. Patty tore my family apart!"

"That's terrible," I say, patting Guinevere's hand.

"Not only that! For years Patty has said she wanted to get revenge on me."

I scratch my head. "Revenge? For what?"

"She is pure evil," Guinevere says, avoiding the question. "You must talk to Patty! Right now! Go see her. And make sure you get her to confess. I know it was her."

Eliza grabs Frank by the hand. We all stand up. "Don't worry, Mrs. LeCavalier," I say. "We'll go investigate. She lives in the house across the street that looks like yours, right?"

"Absolutely not!" Guinevere huffs. "My house is *special*. My husband built secret passageways and rooms that can only be entered if you solve a puzzle!"

The thought of puzzles—especially any that might have to do with math—makes me a little squirmy, but Eliza puffs out her chest.

"No puzzle is too hard for us," she says.

And we all march out of the room.

In the hallway, Eliza smiles with teeth, which is rare for her. "How exciting! A real mystery!"

"Can we go now?" Frank complains.

"Yeah," I answer. "To Patty's house."

We leave Guinevere's place and head toward Patty's house. Across the way, Patty's home is big and beautiful—just like *all* the mansions in this fancypants neighborhood—with enormous columns and Yorkie-shaped hedges. I wonder if that person in the window is still watching us. . . .

"I already told you kids! Feet off the grass!" says a voice from up above.

Otto is in a big tree that's on the border of Guinevere's lawn.

"What are you doing up there?" I shout at him.

"Clipping branches. I don't want them to shake loose during a storm."

I almost snort out loud. *What* storm? Doesn't he realize it's the middle of a dry, hot summer?

"Take the driveway!" Otto says. Then he turns back to his work.

I roll my eyes. I trample grass all the time when I play baseball. But I don't want to be yelled at again, so we move over to the driveway, and it takes us two minutes to walk up to Patty's polished wood door.

When we ring the doorbell, the door flings right open. There's no butler. There is only a short woman with poufy hair, thin lips, and horribly messy makeup. Her makeup is smudged all over her face and makes her look like a sad clown.

I wonder if this woman is the same person who was watching us this morning from the window.

"Are you Patty Schnozzleton?" I ask.

The woman nods. "Who are you?" She has a weird accent. She says her *A*s all funny.

"We're detectives," Eliza says. "We're trying to figure out who's been sending Guinevere LeCavalier threats."

"She thinks *I* did it?" Patty demands. "Well, I didn't do it, but I wish I did. That old bat has had it coming to her for years."

"Can we come in and ask you a few questions?" I say.

Patty leads us inside. Her house is kind of like Guinevere's house, only her walls have a very weird collection of self-portraits. It looks like there are a hundred Patty Schnozzletons, just staring at me. CREEPY.

And it smells *horrible*. Like wet dog. Probably because there are five tiny, yipping dogs running around Patty's feet. Mom refuses to get a dog because she doesn't want our house to smell. I always fought her on it, but after taking a whiff of Patty's place . . . Mom might be right.

We reach Patty's living room, where the couch—still inside its plastic cover—sits next to a dusty fireplace. The walls feature many more paintings of Patty and her dogs. Weird.

I sit down on the couch, and it sticks uncomfortably to my legs—and boy, it's *painful* when I try to peel myself off. Frank wriggles around, and I think he's having the same problem.

"So what do you want to know?" Patty says, picking up one of her dogs. It starts licking Patty's face: her forehead, her nose, her cheeks. Then it licks her lips, and Patty opens her mouth to receive a sloppy dog kiss.

Gross! I bet her breath smells like dog drool. "I'll tell you everything. I have nothing to hide."

We'll see about that.

"What do you know about Guinevere LeCavalier's treasure?"

"Treasure? What treasure?"

"The secret one!" Frank says. "IT'S A SECRET!"

Her eyebrows come together in the middle of her forehead. "Secret treasure? You're joking, right?"

Hmmm. She could be lying. But if she is *telling the truth—and she really* doesn't *know about the treasure—then there's no possible way she could be our culprit. But Guinevere is convinced Patty is guilty. . . .*

Suddenly Frank sinks down to the floor and makes carpet angels in Patty's rug. Then a dog licks his face, and he giggles.

I clear my throat and try to talk over the sound of Frank's chortles. "Tell us about your fight with Mrs. LeCavalier."

Patty's nostrils flare; she looks like an angry lizard. "A long time ago, Guinevere and I were part of the same club, and we had to plan a benefit ball for unextincting and repopulating dodo birds together. But I did *all* the work, while Guinevere just laid there on a chair and had Smythe fan her with a giant leaf. In the end, I got awarded for my efforts, and Guinevere got jealous. She gossiped about me to everyone. She said awful, nasty things about me and got all of our friends to stop talking to me."

One of Patty's dogs rubs its face on her ankle, and she pats the top of its head. "I got these dogs to keep from getting too lonely in my big house."

"So you want revenge on Guinevere," I say, "because you're lonely?"

"Wouldn't you want revenge for that?" Patty shouts. "The woman stole my friends from me! She said horrible things about me behind my back! She said I didn't deserve my award. She poisoned people against me. She embarrassed me. She hurt me. I just want to see her suffer a little . . . is that so bad?"

"Yes," Eliza says, and I stomp on her toes. We can't say that! Detectives are supposed to be nonjudgmental. Even though it *is* weird how obsessed Patty is with getting revenge on Guinevere.

Wait a second! The spying this morning . . .

We thought Patty was snooping on us, but she doesn't care about us. Her binoculars were pointed straight at Guinevere's house, *behind* us! She was looking for an opportunity to get revenge.

"So, let's talk about how you've been spying on Guinevere," I say.

Patty turns pale beneath her layer of thick makeup.

276

"I didn't realize you saw that," she says, squirming awkwardly. "Look, I just watch her house sometimes to see if there's an opening."

Eliza pops up off the couch, clearly excited. "An opening! To go get your revenge? So you sent her those death threats?"

"Of course not!" Patty snaps. "I want to see her humiliated and upset, not dead! Dead would take all the fun out of revenge."

TO ASK PATTY IF SHE KNOWS WHO MIGHT HAVE A PROBLEM WITH GUINEVERE, TURN TO PAGE 89.

←—→

TO ASK PATTY MORE ABOUT HER REVENGE PLAN, TURN TO PAGE 360.

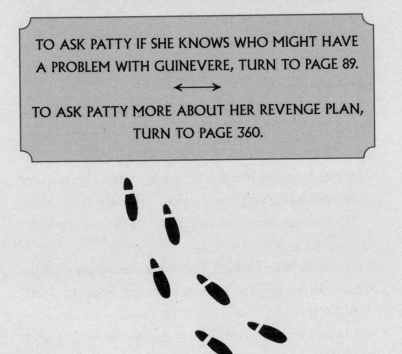

"QUICK!" I HISS. "In a laundry basket!"

We jump into separate laundry baskets and cover ourselves with clothes. Except . . . I think my laundry basket is full of dirty clothes, because it smells like an old armpit.

But no more than a second after I'm covered, Patty enters the room.

"It's this very afternoon," Patty says. There's a pause. "Yes, casual wear is fine. Remember, don't spoil the surprise."

And then I realize . . . she's on the phone.

Through a set of pajamas, I can see the shape of Patty Schnozzleton walking toward Frank's basket and lifting it up, while pinning the phone between her ear and her shoulder.

"Oooooof!" she grunts. "This is *heavy*. Hold on, Marge. I'll call you right back." She puts the basket down and leans out the door. "Maddock-moo-moo? Can you help me carry a basket up from the laundry room? We had more clothes than I thought!"

My heart pounds as Maddock stomps into the laundry room.

"Take the blue basket? Thank you, snookums," Patty Schnozzleton says, and it sounds like she smooches him.

BLECH!

Maddock comes over and picks up the basket with Eliza in it.

"Ugh!" he says. "What did you wash, a bowling ball?"

Patty picks up the white basket again—the one with Frank in it.

And they both leave the laundry room.

As soon as they go, I burst out of the dirty clothes pile and try not to panic. Eliza and Frank are headed *upstairs* with two potential criminals, who are probably going to find them the very second they start folding clothes. If not sooner. What should I do?

The only thing I know is that I can't leave them alone.

I creep down the hall, through Patty's messy kitchen, past a passageway covered with a hundred pictures of Patty and her dogs, up the wooden stairs, and—

"YOU!" Maddock shouts, pointing at me. He's standing across the upstairs landing, in front of double doors to what looks like a bedroom suite. "What are you doing here?!"

Patty pokes her head out of the room. "What are you doing in my house?"

Oh, shoot! Caught!

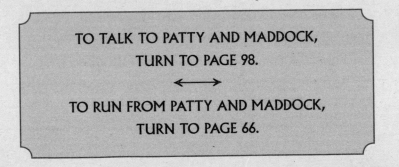

TO TALK TO PATTY AND MADDOCK,
TURN TO PAGE 98.

←——→

TO RUN FROM PATTY AND MADDOCK,
TURN TO PAGE 66.

I HATE TO admit it, but I'm in over my head. I need help.

I inhale deeply and scream, "HELLLLLPPPPPPP!!!!"

"HELLLLLLP!!!!!" Eliza shouts.

"AHHHHHHHHHHHHHHH!!!!!" Frank hollers.

Suddenly, the bookshelf door that leads back into Mr. LeCavalier's fake study starts to move, and I could cry with relief. Someone is opening the bookcase and coming to help!

Crrrreeeaaaaaaaak.

The bookshelf swings open, and we are staring face-to-face with Otto.

My heart starts pounding.

"HELP HELP HELP!" Frank screams.

But Otto just grins. "No one is coming to help y—"
Thunk!

A book comes slamming down on top of Otto's head, and he collapses in a heap.

And standing behind Otto, with a book in his hand . . . is *Smythe.* "I thought I heard you screaming."

I don't even know what to say—I *never* thought Smythe would save our butts!

"Th-thank you," Eliza says, her mouth open wide.

"It was my voice Smythe heard," Frank boasts. "Why don't you thank me, too?"

"Thanks, Frank," Eliza and I say with shaky laughs.

280

Otto is crumpled over on the floor. "He's not . . . dead, is he?"

For the first time ever, Smythe smiles. "I'm strong, but I'm not *that* strong." He bends down, picks up Otto, and tosses him over his shoulder like a doll. "Come on," Smythe says, ushering us out of the secret study. "Let's have some snacks while we wait for the police. And, of course, the missus and miss can return from the hotel, now that the house is safe."

"One more thing," I say with a wince. I can't believe I'm about to say this, but it's finally time. "You need to call my mom, too."

An hour later, things are *chaotic* at Guinevere LeCavalier's house.

First, the police come over to arrest Otto, who is still unconscious. And, since we didn't have any handcuffs or rope, Otto is wrapped up in a whole bunch of cellophane, thanks to Smythe's quick thinking. It takes six officers to lift him up and carry him out, still wrapped up like a present for the nearest prison. The only thing missing was the bow!

Then, as two officers are taking our statements, Guinevere LeCavalier and Ivy return home from the hotel, both looking happy as clams. (Which is something my mom says, but I still don't understand because it doesn't seem like clams have emotions.)

And no more than a minute later, a bundle of blankets bursts into the room.

"A monster!" Frank shouts, pointing at the blankets.

"No, a *mom*ster," I reply.

From underneath the pile of blankets, my mom emerges, looking dazed and sick and worried and angry all at the same time.

I gulp, and Eliza winces.

"CARWOS!" Mom says, snot dripping out of her nose. "EWIZA! FWANK!"

"Oh, you poor dear," says Guinevere. "Sit down, and have some tea."

Guinevere guides my mom into a seat and pours her some tea. Poor Mom—she's too sick to even notice that Guinevere filled her teacup halfway up with jelly beans.

We finish telling our statement to the cops, and then when they leave, we start the story over again with Guinevere, Ivy, Smythe, and Mom. Eliza, Frank, and I take turns sharing everything we know about Otto—I mean, Preston LeCavalier. His story is heartbreaking, sure. But there's no excuse for sending death threats to anyone, no matter what they've done.

As we end our story of the investigation, Guinevere LeCavalier pulls out her checkbook.

"So, from what I understand," she says, "you children

aren't *actually* the detectives on this case at all? And you lied to me?"

"Yes," I say, hanging my head in shame. "But we did it for my mom! To save her agency!"

Guinevere hmms. "Because you lied, I'm going to have to rethink your payment."

"WHAT!" Eliza, Frank, and I all shout.

But Guinevere LeCavalier flashes a toothy smile, and she hands a check to Mom. Mom takes one look at it and faints straight into her tea.

"Oh dear!" Guinevere yelps. "She's taken ill again. *Smythe!* Fetch the smelling salts!"

Smythe gets up from the table and rummages around in the other room.

Guinevere reaches forward and pats my hand. "Well, when your mother comes to again, you can tell her that her agency is saved . . . all because of you three."

Eliza bursts into happy tears, and she and I high-five. Frank gets up out of his chair and whoops as he runs laps around the table. And me? I can't stop smiling!

"Don't tell your mother," Guinevere continues in a hushed voice, "but if ever I need a detective again, I know which three I'm going to call."

"Then we'll be waiting by the phone," I say with a grin.

CASE CLOSED.

I UNPLUG WIRE B. The next thing I know, I'm so dizzy and tired I can barely see, and—*smack*. I fall off the desk. My cheek rubs up against the rough carpet, and that's the last thing I remember. . . .

With a start, I wake up on a deserted island. And I mean *completely* deserted. It's just me, Eliza, Frank, two coconuts, a pelican, and a palm tree. And there in the ocean—zooming away from us on a speedboat—is Otto, wearing a Hawaiian shirt and holding a treasure chest.

"Help!!!!!!!" I cry.

"Come back!!!!!!!!!" Eliza wails.

"SURF'S UP!!!!!!" Frank calls.

Otto turns back around to face us on his speedboat, but he's still so far away. "Couldn't have done it without you! Thanks!" he says before he zips away again. And then he's gone.

Frank, Eliza, and I spend a month on the island, training dolphins to fetch us food. After we win the dolphins' trust, we hitch a ride back to the mainland on three of them. But by the time we get back home, we're *months* too late to save my mom's agency . . . and worst of all, we let the bad guy get away with the treasure.

CASE CLOSED.

ELIZA PICKS UP a letter and lays it by the dripping candle. The light flickers softly, and I peer over to get a look at the loopy cursive handwriting.

Eliza bends over the letter and reads it out loud.

> Dear Father,
> This is the last letter I'll be sending. I have nothing more to say to you, except this: you are no father to me.
> When we meet again, you'll be sorry.
> Preston

"Yikes," I say. "That's very threatening."

Eliza's gray eyes widen. "Yes, it is," she says.

I forgot . . . or I guess it didn't seem like an actual clue . . . but Guinevere *did* mention that Mr. LeCavalier's son from his first marriage had sent threatening letters years ago. Is it possible that history is happening again?

"Read another," I tell her.

> Dear Father,
> I don't understand why we had to leave. Mom says you fell out of love with her. But did you fall out of love with me too? Why won't you contact me? Is that Guinevere woman forbidding

you? Did I do something wrong? Don't you love me anymore?

Forever and always,
Your faithful son,
Preston LeCavalier

I feel a twinge of pity for poor Preston. I just couldn't even imagine Mom cutting me off like that.

Eliza hums as she skims more letters. "They're all like this," she says. "Very sad."

I take the first letter and look at it. The handwriting looks so familiar. Where have I seen loopy cursive like this before?

Eliza pulls out the first clues we ever got from Guinevere LeCavalier. There's a copy of the first death threat she got: the letter written in magazine clippings. And there's a photograph of the second death threat: a picture of the library with toppled shelves and a message in red paint on the wall.

Red paint written in LOOPY. CURSIVE. HAND-WRITING.

I gasp.

"Look at this!" I shout. And Eliza yelps from surprise and nearly drops the candle. Ooops! I lower my voice and say, "Look at this picture of the second death threat—on the wall of the library. It's the same cursive that's in these letters from Preston!"

"Let me see!" Frank yelps, pulling on my shirt. "Let me see!"

She and Frank bend over the letter. "You're right," Eliza whispers. "They do look similar."

"So," I say excitedly, my hands shaking, "do you think that Preston is the one behind—"

KA-*THUNK*.

The bookshelf closes completely.

Eliza and I look at each other for a second. Then we both run to the door.

It's locked.

"Locked!" I'm trying not to panic, but I can barely breathe. Will someone discover the secret entrance in fifty years and find our skeletons in here? Will we have to eat old letters to survive? Is it possible to survive on old letters?

"This is both terrifying and interesting," Eliza says, her voice quiet.

"Interesting *how*?"

Eliza drops down to her knees and pats her brother's head, but Frank is totally fine. He doesn't seem freaked out at all.

"Smythe," I choke. "Smythe is the only one who knows we're in here. Do you think . . . do you think he led us into a trap?"

"It's possible," Eliza says.

"Anything is possible if you just *believe*!" Frank says. "That's what Walt Disney taught me!"

I try the door again. The bookshelf won't budge. "Well, I *believe* we're in huge trouble."

"Dream it and believe it!" Frank replies.

Eliza grabs my arm. "You know what this means, right?" she says. "Someone doesn't like what we're finding. We—we must have stumbled upon something important. Something incriminating."

I lean against the small desk. "What makes you so sure?"

"Hey!" says Frank. "Look at this!"

Eliza looks at me with a knowing smile. "Clearly someone—"

"Smythe," I interrupt.

"—is watching us." Eliza lowers her voice. "*Someone*—"

"Smythe," I say.

"—wants to know what we're finding." Eliza chuckles. "That always happens when there's an ongoing investigation! Criminals often get very nervous when people get too close to the truth. And they *always* get antsy being far away from the action. So they keep close tabs on the investigation, and when it starts going sour . . . *bam*! They attack."

"Look at this!" Frank yells.

"But what did we find that could make someone

panic?" I wonder aloud. "Nothing that solves the case, right? Let's take another look at the letters—"

"NO!" Frank shouts. "NO NO NO NO NO NO NOOOOOOOOOO."

Eliza and I exchange a glance—then we look at Frank, who's pounding his fists on the floor.

Oh boy. Here comes a tantrum.

"What's wrong?" Eliza says quickly.

"You aren't LISTENING to me! I *said* LOOK!" And he reaches under the desk—where it's too dark to see in the candlelight—and pulls out a small box.

"Is this . . . the treasure?" I say. Could this small thing really be it?

"It's got a puzzle on it," Frank says. "And I. HATE. BORING. PUZZLES. BLECH."

On top of the box, there's a dial with two numbers filled in. I feel around the box, and underneath, I find a taped piece of paper with some sentences on it.

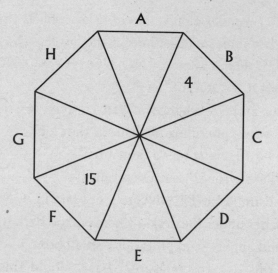

A plus A equals B.
F divided by 3 is C.
C times A is D.
D times A is G.
H minus G equals D.
B plus B plus B equals E.

IF YOU KNOW THE ANSWER, ADD UP A, B, C, D, E, F, G, AND H. ADD ONE HUNDRED AND TURN TO THAT PAGE.

←→

TO GET A HINT FROM ELIZA,
TURN TO PAGE 212.

I LOOK BETWEEN the books and my scrap of paper. I tap my forehead with my pencil. I just don't get this.

"Eliza, can you help?"

She grabs the pencil and paper from me.

Frank tries to crawl onto my lap, but I push him off—so he hangs on my other shoulder.

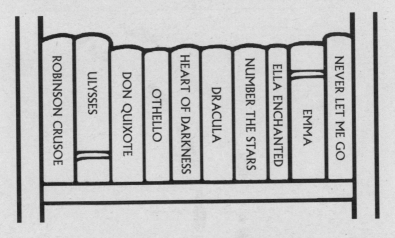

ROBINSON CRUSOE · ULYSSES · DON QUIXOTE · OTHELLO · HEART OF DARKNESS · DRACULA · NUMBER THE STARS · ELLA ENCHANTED · EMMA · NEVER LET ME GO

"Hmm," she says. She always talks through puzzles out loud, even when we're in school. She says it helps her think better. "If we write down the first letter of each book title, we have . . ."

She scribbles down:

RUDOHDNEEN

"So all we have to do is unscramble this, Eliza?"

"It says BUTTERNUT SQUASH!" Frank cries.

"That is a great effort, Frank," Eliza says.

"I see the word ONE in there," I say.

"Yes, I see that too. In fact . . . I think I see an even bigger number hidden in these scrambled letters."

THE SOLUTION TO THE PUZZLE WILL LEAD YOU
TO YOUR NEXT PAGE.

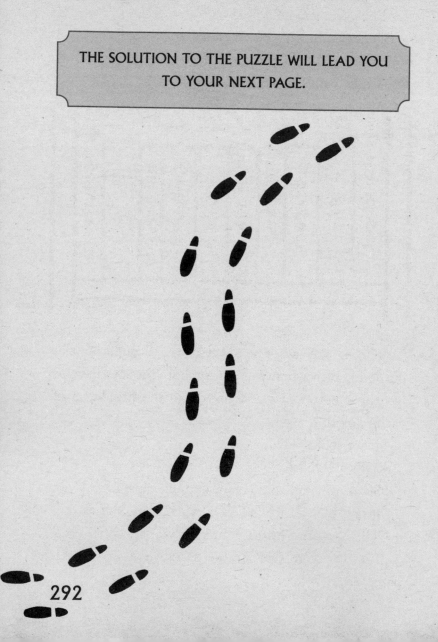

"WHY WERE YOU bullying Guinevere? What has she ever done to you?" I say through the crack at the bottom of the door.

"Hehehehehe!" Otto wheezes, and it sounds like a squeaky squirrel choking on an acorn.

"I don't get it," Frank says. "What's so funny?"

"The idea that *I'm* the bully and *Guinevere* is the victim!" He snortles again and explains. "I used to live in this house with my mother. When my parents separated, my mother and I were thrown out like garbage. We had to find another place to live. When Guinevere moved in less than a year later, suddenly my father didn't return my calls or lett—"

"Your father?"

"Yes, that's right. Mr. LeCavalier is my father."

My mind is spinning, and I think back to the first conversation we had with Guinevere. She *did* mention that Mr. LeCavalier's first wife and son had sent him threatening letters in the past. Only she hadn't heard from them in years. Or so she thought!

Otto sniffs. "I hadn't talked to my father since I was your age, all because of Guinevere."

"That's terrible," I say.

"Of course it's terrible!" Otto snaps. "That's why Guinevere deserves to be hurt. Just like I was hurt!"

"No one deserves that," Eliza says. "Yes, Guinevere treated you horribly, but you shouldn't be horrible back."

"The Golden Rule!" Frank says, perking up. "Treat others the way you want to be treated!"

"Hehehehehe!" Otto giggles again. "How naive! But I couldn't expect anything less from children!"

I fold my arms. "So you're mad at Guinevere. She treated you badly, and she cut you out of Mr. LeCavalier's life. That's why you threatened her."

Otto coughs. "Yes. That's true. But also, I need her to hand over the treasure. My father told me about a secret treasure beneath the house, long before he even met Guinevere. It belongs to me. I know—in my heart—that my father would've wanted me to have it."

"If he wanted you to have it," Eliza says, "wouldn't he have left it to you in his will?"

"For years," he growls, "I knew the day would come when I could return to my house, collect my treasure, and get my revenge. I wish I had time to answer more of your pointless questions, but I have a treasure to collect. Bye-bye!"

His footsteps get more and more distant, and then he is gone.

TURN TO PAGE 196.

 294

"CAN WE SEE the first clue of the treasure?" I ask.

"Of course," Guinevere says. "We've figured out what it means, but we don't know what to *do* beyond that. *Smythe!* My lockbox!"

Smythe storms off, grumbling under his breath. I remind myself to talk to Eliza about questioning him later.

He returns with a little safe, and Guinevere LeCavalier opens it up with a key hanging around her neck. She pulls out a crumpled-looking loose-leaf paper that reads:

The red house is made of red bricks.
The blue house is made of blue bricks.
The white house is made of white bricks.
The gray house is made of gray bricks.
What is the green house made of?

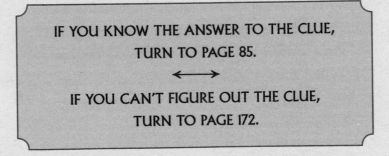

IF YOU KNOW THE ANSWER TO THE CLUE,
TURN TO PAGE 85.

←→

IF YOU CAN'T FIGURE OUT THE CLUE,
TURN TO PAGE 172.

AS SUSPICIOUS AS Patty and Maddock are, I shouldn't accuse them yet. We still don't have hard proof that they did it.

"We don't know who's guilty yet," I say to Ivy.

"Well then, what are we paying you for?" Ivy cries.

Eliza puts her hands up peaceably. "We don't want to jump to—"

"I've seen what my mom is planning to pay you," Ivy interrupts, "and it's more than I got from my own father's will! But you're not even doing your job. You play tag, wrestle with Maddock, run giggling through our house—"

"Hey!" I say. "Wait a min—"

"No," Ivy says. "You are done here. Take your things and leave."

My stomach drops. Is she . . . is she really firing us? This *can't* be happening! "Ivy, no! Please—"

"GET," she breathes, "OOOOOUUUUTTTTTTT!"

Her voice is like an earthquake, a tornado, a hurricane, all rolled up into one massive force.

I plant my feet on Patty Schnozzleton's floor and say, "We're not going anywhere."

But then Smythe takes two lumbering steps toward us, picks us all up in his arms like a bouquet of three wriggling flowers, and tosses us onto Patty's lawn.

296

"And good riddance," Smythe gloats as he slams the door in our faces.

CASE CLOSED.

"LET MRS. LECAVALIER go!" I demand. "RIGHT. NOW."

Otto laughs, and it sounds like a whoopee cushion filling up with air. "Oh, that's rich! Let her go! Oh boy, you are the funny one, aren't you?"

"No," Frank says, putting his hands on his hips. "*I'm* the funny one. And the smart one. And the nice one. And the one who hates vegetables—"

"Okay," Eliza says to Frank. "We get it."

I glare at Otto. "Seriously! Let her go!"

"Never," he says. "I've waited more than twenty years to get my revenge on Guinevere, after she stole my father from us. My mom and I were kicked to the curb, and my father cut me off from his life completely."

Eliza gasps. "You're Preston LeCavalier, aren't you? Mr. LeCavalier's son from his first marriage?"

"Very smart," Otto says. "You've always been very smart. Anyone can see you're the brains of this little team. And it *just so happens*, we're stuck on this next puzzle." Otto's eyes shine with an evil twinkle. "Come here and help me solve this next puzzle."

"No!" I shout.

Eliza doesn't budge.

"Maybe you didn't understand. That wasn't a question. Help me solve this next puzzle, or say good-bye to Guinevere." He tightens his grip around her neck, and Guinevere winces.

298

We have no choice. Guinevere's life is in Otto's hands . . . literally. And we can't risk her melon being squashed in Otto's grip.

Eliza helps Otto with the next puzzle, and the wall opens up. He forces us to go with him, puzzle after puzzle, until we finally reach a treasure chest. He tosses Guinevere LeCavalier at us, picks up the chest, and bolts away before we even realize what's happening.

We search the caves for him, but he and the treasure are long gone.

CASE CLOSED.

"NOTHING!" I SAY quickly. "Never mind!"

"Seriously," Otto says. "I want to help."

How do I know that's true? I can't just go around discussing the case with anyone who comes by.

I frown. Eliza folds her arms.

"Eliza! Carlos! COME PLAY!" Frank shouts from across the yard.

But I ignore him and look up at Otto. "You should mind your own business," I say.

Otto frowns. He seems hurt, and for a second I feel bad. He *has* been nice to us. But as Mom likes to say, we have to hold our cards close to the chest. Which I think is a poker reference. But I don't know for sure, because the only card game I know how to play is 52 Pickup.

At long last, Otto walks away, leaving us to whisper about Ivy and the treasure until we're ready to walk home.

GO HOME FOR THE DAY. TURN TO PAGE 32.

I **ENTER THE** number one into the keypad on the bottom of the drawer. With a click, the bottom of the drawer pops up, and I reach into the false bottom. But there's only one thing in this secret compartment: a letter addressed to Patty . . . from Smythe:

> *To Patricia Nicole Schnozzleton,*
> *I am writing in the hopes that you'll hire me to be your butler. I am looking to leave Guinevere LeCavalier's service due to egregious dissatisfaction and irreconciliable differences. As I've been with the LeCavaliers for thirty years, I know you have been looking for a way to get revenge on Guinevere, and I think stealing her butler might be the perfect solution.*
> *Please let me know if you are interested in my services, and we will discuss my salary and start date.*
>
> Sincerely,
Samuel S. Smythe

I read over the letter a few times, tripping over some words I don't know. What is *egregious dissatisfaction? Irreconciliable differences?* What good is finding a secret letter if I can't even understand what it says?

301

I need to share it with Eliza. I bet she'll know what it means.

"Eliza!" I shout, running through the house. "Where are y—"

I turn a corner and collide with Frank, who falls to the ground and skins his knee. His eyes fill with tears.

"Oh no! Frank, please don't cry!"

But it's too late; he starts to howl.

I scoop him up in my arms and carry him around. "Eliza?"

"In the living room!"

Living room? That wasn't one of the places we agreed to search.

I find Eliza with her knees on the couch, staring out the window with Patty's binoculars.

"Come look at this, Carlos!"

I put Frank down, hop onto the couch, and look through the binoculars—but I don't see anything unusual. Just Otto in the yard and Smythe in the window.

"I don't get it. What were you looking at?"

"Patty can see everything. Every little detail—she has the perfect spying view of Guinevere's house. And look at this!"

She kicks her foot toward a can sitting on the

carpet . . . a can of deep red paint.

"Paint?"

"Don't you remember, Carlos? Red paint was used to write the death threat in Guinevere's library. Suspicious, right?" she says.

I pull the photo of the crime scene out of my pocket and look at it. Could it be the same paint? And if it is . . . we've solved our case! "We have to compare this paint to the threat on Guinevere's wall."

"I found the jackpot," Eliza brags.

"Maybe. But look what *I* found."

I hand Eliza the letter from Smythe, and she reads it aloud. Her eyes grow wider and wider as she reads, and by the time she finishes, her mouth is a perfect round circle.

"Do you understand it?" I ask.

"Well, I don't know all the words, but I get the point. Clearly, Smythe is miserable working for Guinevere and was looking to leave. He wanted to work for Patty. If Smythe is unhappy with Guinevere—"

"You think he could be mad enough to send her death threats?"

"It's possible," Eliza says, her eyes twinkling with the thrill of a good mystery. "This is our best clue yet!"

"They both are," I say, jerking my head toward the paint can. Should we compare the paint in Patty's house with the paint at the crime scene? Or should we go straight for Smythe?

TO COMPARE THE PAINT COLORS,
TURN TO PAGE 153.

←——→

TO CONFRONT SMYTHE,
TURN TO PAGE 264.

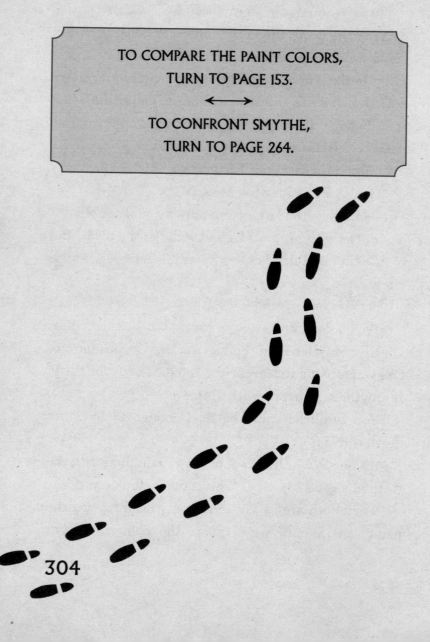

AFTER MUCH THINKING, I decide we should investigate Ivy.

We find her lounging in the lounge. Then we stick to her like tape, like glue, like gum that gets tangled in your hair. We follow her like a shadow. We track her like a bloodhound.

"Are you following me?" Ivy says at last, as we try to get into her car with her.

"No," I say too quickly.

"Please get away from me."

"No can do," Eliza says. "This is our job."

"Fine!" Ivy huffs. Then she drives and drives. From the time I started paying attention to the clock until now, it's been at least two hours. It's like the car ride that never ends! Where could she possibly be going?

I'm just about to complain when Ivy finally stops at an open field with lots of big red tents.

"HOORAY!" says Frank. "You brought us to the circus!"

"Actually," Ivy says, "I enrolled you in clown school. At least now when you pester someone, you'll get paid for it. Or not. I don't know the rules of clowning."

Then she rolls off in her car, leaving us behind.

CASE CLOSED.

"THE RED DOOR!" I shout. "It's the only one that makes sense!"

Eliza hums. "I haven't finished solving it yet."

I tap my foot impatiently. "Eliza, come on! We don't have time! I promise—I solved it!"

"Let's GOOOOOO!" Frank hollers, and he hops through the red door.

I follow him, dragging Eliza behind me. It's really dark, but as soon as the lock from the red door clicks behind us, the room lights up.

My eyes bug out. "What the . . . ?"

We're in a room exactly like the one we came from. With four doors and the same message:

ON EACH DOOR, THERE IS A SENTENCE.

THREE OF THE SENTENCES ARE FALSE, AND ONLY ONE IS TRUE.

But the sentences on the doors are different. And when I read them, my stomach drops like a stone:

YOU ARE ON YOUR WAY TO THE TREASURE.

ALL OF THESE DOORS AREN'T FAKE DOORS THAT HAVE BRICK WALLS BEHIND THEM.

306

YOU SUCCESSFULLY SOLVED THE
PREVIOUS PUZZLE.

YOU HAVE FAILED THE PREVIOUS PUZZLE.

CASE CLOSED.

"WHEN'S THE LAST time you saw Ivy?" I ask.

"It's been too long," Guinevere says, flicking her wrists.

"Could Ivy be sending you the death threats?" Eliza says.

Guinevere laughs. "Tee hee! Ivy? *My* Ivy? That's a preposterous suggestion! She positively *adores* me!" She scrunches her face, like she's about to say something else, but then she looks up and blinks. Her cheeks are a little flushed.

It doesn't seem like she's lying. But then again, she's definitely holding *something* back.

"If Ivy adores you," I say, "why haven't you seen her recently?"

Guinevere scowls into her tea. "Her husband."

"You don't seem to like Ivy's husband very much. What's his name?"

"Walter," Guinevere says distastefully. "And you're correct. I don't like him very much."

"Why not?" Eliza asks.

"Well, I don't see how this is relevant, but if you must know, it's because he took my Ivy away from me. And because he can't seem to hold down a job, because he keeps having lofty ideas about opening a ridiculous restaurant called Noodles, Strudels, and Poodles—"

Frank's eyes grow wide. "They don't *eat* poodles, do they?"

308

"Of course not," I say. I elbow Frank, then look at Guinevere. "Er . . . they *don't* eat them, do they?"

"No, no! It's some silly restaurant that serves noodles and strudels . . . and allows you to bring in your poodles. But no other dog. Only poodles. Ivy and Walter keep asking me to fund this bizarre project of theirs, but I refuse to waste my money on that."

I glance at Eliza, and she quickly raises and lowers her eyebrows. I can tell we're both thinking the same thing. Ivy and Walter are asking for money. Maybe *they* want the treasure. Maybe they're mad Guinevere won't fund their restaurant and are sending threats!

Eliza twists the ends of one of her pigtail braids. "Do you think Walter is sending you these threats?"

Guinevere sniffs. "I suppose it's possible, but I highly doubt it. He lives very far away. Whoever's sending the death threats is close by. Close enough to destroy my library, anyway."

TO ASK GUINEVERE WHO MIGHT BE
SENDING HER THREATS, TURN TO PAGE 269.

THE TOOLSHED IS small and rickety. The green paint is all speckled and flecked. Honestly, it's hard to imagine Mr. LeCavalier spending a lot of his time in this dumpy little shed when he has a beautiful mansion right across the yard. I mean, if *I* had a mansion, I'd never leave it!

Eliza is leading the charge into the shed, and she pushes on the door.

"Locked," she says.

Ivy shakes her head. "Knowing my father, there must be some trick here."

"Mmmm," Smythe grunts in agreement, and he stands on his tiptoes so that he can peer in through the one tiny window.

"Do you see anything?" I ask.

"No . . . too dark."

"Let's take a lap around," Ivy suggests. "Maybe we can find a way in."

All of us start circling the toolshed, looking for any signs of a puzzle or a secret door or something . . . but I don't see anything other than the shed itself.

"We could lift Frank up through the shed's window, and he can open the door," I suggest.

"And put him in danger? All by his lonesome?" Eliza says.

Fair point.

"Knock knock knock!" Frank says, pounding on the door. "LITTLE PIG, LITTLE PIG, LET ME COME IN!"

"Stop it, Frank!" Eliza says, wrenching Frank away. "Oh no! Frank! Look at your hands!" His palms are covered with some sort of chalky green paint. Eliza groans. "Mom's going to kill me when she sees what you've done to your shirt."

"But I was *playing*," Frank says, like that solves the matter.

Suddenly Smythe taps my shoulder. "Look!" he growls, his droopy eyes growing wide. "Where he was playing!"

There's something written on the door . . . something that had been covered up by chalk or clay or something. Smythe and Ivy dive forward to wipe off the gunk so we can see what's written underneath.

In my garden:
All but two of my flowers are roses.
All but two of my flowers are tulips.
All but two of my flowers are lilies.
How many flowers do I have in my garden?

Ivy scratches her head, and she hums softly. "Daddy was very proud of his garden. He had prize-winning tomatoes for many years. I could count the flowers in Daddy's garden—"

"That won't be necessary," Eliza says. "This is a logic puzzle. Plain and simple. All the information we need is right here on this door."

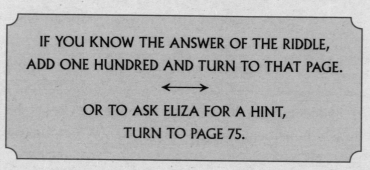

IF YOU KNOW THE ANSWER OF THE RIDDLE,
ADD ONE HUNDRED AND TURN TO THAT PAGE.

OR TO ASK ELIZA FOR A HINT,
TURN TO PAGE 75.

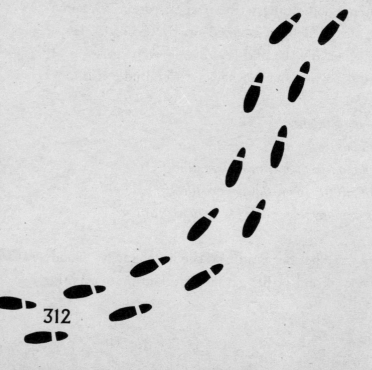

"LET'S SEARCH THE study," I say.

Eliza folds her arms and turns to Smythe. "Will you cooperate with us? Let us look around?"

"PLEASE!" Frank yells. "PRETTY PLEASE! PRETTY PLEASE WITH SUGAR ON TOP?"

"Fine," Smythe mumbles. "I'll let you look around. But the second I hear you making a commotion, I will kick you out of this house." Then Smythe trudges away.

I look around at the study again, and it seems pretty standard. A desk in the center, floor-to-ceiling bookshelves all around, and a ladder for climbing up.

"Where should I search first, Eliza?" I ask. "Eliza?"

She's holding four books in her hands and smiles guiltily. "They were upside down," she says. "I have to rearrange them."

"*Now?*" I say, exasperated. "Can't we do that later? We have clues to find! I think I want to search the desk drawers."

Eliza shrugs. "Sure, that sounds good."

"Noooooooo, *up!*" Frank says, pointing at the ladder. "Up like a plane! Up like a rocket! Up like a push pop!"

I hesitate. Should I listen to my gut? Or follow Frank?

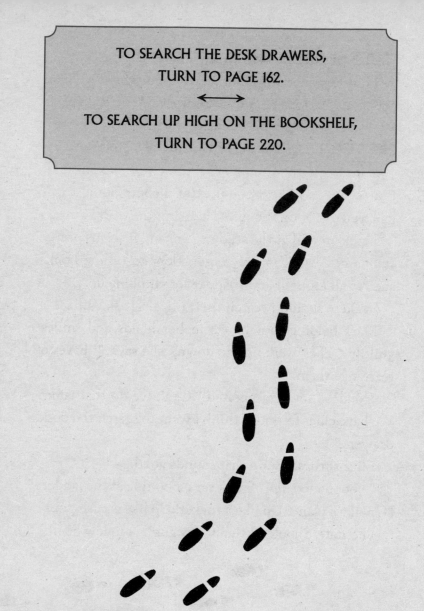

TO SEARCH THE DESK DRAWERS,
TURN TO PAGE 162.

←——→

TO SEARCH UP HIGH ON THE BOOKSHELF,
TURN TO PAGE 220.

314

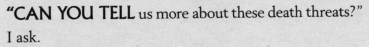

"CAN YOU TELL us more about these death threats?" I ask.

Guinevere LeCavalier strokes her chin and stares at Frank, who is now trying to balance a silver spoon on his nose. Eliza elbows him.

"I'm bored," Frank complains.

Eliza elbows him even harder.

"Sorry, ma'am," I say. "Now, about that first threat."

"Right," she says. "Hold on. . . . *Smythe!* The first threat!"

Smythe folds his arms. He does *not* look happy. He stomps over to a drawer that Guinevere LeCavalier easily could have reached herself.

Smythe grunts, glaring at his employer. I can practically see the lasers coming out of his eyes. He lays the paper on the table, then storms off.

The threat is made of cut-up magazine clippings. I read it aloud.

> *"The treasure does not belong to you.*
> *It belongs to me.*
> *You have seven days to find it.*
> *Or else."*

"Yikes," Eliza says. "Can we keep the note? For reference?"

Guinevere nods, and Eliza tucks the note into the

front pouch of her backpack.

"What about the second threat?" I ask Guinevere.

"Three days after that *dreadful* letter, I found a message in red paint on the wall of my library. It said, '*You are running out of time. Find that treasure, or MEET YOUR DOOM. HA HA HA HA HA HA HA HA HA HA HAHAHAHAHA.*'" I can't remember how many *HA*s there were, but it was at *least* seven." Guinevere pauses to dig in her pocket. "Here—you can have this picture of the crime scene, too. For your records."

Eliza slips the picture into her bag.

Guinevere looks between me, Eliza, and Frank with watery eyes and a wobbling bottom lip. "These threats . . . they're serious, yes?"

I nod. "Someone *really* wants that treasure."

ASK GUINEVERE WHO KNOWS ABOUT THE TREASURE. TURN TO PAGE 26.

I HAVE TO KEEP questioning Maddock myself, without Guinevere LeCavalier around. I know I can get him to give me more information.

"What do you know about Mrs. LeCavalier's treasure? Do you plan to steal it?"

Maddock's eyes bulge. Eliza gasps. And Frank sniffs his armpit.

"Steal it?" Maddock snorts. "Kid, I know you just arrived on-scene yesterday, but I've been the LeCavaliers' lawyer for twenty years. And I have no interest in some elaborate scavenger hunt that Mr. LeCavalier set up. The man was a kook! Who knows if there's even a treasure?"

"What do you mean?" Eliza asks.

"I mean the man was a jokester. I wouldn't put it past him to tell the world about a secret treasure but then not have one at all. I have no interest in things that may not even exist."

"So what *are* you interested in?" Eliza says.

"I have three words for you kids. Money, money, and—" He cocks his head to the side with a fake smile. "Hmmm," he feigns. "What's the last word?"

"POTATOES!" Frank shouts.

Maddock looks at Frank like he's stupid. "No, money!" Maddock rises from the couch, and the cologne wafts my way again like a giant gas cloud. "Mysterious treasures don't have any value unless you know what's inside. But money always has value, and I always know exactly what that value is. Can your little child brains grasp that concept?" he sneers.

I do not understand everything he just said, but he's acting snotty about us being "just kids" again, so I nod and pretend I get it.

"Besides," Maddock continues with a grin, "you're missing the bigger picture here."

"What's the bigger picture?"

"Say cheese!" Frank says idly, running his fingers across the piano. He doesn't know how to play, though, so it sounds like a horrible mishmash of notes.

Maddock drops his voice and leans in close to us, and we all ignore Frank as he continues to pound his fist on the piano. "As the executor of Mr. LeCavalier's will, I can tell you things that will make your jaws drop."

"Try us!" I say.

"Let's just say there were many amendments made to the will, just before Mr. LeCavalier's death. One final change eliminated his daughter from the will."

"He . . . he cut Ivy out?" I say.

"On the request of Guinevere LeCavalier."

I gasp. "So . . . you're saying . . ."

Eliza jumps in. "Mr. and Mrs. LeCavalier removed Ivy from their will, just before Mr. LeCavalier died?

And it was Mrs. LeCavalier's idea!"

Maddock smirks. I can tell he loves being able to hold information like this over our heads, the slimeball. "If you ask me, there's old bitterness there," he says. "And speaking of bitterness, have you, for one second, stopped to consider why our dear butler is so angry?"

I try to catch Eliza's eye, but she's not looking my way.

"Of course you haven't," Maddock says. "Because you're just *children*. But before accusing an innocent lawyer, maybe next time you should stop to consider the people who openly resent Mrs. LeCavalier." He sighs. "Oh dear, now I'm late for my appointment with Mrs. LeCavalier. I shall have to blame you. *Good day*," he says.

Then he rustles his papers together, shoves them into his briefcase, and walks out.

I turn to Eliza, whose round cheeks are all flushed. She huffs furiously. "I hate the way he talks to me! Like he thinks I'm stupid or something. But I understand you perfectly, Mr. Snobbish, thank you very much!" Eliza sticks her tongue out in the direction where Maddock left, but he's long gone.

Then she sighs, and in that one breath, all the anger leaves her body.

"So," I say, "he actually gave us a lot of important information."

Eliza nods. "Well, Maddock says he's not interested in a treasure because he doesn't know what's inside and he doesn't want to waste his time. He seems to think Mr. LeCavalier would send people on a wild goose chase for nothing."

"Would he do that?" I say. "*Could* he do that?"

Eliza shrugs. "I don't know."

"Then there's Ivy," I say, my head still spinning with new knowledge. "She was written out of her parents' will! She didn't tell us that!"

"Why would she?" Eliza says. "It makes her look really suspicious. She could still be mad at her mom. I mean, she *did* seem to be mad at her mom this morning."

"And then Smythe—we already knew he was angry and bitter. But *why*?"

Frank burps. "Can we do something fun *nowww*?" he groans.

"Fun like what?" Eliza says.

"FUN LIKE CRAWLING! FUN LIKE SNEAKING!"

Eliza grins. "Do you want to sneakily search someone's room, Frankie? Maybe Smythe's or Ivy's?" she says with a pointed look at me.

Frank's eyes grow really wide, and he starts to hyperventilate with excitement. "Yes! Yes! Yes! Yes! Yes! *Yes!*"

The only question is, whose room do we search? The daughter with the case of lost inheritance? Or the butler with the case of the mysterious grumpy grumps?

TO SEARCH SMYTHE'S ROOM,
TURN TO PAGE 355.

←——————→

TO SEARCH IVY'S ROOM,
TURN TO PAGE 19.

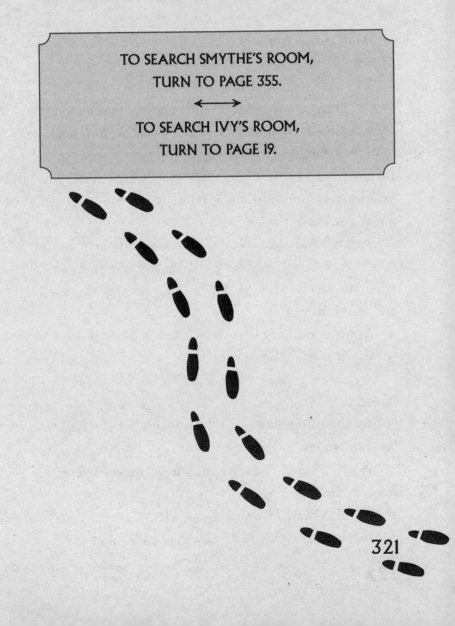

321

"HAVE YOU SEEN anything suspicious around the house?" I ask.

"Suspicious like what?" Smythe asks, raising an eyebrow.

"Well, since you're the butler, I'm sure you see lots of suspicious things."

"I haven't seen anything."

Oh. I can't really come up with a good question to get information out of him. Not without making him mad.

"I find that hard to believe," Eliza says, jumping in to fill my pause. I smack my head. Most of the time, you shouldn't accuse your suspects of lying; they just get angry and defensive.

Smythe folds his arms and scowls. His arm muscles look so huge, bulging out of his suit like that. And when he steps toward us, it takes a lot of effort to stand and face him.

"Are you implying that I'm bad at my job? Or do you think *I'm* guilty?" he growls.

Eliza realizes she's offended him, and she squeaks, "N-neither."

Smythe glares at us. "Maybe it's time for you kids to go home today."

"What?" I say. "But we still have more detective work to do!"

"YEAH! YOU POO-POO BRAIN!"

Smythe glares, his face growing redder and redder

322

by the second. "That's it. You're done for the day."

Smythe escorts us down the hall and shoves us out the front door. Then he slams it in our faces. "Hey!" I shout through the door. "You're getting in the way of our detective work!" But Smythe doesn't respond. How rude!

In defeat, I trudge down Guinevere LeCavalier's front steps and onto the grass. Immediately my feet get wet with sprinkler water, and I realize I forgot my shoes inside!

"My shoes," I say to Eliza. "I left them in the hallway when I was sliding around the floor. I can't walk home in my socks!"

"At least you're not barefoot," Eliza says. "You can get them tomorrow."

I shake my head. I *have* to get my shoes. It's a half-hour walk back to my house, and I can't do it in socks. It'll kill my feet—and I won't be able to do great detective work tomorrow with blisters!

I turn back toward the door to ring the bell.

"I wouldn't do that if I were you," says Otto, examining a tree on Guinevere's lawn. "Smythe looks mad. Best to wait until he cools off. Now, what did you kids do to get him so angry?" He chuckles.

"Nothing," I say.

"Some friendly advice? If I were in your shoes—well, socks—I'd listen to the young lady and head home."

He *really* seems to want us to go home. And if we're home, we're not investigating. Is he trying to get us to leave on purpose?

With all our investigating of Maddock and Smythe, I forgot that Otto is a suspect too. After all, he *is* always around the house.

"Are you *sure* you haven't heard anything about Mrs. LeCavalier's treasure?" I ask him.

"There's a treasure?" he says. "I just thought there was a threat on her life! That's what you said before, right?"

Eliza nods. "That's what we said, yes."

"So there's a threat *and* a treasure? Oh! Is the treasure the reason why there's a threat?"

"Duhhhhhhhh." Frank puts his hands on his hips. "You don't know *anything*, do you?"

Otto shrugs. "I guess I don't."

It's hard to get a read on Otto. His face is as expressive as a brick wall.

"Maybe we should go home, Carlos?" Eliza says. She looks tired, and even Frank yawns, but we made *no* progress today. We aren't any closer to figuring out who is sending the death threats. I'm wondering if we should go back inside. After all, my mom's fate depends on us!

"Well . . . ," I begin.

"Sometimes it's best to call it a day and try again later," Eliza says. She presses her lips together tightly. "We can always continue our work tomorrow."

"You should listen to your friend," Otto says. "Why would you kids want to be here, when you can be comfy at home? By the way, where is home for you?"

Frank's eyes grow really wide. "STRANGER DANGER!" he shouts. "STRANGER DANGER! STRANGER DANGER!"

"Frank!" Eliza scolds.

Is it my imagination, or is Otto awfully quick to suggest we go home? Is he purposely trying to get us away from the investigation? "Why do you want us to leave so badly?"

"I don't care either way," Otto says. "It just seems boring here. If I were you, I'd want to go home. But personally, I'd always rather be at home."

I stare at him, and he stares right back at me. I wonder . . . is he *really* just being nice? Or is he hiding something?

Otto finally blinks, ending our stare-off.

"So what are you going to do now?" Otto says.

TO GO HOME FOR THE NIGHT,
TURN TO PAGE 132.

←——→

TO TRY TO SNEAK BACK INTO THE HOUSE
THROUGH THE BACK DOOR, TURN TO PAGE 194.

I HAVE TO trust Eliza.

Otto clutches his treasure as Eliza guides him back the way we came. Frank silently follows, and I am the caboose.

I hope I'm making the right decision.

Eliza's awesome memory comes in handy, because she takes every twist and turn of the maze without pause. At times I have no idea where we are, but Eliza seems to remember every bend and every corner.

Finally we reach the middle of the maze—and the spiral staircase. Eliza leads Otto up the steps. I don't understand what she's doing. There's no way Otto will be able to fit through the exit in Ivy's closet. It was barely big enough for me!

But she leads him that way anyway.

We get to the bottom of the slide—the one that leads up to Ivy's closet.

"At the top of the slide is the exit," says Eliza. "Want to go first?"

"No," Otto says warily, and I'm beginning to think he doesn't trust Eliza. "You first."

Eliza climbs up the slide. Otto follows, and Frank is behind him. I go last.

"Okay," says Eliza. "I'm slipping out the exit."

And then she's gone. Otto eagerly scoots up the rest of the slide, slips the treasure chest through the exit, and sticks his arms, head, and shoulders through.

Oh no!

He's about to escape—and Eliza led him right to it!

Otto thrusts his body farther into the exit.

"Uh-oh," he says. He tries to wiggle himself back into the tunnels, but he can't. He's stuck in the tiny door. Just like that time Frank got his head stuck in between two bannister poles.

I laugh. Eliza was just trying to trick Otto this whole time. Of course!

I hear shuffling coming from the other side—in Ivy's room. The police are here. They slap handcuffs on Otto before they take an ax and chop up Ivy's closet to get him unstuck. Once the police cart him away, Frank and I can finally crawl up the rest of the slide and escape the tunnels too.

And once I am in Ivy's room again, I feel like cheering! We actually got Otto!

Then Guinevere hands me a check for more money than I've ever had in my whole life (which I guess isn't saying much, because I've never had more than ten dollars at a time), and I *really* feel like cheering.

But the good feeling goes away when Smythe drives me home. I part ways with Eliza and Frank and head into my house. I try to sneak in, hoping that Mom's flu has her knocked out. . . .

"WHERE HAVE YOU BEEN?" Mom bellows from the living-room couch the moment I open the screen door. Then she folds over into wheezy, chesty coughs.

"Don't get mad," I say. "But Eliza-Frank-and-I-may-have-investigated-your-Guinevere-LeCavalier-case-and-solved-it-which-was-stupid-and-dangerous-but-I-wanted-to-help-you-and-your-agency," I say all in one breath, and I pull out the check from my pocket.

My mom splutters on another cough. "Wh-what is this?"

"Money," I say quickly. "For you. And your agency. We did this for you. You'll be able to hire more detectives and assistants with this kind of money. You could even get yourself a better office."

Mom's eyes fill up with tears, and she starts wailing. She pulls me into a slobbery bear hug and sobs into my hair. Nothing like snot-and-tears shampoo, am I right?

"So, I take it you're happy right now?"

Mom nods.

"And I take it I'm not grounded?"

Mom snorts. "You wish."

I grin. It was worth a shot. But hey—even a summer's worth of chores and groundings would be worth the look on my mom's face right now. Worth it for that feeling of saving Mom's career and making her happy. Because when it comes down to it, I did this all for her.

I think I'm ready for my next case. (Just don't tell Mom.)

CASE CLOSED.

"CLEARLY THERE ARE five rectangles," I say, staring at the engraving.

"Hmm . . . I think you're missing all the rectangles inside of other rectangles."

Eliza starts to trace her finger around some of the other rectangles.

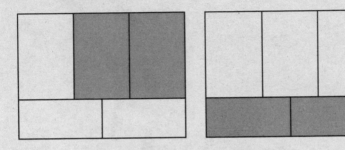

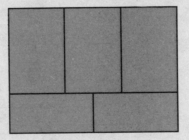

"WOW!" Frank says.

"Eliza," I breathe, "you're a *genius*! How did you know that?"

She blushes. "I just really love math. So far, with the five rectangles you saw and the three I found, we have eight. Can you see any others?"

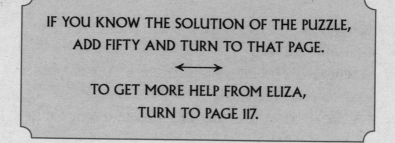

IF YOU KNOW THE SOLUTION OF THE PUZZLE,
ADD FIFTY AND TURN TO THAT PAGE.
↔

TO GET MORE HELP FROM ELIZA,
TURN TO PAGE 117.

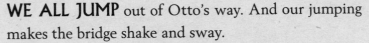

WE ALL JUMP out of Otto's way. And our jumping makes the bridge shake and sway.

The wooden planks make crackling noises like they're about to splinter. Maybe they *will* splinter under the weight—Otto is heavy, and that treasure chest looks heavy too.

And just like that, I have the perfect idea.

"Hold on to the rope and keep jumping!" I tell Eliza and Frank.

I grip the rope so tight that it's giving me a burn on my palm, and I jump up and down on the bridge until it's wobbling wildly. Otto is running fast, and—*CRACK!*

A wooden plank snaps in half, and Otto's foot goes right through.

Frank chortles with glee, and all three of us bounce so hard that Otto can't seem to get a grip on the bridge and hold on to the treasure chest at the same time.

He fumbles around with the chest, and then—like in slow motion—the chest flies out of his hands, off the bridge, and down into the netting above the alligator pit.

"NOOOOOOOOOOOO*ooooooo*OOOOOOO*ooooo*
OOOOOOO*ooooo*OOO!"

Otto swan dives off the bridge, plunging headfirst after his treasure.

He bounces in the net and rolls around. Then he crawls over to the treasure and cradles it like a baby to his chest.

"Treasure treasure!" he coos. "Treasur—OUCH!"

With the added weight of the treasure chest, the netting sinks lower than it did when we were caught in it. His butt is within reach of the alligators.

"YOW!" he cries as the alligators nip at the net and—from the looks of it—Otto's pants. His polka-dotted boxers are exposed. He tries to juggle the treasure *and* keep the alligators at bay, but he loses his hold on the treasure again, and it tumbles into the alligator pit.

The top flies open, and I gasp: the treasure chest is filled to the brim with bouncy balls. They start rebounding all over the place, and the alligators snap at them.

A piece of paper also rolls out of the treasure chest, into the pit, but an alligator swallows it up. I guess we won't ever know what it says . . . unless we sift through alligator poop in a few days.

As Otto battles three alligators, we wander through the tunnels until we find an exit. We emerge where Guinevere LeCavalier's grandfather clock is, in the hall.

"MRS. LECAVALIER!" we shout at the top of our lungs, even though it's two in the morning, and everyone's sleeping.

When she appears, bleary-eyed and wearing a green face mask, we urge her to call the police *immediately*, and after she hangs up, we tell her everything—about Otto, about getting locked in the closet, about finding the tunnels in the basement and following the clues.

And before we're even done with our story, the police arrive. We take them underground and weave through tunnels until we reach the alligator pit. Otto is still battling the beasts, but now he's only wearing underwear! The rest of his clothes seem to have been eaten.

Then the police hop into the pit, wrangling alligators and capturing Otto.

And then, after we tell Guinevere the truth about how we're not *really* detectives from the agency, my mom comes to capture *us*, which is a lot less fun.

"Carwos!" my mom cries, tissues flying everywhere like snotty confetti. "When you neber came home, I was so wowwied! You—you awe gwounded!"

"Sorry, Mom."

"Sowwy isn't good enou—"

"Here we are!" Guinevere LeCavalier says in a sing-songy voice, and she enters the room carrying a check.

Guinevere hands it directly to Mom, whose jaw drops.

"Close your mouth, dear," Guinevere says, "or you'll let the bugs in."

Mom closes her mouth and hugs the check to her chest. "F-fank you! Fank you so much!" Suddenly she starts to wail. "Wahhhhhhhhhhh!" Mom blubbers onto her sleeve, and then she howls and sneezes and coughs all at the same time.

When she finally stops bawling, Mom drives us home

in silence. Eliza and I nudge each other in the backseat, but we're both too afraid to say anything. Sooner than I'd like, Mom drops Eliza and Frank off at their house. Their light is on, which means they're about to be in major trouble, too.

Mom and I continue down the road toward our house. As we pull into our driveway, I turn to Mom. "Hey," I say, trying to break the angry silence that hangs between us. "I was just trying to save your agency. Because I know how much you love your job."

She turns to me and grabs both my cheeks between her cold, clammy hands. "Don't you know?" she shouts hysterically. "Carwos, I wuv you more than my job—more than anyfing ewse in de world! I cawe about youw safety more than anyfing!" She has real tears in her eyes.

"I'm sorry! I didn't mean to make you worry. I was just trying to help."

"I know," she says, hugging me close to her chest. "Fank you. But don't you *dawe* do it again."

SIX WEEKS LATER.
Punishment is the worst. I am sooooo bored. Mom has me picking up garbage in the parks with other volunteers and answering phones at her new office and—worst of all—cleaning the house. Ughhhh. I never want to clean anything again!

It's especially bad because while I'm being punished

all day long, Eliza and Frank are having fun at camp. Lucky ducks!

I guess Mom starts to feel bad for me, because she drives us to Guinevere's house. Guinevere must have been expecting us. When we arrive, she answers the door with a wildly enthusiastic "WELCOME BACK!"

"What's this?" I ask, turning to Mom.

"A debrief," she says. She pats my head as we follow Guinevere through her house. "It's the final meeting after a detective wraps up a case."

At last we arrive in the living room, and Guinevere hands us empty teacups and a jar of jelly beans.

"Sorry," she says, "but I've never had to make tea for myself before. I don't know how."

"Smythe quit?" I ask.

"Unfortunately. He's gone and joined the circus."

"As a strong man?" I say, thinking of Smythe's gigantic muscles.

"As a clown."

I laugh. There's no one grumpier than Smythe. It's funny to picture him with a permanent smile painted on his face.

"I apologized for not appreciating him all these years," Guinevere said. "We had a nice long chat, and he decided he didn't want to be a butler anymore, so he ran off to the circus. Ivy and I are getting along great—we're closer than ever. And . . . I even apologized to

Patty. For that whole fiasco with the police at her house. We've even started meeting for weekly gossip sessions—I mean, dinners."

"What about Otto?"

Guinevere shrugs. "Well, his alligator bites have healed quite nicely. His trial is in a few months. But I do feel bad. I didn't mean to come between him and his father. Maybe I can apologize somehow."

My mom coughs. "Speaking of apologies," she says, looking bashful, "I'm sorry Carlos and his friends tricked you into thinking they were the detectives for this case while I was sick."

"Yeah," I say, staring down at my sneakers. "I'm sorry."

When I raise my head, Guinevere LeCavalier looks me square in the eye and says, "I'm not sorry. Not one bit. You and your friends are the best detectives I've ever met."

Ha! That's not what Mom wanted her to say. But you know what? Guinevere is right! Eliza, Frank, and I make a great team—all three of us.

I grin. "Let us know if you hear about another case. We're on the lookout."

Mom shakes her head . . . but underneath it all, I can tell she's proud. I know *I* am!

CASE CLOSED.

"WHERE SHOULD WE look now?" I say.

Eliza jumps in. "We're trying to learn more about the LeCavaliers' past," she explains. "We feel that studying their past can help us get more information about what's happening now—and maybe even point the way to Mr. LeCavalier's treasure. So, were there any places that were important to Guinevere or Winston? Places in the house where they hid stuff—"

"Or even where they spent a lot of time," I interrupt.

Smythe licks his lips, and his gaze drifts up to the ceiling as he thinks. "Would you believe," he finally says, "that Mr. LeCavalier actually spent a lot of time in this very study?"

"Why?" Frank says.

Smythe shrugs. "He used to spend hours in here. And when he wasn't here, Mr. LeCavalier was in the toolshed in the backyard. He loved to garden."

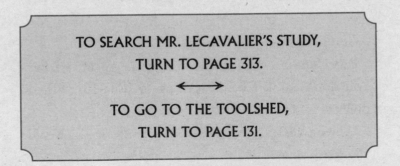

TO SEARCH MR. LECAVALIER'S STUDY,
TURN TO PAGE 313.

←——→

TO GO TO THE TOOLSHED,
TURN TO PAGE 131.

WE DECIDE TO start with Patty Schnozzleton. She seems to have a motive for threatening Guinevere LeCavalier, and she's the only person we haven't talked to yet.

We let ourselves out of Guinevere's house and step into the blistering sun. It's so hot out here, I *swear* the bottom of my shoes are melting.

When we arrive at the yellow mansion across the street, I knock on the door, but Frank goes straight to the doorbell and presses it over and over again. I hear a groan from inside Patty's house, and a woman opens the door a crack, just enough for us to see her face, which is wrinkly and full of gloopy makeup. A bunch of dogs are trying to dodge around her feet and run outside. "Hush, puppies! Hush!"

"HUSH PUPPIES!" Frank says.

"Are you Patty Schnozzleton?" I ask, and when she nods, I continue. "We are detectives from Las Pistas Agency. We're investigating the death threats at Mrs. LeCavalier's hou—"

Patty squints at me. The dogs still yip at her feet. "You don't think *I* had anything to do with this, do you?"

"Maybe yes! Maybe no! Maybe sometimes! Maybe so!" Frank sings.

"I mean," adds Eliza, "if you look at the facts, you *do* look suspicious."

338

Patty's face goes white. Deathly white. Whiter than a bedsheet. Whiter than seafoam. Whiter than a moldy tomato. "Spotty, Shaggy, Waggie, Barkie, Mo! *ATTACK!*"

She opens the door wide, and her dogs lunge at us, their mouths twisted in five horrible snarls.

"*AHHHHHHHHHHHHHH!*" we scream as the dogs chase us off Patty's lawn. Down the street! Out of the neighborhood! Across town! Beyond state lines! We run, run, run, run, run! The dogs are behind us, nipping at our heels, every step of the way. We run for two full weeks before the dogs find a colony of squirrels and finally start chasing them instead.

Hungry, tired, shaken, and having completely flaked on the mystery, we have no choice but to return home with our tails between our legs.

CASE CLOSED.

"BRAID!" I SHOUT, holding on tightly to the ladder. "The answer is *braid*!"

Below me, more rungs of the ladder come out from the wall, and I'm finally able to climb down. It's too dark to see where I'm going, so I go slowly until I reach solid ground. I help Eliza down after me, and then grab Frank.

We're in a dark pit, like what I imagine the bottom of a well to look like.

A high-pitched scream interrupts the darkness.

Eliza grabs on to my arm and whispers, "Where is that coming from?"

"Up your BUTT and around the corner!" Frank says.

I can barely see Frank in the darkness, but he seems unfazed. He either has no idea what's going on, or he's very brave.

"Shhhhh, Frank," Eliza says. "You have to be very quiet now. If you're completely silent, I'll give you candy."

"Candy!" Frank tugs on Eliza's arm. "Do you have candy with you *now*?"

Eliza shushes him again. "No—ouch, Frank, get off me. I only have raisins and granola bars. But when we get home, I promise."

"HEEEEEEELLLLLPPPPP!" shrieks the voice again. It's Guinevere LeCavalier! Only she sounds far away.

We walk toward a soft light in the distance, and as we get closer, I realize it's coming from a gas lantern, left in the middle of the dirt path. It must belong to

Otto and Guinevere. Maybe they forgot it? Or maybe Guinevere left it behind on purpose—to leave a trail! Like Hansel and Gretel!

The lantern illuminates a wall with a giant tapestry on it. The tapestry is red and gold and royal blue, and it looks very majestic. But unlike the tapestries inside the LeCavalier house, this one doesn't have a picture of anything on it. There are just a whole bunch of random circles.

"GET AWAY FROM ME, YOU WRETCHED MAN!" Guinevere says, and her voice is closer than ever. It's pretty much *right* behind the tapestry.

"Quiet, or I'll shut you up myself," Otto snarls. His voice gives me shivers.

I hold up the lantern while Eliza and I try to peek behind the cloth. I'm hoping there is a door, so that I can get to Guinevere before Otto does something horrible.

But instead of a door, the wall has a message:

The shortest distance between two points is a line.
The shortest and longest line is a circle, for a circle has
      no beginning and no end.
How many are on my tapestry?

The second sentence gives me a headache, but the task seems straightforward enough. But then I look at the tapestry again, and sigh. There are a *lot* of circles.

"Maybe we can shade each circle when we're done

counting it," Eliza says, digging into her backpack and pulling out a piece of chalk. "That way, we can keep track of the ones we've already counted."

I take the chalk from her. "Got it."

"And I think we should start with the smaller circles first, since the small circles are inside bigger circles. Save the bigger circles for later. That should help."

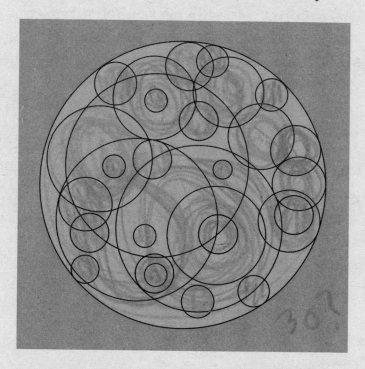

ADD TWO HUNDRED TO THE SOLUTION OF THIS PUZZLE AND TURN TO THAT PAGE.

"WHAT DOES THIS mean?" I ask Eliza. "Tune tune tune tune?"

Eliza licks her lips. She's got that look in her eyes again—that hungry gotta-solve-everything kind of look. "I think they're picture puzzles."

TUNE
TUNE
TUNE
TUNE

TO THE

"There are four tunes," she mumbles to herself. "Four tune. For-tune. Fortune."

I smack my head. "Ohhhhh! So the second one . . ." I stare at it blankly.

"TO THE," Frank says loudly. "To the . . . tothe . . . TOOTH!"

Eliza shakes her head no. "I don't think that's it, Frankie. I'm pretty sure the key to this one is the placement of the words *to the*. Now, we have two choices. We could go to the left, or we could go to the right. Which way is best?"

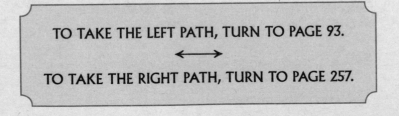

TO TAKE THE LEFT PATH, TURN TO PAGE 93.

←——→

TO TAKE THE RIGHT PATH, TURN TO PAGE 257.

WE CAREFULLY FOLLOW the maze. It reminds me of the corn mazes that Mom takes me and Eliza to every Halloween, only this is a lot harder and a lot larger, and we have to move a lot faster. We're practically running around the thick stone walls. But I guess those corn mazes were good practice, because we reach Exit Three, no problem.

Exit Three leads into a small cave with stalagmites and stalactites. I can't really remember which one's which, but they're sticking up from the ground and hanging down from the ceiling. There's a weird glow to the hall, like it's being lit by fireflies or glowworms. A *drip-drip-drip* sound echoes, and it smells musty, like my sports socks.

Eventually, the cave gets smaller, and I have a sinking feeling in my gut that we're about to hit a dead end.

Frank crawls toward the back of the cave.

"Frank," Eliza calls. "Come back! Otto might be—"

"Boo!" shouts Otto, emerging from the shadows up ahead.

"Eeeeeeeeeeeek!" we scream together.

He's holding the treasure chest and looking around the cave shiftily.

"Get out of my way, kids. I'm not playing around here."

"Neither are we!" I say. "Hand over the treasure!"

"Never! Now *move*!"

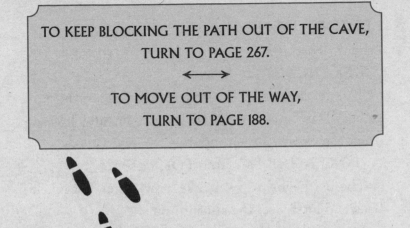

TO KEEP BLOCKING THE PATH OUT OF THE CAVE,
TURN TO PAGE 267.

←——→

TO MOVE OUT OF THE WAY,
TURN TO PAGE 188.

345

I DECODE THAT cipher in record time! With pride, I shout, "Forty-six!"

KER-*THUMP*.

The net drops a little, dangerously close to the alligators. They smack their jaws together, and I *swear* drool comes out of their mouths.

"FORTY-SIX!" I scream. "FORTY-SIX!!!"

The net begins to sway, like a swinging hammock. Back and forth over the alligator pit.

I haven't been this nervous since my last math test. No, wait—since the time I was sent to the principal's office for stepping on Sherri Fischer's diorama (it was an accident, but no one believed me). No, wait—since the last time I was at bat with two outs and bases loaded.

But honestly, none of that even compares to possibly being eaten by alligators.

Air swishes through the net as it swings higher and higher. I lace my fingers through the holes between the rope. Then, with one GIANT swing, the net dumps us on a ledge, high up on the ragged, rocky wall.

Eliza brushes herself off, watching as the net sinks back down to the pit where the alligators are. "Let's get out of here."

"WEEEEEEEE! Let's do that *again!*" Frank says. He almost leaps off the ledge back onto the net, but Eliza yanks him by his shirt. As she tries to restrain her brother, I hug the solid, rocky wall opposite the steep edge and the alligator pit. There's a path, and only one direction to walk.

The crooked trail snakes between tall walls, and the space to walk is so narrow that we have to squeeze through real tight. Thankfully, the sounds of the alligators get fainter as we walk forward, and we eventually find ourselves walking into a circular room, facing a solid, curved wall with four doors—one hot pink, one bright blue, one deep green, and one dark red. Above the doors, someone has painted a message on the wall.

ON EACH DOOR, THERE IS A SENTENCE.

THREE OF THE SENTENCES ARE FALSE, AND ONLY ONE IS TRUE.

WHERE IS THE TREASURE?

Eliza and I hop between the pink door, the blue door, the green door, and the red door, reading all the sentences.

PINK DOOR

THE TREASURE IS EITHER BEHIND THE PINK DOOR OR THE GREEN DOOR.

BLUE DOOR

THE TREASURE IS EITHER BEHIND THE PINK DOOR OR THE BLUE DOOR.

"Three of these sentences are false." Eliza hums, a smile twisting at the corner of her mouth. "And only one of these sentences is true."

"A logic puzzle," I groan.

"A logic puzzle!" Eliza squeals.

GREEN DOOR

RED DOOR

THE TREASURE IS NOT BEHIND THE GREEN DOOR.

THE TREASURE IS BEHIND THE RED DOOR.

TO GO THROUGH THE PINK DOOR,
TURN TO PAGE 78.

←→

TO GO THROUGH THE BLUE DOOR,
TURN TO PAGE 160.

←→

TO GO THROUGH THE GREEN DOOR,
TURN TO PAGE 253.

←→

TO GO THROUGH THE RED DOOR,
TURN TO PAGE 306.

"HIDE!" I **WHISPER** at Eliza, and I gesture at the door in panic. "Please!"

Eliza doesn't look thrilled, but she crawls under the desk. I look for another spot to hide—but there isn't much else in the room. So I decide to crouch behind the trash can. Frank rolls behind a row of books on the bookshelf.

Not a second later, Smythe thumps into the study. He breathes heavily through his nostrils, while I'm frozen like a statue.

Thump.

I can't panic. Stay calm. Eliza is still, but Frank fidgets in his hiding spot. We are dead!

Except . . . Smythe turns around and walks away, his footsteps growing fainter and fainter until I can't hear them anymore.

"Phew!" I say, standing up. I tiptoe across the room and lock the glass door of the study. "I can't believe that worked! We did it!"

"*You* did it," Eliza says.

"I did it!" Frank says.

"No you didn't."

"Well, I did *something*," Frank says. "Otherwise, why else would I be your boss?"

I roll my eyes. "Frank, you're not anyone's boss."

"I AM THE BOSS!" Frank shouts. "I AM, I AM, I AM!"

"Frank, please! Be quiet!"

"Aha!" Smythe bellows from the doorway. "I knew you were hiding in here! Now out, out, *out*!" He runs to the glass door and jiggles the knob. "Unlock this! Now!"

I shake my head.

Smythe bangs on the door and pulls on the doorknob. His face is red, and his droopy eyes bulge. "When I get in there, you kids are in *so* much trouble!"

Eliza flinches every time the doorframe rattles. But then she swallows her fear and says, "If you don't let us poke around, we're only going to assume you have something to hide. Don't incriminate yourself, Smythe."

Smythe stops knocking. "If you make a mess, you're done. No second chance." His nostrils flare. "I'm going to get the key, and I *will* be back to unlock this door." Then he turns on his heels and clomps down the hall.

Eliza sighs when he leaves. "Was that a yes or no to letting us investigate?"

"I don't know," I say. "But we better hurry. Let's look around Mr. LeCavalier's study. There has to be something to find in here."

"Stop being bossy," Frank says. "Remember, *I'm* the boss. No . . . wait! I want to be the captain."

"Okay." I sigh.

"NO! NOT O*KAY*! IT'S AYE AYE, CAPTAIN!"

"Aye aye, Captain," Eliza and I say in monotone mumbles.

"I CAN'T HEAR YOU!"

"AYE AYE, CAPTAIN!" we shout.

"And as your captain, I command you look up high on the bookshelf!"

I really wanted to look inside the desk drawers, to maybe read some papers. I don't know whether to let Frank get his way right now . . . or to try to get my own way.

I look at Eliza to get her opinion, but she isn't even paying attention. She's busy pulling books off the shelf and moving them around. "What are you *doing*?" I ask.

She smiles guiltily at me. "Just . . . rearranging."

"You can't rearrang—"

"But the spines of these books are upside down," she groans. "It's unorganized, unmatching, un . . . unbearable!"

"Well, if you stop that for a second, help me decide where to search."

"I ALREADY TOLD YOU," Frank whines.

"I can't stop mid–organization session!" Eliza says, scandalized.

I guess it's up to me.

TO SEARCH THE DESK DRAWERS,
TURN TO PAGE 162.

←——→

TO SEARCH UP HIGH ON THE BOOKSHELF,
TURN TO PAGE 220.

I **DECIDE TO** keep the information about Ivy a secret for now. Sometimes it's better for the investigation not to let anyone know what you know. Mom always says that when she pores over her case files at dinner. Thinking of her, bent over her papers with a smile, makes me worried. Two days of investigating, and we're no closer to saving her agency. What if we fail? What if her company goes bankrupt?

"What's wrong, Carlos?" Eliza says.

"What? Nothing!" I say too quickly. "Why?"

Eliza gives me a funny look, but she doesn't say anything. We walk out of Guinevere LeCavalier's house in silence.

"Are you thinking about Ivy?" Eliza asks.

"She's guilty, right?" Frank says, but then he doesn't wait for the answer. He runs into the middle of the lawn and starts rolling around.

"We don't know enough," Eliza says to me. We both sit down on Guinevere's front step. "I think we need some really hard evidence. Until then, I'm not sure we can know *for sure* whether Ivy's the one behind all this—"

"Did you say something about Ivy?" Otto says, popping out from around the house.

I stand up. "How long were you listening?"

Otto's smile wavers. "Just long enough to hear you say something about Ivy. Should I be concerned about her?"

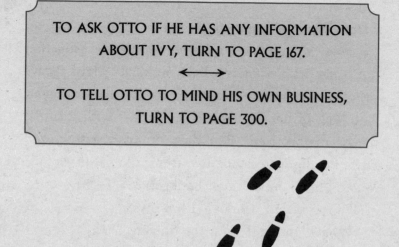

TO ASK OTTO IF HE HAS ANY INFORMATION ABOUT IVY, TURN TO PAGE 167.

←——→

TO TELL OTTO TO MIND HIS OWN BUSINESS, TURN TO PAGE 300.

354

THERE'S A BIG wooden door at the end of a long hallway leading to Smythe's room. And on that door is a sign that says STAFF ONLY. The door is locked, but—weirdly enough—there's a keyboard under the doorknob.

Frank goes over to type something in, but I hold him back.

"We can't just try random passwords."

Frank deflates, and his lip juts out in an enormous pout. I put my hand on his shoulder and look him square in the eyes. "Don't worry. If we crack this access code, you can do all the sneaking you want in Smythe's room." I pause. "But how do we find the password?"

I run my hand across the door, but it feels normal. Eliza's feeling along the wall, and Frank's searching on the floor. We don't really know *what* we're looking for. But there must be a way in.

I touch the hinges. "Hey!" I say, leaning in for a closer look. One of the hinges is a little loose, and wedged in there is a small scroll. "Frank, I need your tiny fingers."

Frank yelps in delight and sticks his fingers into the hollow space in the door hinge. After a minute of prying, he finally pulls out a yellowed piece of curled-up paper.

HINK PINKS

Hink pinks are one-syllable words that rhyme. I shall give you the clue, and you will come up with the hink pink.

For example:

A heavy feline: FAT CAT

Steak stealer: BEEF THIEF

Sobbing without any tears: DRY CRY

Got it?

Now, to get through this door, you'll have to figure out these hink pinks:

1. Depressed father: _____ _____
2. A painting that makes you think: _____ _____
3. Sky-colored sneaker: _____ _____
4. A bald rabbit: _____ _____
5. Thief of literature: _____ _____

Take the highlighted words, put them in alphabetical order, and you will have your passcode into the servants' quarters. Good luck!

WSL

"WSL?" I say.

"Winston Something-something LeCavalier," Eliza replies. "Oh, this is just like Guinevere LeCavalier said." She beams. "To get to Smythe's room, we'll have to get through this hink pink!"

"Do you think we can?"

"Why not? Everyone's good at one-syllable rhymes!"

"YOU TOO!" Frank shouts.

"Yes, yes, very good, Frank," Eliza says, patting him on the head.

I stare at the hink pinks and try to figure out the password.

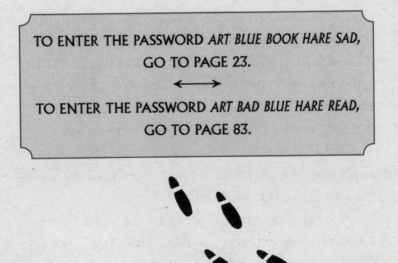

TO ENTER THE PASSWORD *ART BLUE BOOK HARE SAD*, GO TO PAGE 23.

←→

TO ENTER THE PASSWORD *ART BAD BLUE HARE READ*, GO TO PAGE 83.

"**YOU SEEM SAD** about your daughter, Ivy," I say. "Are you upset she's living in Whatsitcalled with her husband?"

"Wichita," Eliza whispers.

"Bless you!" says Frank.

Guinevere LeCavalier frowns. "Of course I'm sad. I miss my Ivy."

"Why haven't you seen each other in five years?" Eliza says. "That's an awfully long time not to visit your beloved daughter—and for her not to visit you. Are you fighting?"

"W-w-what?" Guinevere splutters. "Who do you . . . how do you—how *dare* you—"

"HOW DARE *YOU*?" Frank screams, standing up on his chair. "HOW DARE YOU AND YOU AND ALLLLLL OF YOU!" He beats his hands on his chest.

Guinevere looks at Frank like he's crazy. (Which he is.)

Okay, maybe I should play peacekeeper.

I hold up my hands soothingly. "Apologies, Mrs. LeCavalier. What we meant was, does Ivy have a reason to want to threaten you?"

"No! Of course not! Ivy and I are on great terms!" Guinevere says, clutching her necklaces. Beads of sweat form on her forehead, and a kicking instinct in my gut tells me she's lying. But I can't accuse her of lying without making her mad. And I should never upset the client.

But I don't think Eliza knows that rule, because she keeps nudging Guinevere. "But Ivy *could* be threatening you. Logically. Since she knows about the treasure."

Guinevere's eyes dart toward the door, as if she's hoping Smythe will burst in and interrupt. "Ivy would *never* threaten my life!" she howls. "Those death threats were gruesome and vulgar and uncouth! Besides, many other people know about the treasure as well!"

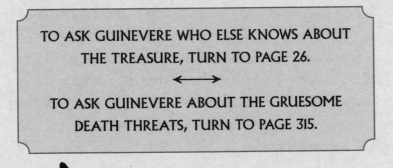

TO ASK GUINEVERE WHO ELSE KNOWS ABOUT
THE TREASURE, TURN TO PAGE 26.

←——→

TO ASK GUINEVERE ABOUT THE GRUESOME
DEATH THREATS, TURN TO PAGE 315.

"WHAT KIND OF revenge do you have in mind?" I ask.

"Oh, it has to be something very public and very embarrassing. Hmmm . . . what if I switch her meal at the next charity ball? So instead of lobster, she'll be eating filet mignon! Or I could switch out her speech with a rap song. Or perhaps I could steal her shoes while she's dancing and replace them with doll-sized shoes. Or clown shoes." Patty giggles.

I look at Eliza, and we both wince. No offense to Patty Schnozz, but her revenge ideas sound kind of lame. Maybe grown-ups just don't understand good pranks.

And someone with such dumb prank ideas doesn't seem capable of sending death threats—at least in *my* professional opinion. Maybe we should just end the interview now. Though, I guess I should see if she knows anything else. . . .

ASK PATTY IF SHE KNOWS WHO ELSE HAS A PROBLEM WITH GUINEVERE. TURN TO PAGE 89.

ELIZA, FRANK, AND I refuse to move. As Otto crashes into us, he knocks us over like bowling pins. We fly off the bridge and plummet down into the netting above the alligator pit.

Only this time, the netting doesn't hold up. It sinks down so low that the alligators get a good bite out of it, and we go rolling into the pit.

The last thing I see is the pink inside of an alligator's throat . . . before it swallows me whole.

CASE CLOSED.

THERE ARE MANY screams now. Echoing all through the halls.

We sprint to the source of the sound: the foyer of Guinevere's enormous house. When we arrive, I gasp at the scene.

The chandelier has shattered all over the floor, with sharp glass pieces everywhere. In the middle of the circular room is a giant doll, dressed up in necklaces and gems. It's made to look like Mrs. LeCavalier, I think. But the scariest part is that the doll's eyes have been scratched out, and there's a knife in the doll's heart.

For the first time since we stole this mystery from my mom, I think that maybe we *should* have let adults handle it. This is really, really scary.

Everyone is statue still. Smythe is on the other side of the foyer, openmouthed. Guinevere is standing near the front door with a woman who looks exactly like a younger version of her. It must be her daughter, Ivy.

And standing in the shadows is a middle-aged man I've never seen before. He has dark, slicked-back hair and a greasy goatee.

"Detectives!" Guinevere cries. "Thank goodness you're here!"

"Who's that?" I say, pointing to the oily man.

The man smirks at me. "Joe Maddock, attorney-at-law."

Right. Guinevere's lawyer.

362

"Carlos, look," Eliza says in my ear. "What's around the doll's neck?"

I take a tiny step forward. Then another. Then another—

"STEP ON THE GLASS AND YOU BREAK YOUR MAMA'S BACK!" Frank calls.

"That's *crack*, not glass," Eliza corrects, and Frank just sticks his tongue out at his sister.

When I reach the doll, its scratched-out eyes make me shiver. Around its neck is a tiny bottle with a note inside. I tip the bottle, and the note flutters into my palm.

LAST CHANCE.
ALTHOUGH . . .
DEATH LOOKS GOOD ON YOU, GUINEVERE. ☺

A chill prickles up my spine. Creepy!

"What happened here?" I ask Guinevere.

Guinevere clutches her daughter. "As soon as we walked in the door, the chandelier came crashing down."

"Mrs. LeCavalier," Maddock says. "My legal advice is that you should prepare to meet this criminal's demands."

Guinevere wails, "I would . . . if only I knew how to find the treasure!"

"I could help you, Mom," Ivy says, patting her

mother's shoulders. "We could search the house together again."

"What we need," Smythe grumbles from across the room, "is to catch the culprit. What have you kids—I mean, *detectives*—found? Anything useful?"

Eliza gulps and looks at me, and I know she's waiting for me to speak. It's weird and new and different to be the leader.

We have two major suspects, and all I have to do is accuse one. But which one?

TO SHARE SUSPICIONS ABOUT SMYTHE,
TURN TO PAGE 111.

←——→

TO SHARE SUSPICIONS ABOUT
PATTY SCHNOZZLETON, TURN TO PAGE 215.

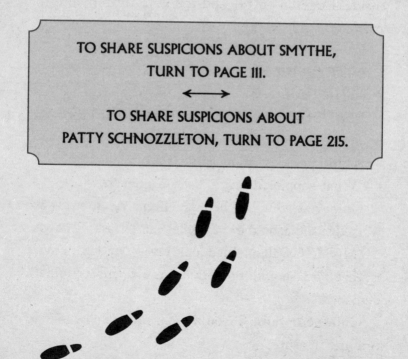

"I CAN'T THINK of any more questions," I say.

"Good, then am I free to go?" Patty says, looking longingly at her own house. "My wittle doggie-woggies are waiting. They probably miss me oodles."

"If we have any more questions—" I start to say.

"Yeah, yeah, you'll come find me," Patty says. "But the more you investigate me, the more Guinevere'll be in trouble. . . ." She pauses. "On second thought, come over for as long as you want!"

"GOOD-BYE!" Frank shouts as he tackle-hugs her around the middle.

"Oh dear!" she says, patting Frank on the head. "Get off now, that's a good boy."

"Frank!" Eliza says—and it takes both her and me to pull Frank off.

The moment she's free, Patty walks the length of the bushes and waddles down Guinevere LeCavalier's lawn.

"Adults are weird," I say when Patty is out of earshot.

Eliza nods. "What are we going to do now?"

But then Frank tugs on her shirt. "Aren't we going to look at this?" He holds out his hand. In his palm is a bright pink phone.

"Whose phone is this, Frank?" I ask, even though I already know what he's going to say.

"Patty Schnozzlepoop's, duhhhhhhhhh! I stole it!"

I look at Eliza. "Should we?"

"On the one hand, a person's phone is very private . . . on the other hand, we *have* to look."

I peer over the bushes, and Otto is nearby, mowing the lawn. "Come on," I hiss, and we crawl along the hedge—once we reach the very end, we turn right, so that we're hiding near the garage. We're covered by the shade from the house's enormous shadow, which is nice because it's sticky hot outside, and even *hotter* on the blacktop.

I peer around, just to make sure we're alone. The garage doors are open, but there's no one around, and we can't see Otto anymore from this angle.

Okay, phone time!

I pull the phone out of my pocket and try to wake it up, but there are some weird boxes on it with some numbers and blank spaces. I've never seen a password like this before!

3			2
	4	1	
	3	2	
4			1

"What in the world is *this*?" I ask Eliza, passing her the phone.

"Sudoku!" Eliza exclaims.

"And . . . how do we solve it?"

Eliza points to the screen. "Each column and each row *must* contain the numbers one through four. But you can't repeat any of the numbers in the same row or column."

"Okay?"

"Take the first column. There's a three at the top corner and a four at the bottom corner. We know the remaining two numbers in this column have to be one and two."

I nod. I think I'm getting it so far.

"So then we look at the rows. Since there's a one in the second row, we know we can't repeat it in the same row. So that box *has* to be for the number two." She types it into the box.

3			2
2	4	1	
	3	2	
4			1

"Okay, I think I got it now!" I grab the phone from her. Then I bite my lip and think. Every row and every column has to contain a one, two, three, and four. So if we already have two, three, and four in the first column, then the last number has to be . . . "One!" I say out loud. "We'll crack this in no time, Eliza!"

WHEN YOU HAVE SOLVED THE PUZZLE,
ADD UP THE NUMBERS IN THE HIGHLIGHTED
BOXES AND MULTIPLY THE SOLUTION BY TWO.
TURN TO THAT PAGE.

←——→

TO GET A HINT FROM ELIZA,
TURN TO PAGE 230.

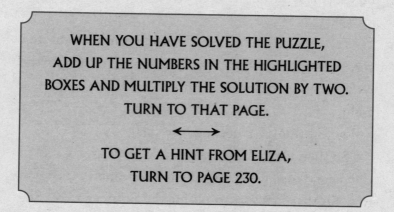

I UNPLUG WIRE C, and immediately the air vent goes ka-*thunk* and turns off.

"HOORAY! YOU DID IT!" Frank and Eliza shout, and they both start dancing around the tiny room, linking elbows.

I wipe my wet forehead with my wet T-shirt. I think I'd be drier if I'd just taken a dunk in a swimming pool.

Eliza coughs, clearly trying to get my attention. When I look at her, she seems nervous. "We don't have a lot of time," she whispers. "We don't know whether Otto—I mean, Preston—is lurking outside the room. He could attack again."

Now that the heat is off, we could send Frank through the air vent to go get help. Or we could search for a key. Or maybe we could just scream until, hopefully, Smythe hears us.

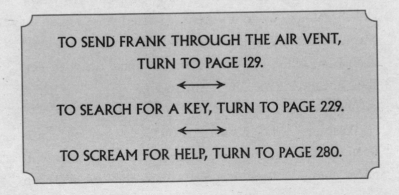

TO SEND FRANK THROUGH THE AIR VENT, TURN TO PAGE 129.

←——→

TO SEARCH FOR A KEY, TURN TO PAGE 229.

←——→

TO SCREAM FOR HELP, TURN TO PAGE 280.

"QUICK, IN HERE!" I wheeze, and I pull Eliza and Frank into Ivy's closet with me. I shut the door just in time.

"I *know* we need the money. I know we're broke! Don't you think I know that?" Ivy's voice shouts. "I'm working on it!"

I almost gasp. Her voice isn't the sweet, soft voice that it was before. Now her voice is loud, angry, and bossy.

"Look, Walter!" she says, and I realize she's talking to someone on the phone. "I will *get* us the money for your restaurant. But Mom still refuses to give me a dime unless I divorce you, just like last ti—NO! Walter! That would never happen, baby! I love you!"

Silence . . . except for the sound of Ivy pacing the room. Frank starts to fidget behind me, and Eliza holds him tight.

"Walter, she cut me out of her will. Remember how she threatened to do it when I married you? I thought she was bluffing, but she really did cut me out. And even now, when I'm pretending to make up with her, she's not letting me touch any money."

A pause.

"Walter . . . I'm figuring it out! My only chance is to find the treasure before anyone else does. Mom will never know it went missing, since she doesn't even know how to get it."

370

The floorboards creak under her feet.

"Of course I didn't tell those kids where the entrance to the tunnels is," she says.

I freeze. She knows where the entrance to the treasure tunnels is? And she *lied* to us!

"Don't worry, baby," Ivy says. "I got this. Love you! Bye!"

My brain is shouting. She's after the treasure! It's her! It's her! It's her!

TO HIDE IN THE CLOSET UNTIL IVY LEAVES, TURN TO PAGE 251.

←——→

TO FACE IVY NOW, TURN TO PAGE 234.

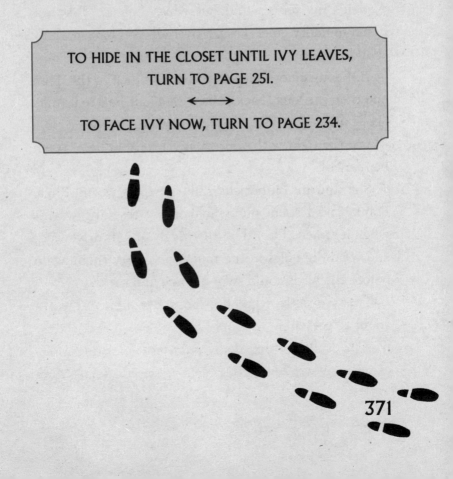

371

"WHAT WAS THE fight between you and your mom about?"

Ivy's hands tremble around her teacup, and it clatters against the saucer.

"When I said . . . I didn't mean . . ." She coughs, very daintily, into a handkerchief she's pulled from her pocket. "Let's not dwell on the past."

"No, we should dwell," I say. Judging from her response, it seems like she wants to hide *something*. And it's my job to find out what that is. "Take me down memory lane," I say. "After all, you have nothing to hide, right?"

"Of course not!" she says. Her eyes dart to the door, and then she looks back at us with a half-hearted smile. "I . . . uh . . ."

"So the fight with your mom," I remind her. "What happened?"

She squirms on her chair like a wiggly worm. Eliza, Frank, and I spent our whole spring rescuing worms when it rained. They'd be all wriggly on our driveways, and we'd dig holes in the mulch and bury them again before the birds could swoop down and eat them.

That's exactly what Ivy looks like now. A worm about to get eaten.

"Oh, well, nothing really *happened*. Nothing interesting, anyway." Ivy titters. "Long story short? Mom and I just don't talk much anymore."

"Why?" Frank asks.

"Well, she didn't really like my boyfriend—now husband—at the time."

"Why?" Frank asks.

"B-because he isn't very wealthy."

"Why?" Frank asks.

"Because he is unemployed, and his mom is a receptionist, and his dad is a plumber."

"Why?" Frank asks.

"I suppose . . . because they like it?"

"Why?" Frank asks.

"Okayyyyy!" Eliza interrupts, putting her hand over Frank's mouth. "That's enough of the why game."

"I—I just can't discuss this anymore," Ivy says dramatically, putting her hand on her forehead. "It's very upsetting."

I don't know. It seems phony to me. A well-rehearsed act . . .

I'm not sure what to do next. On the one hand, this is important. What if the fight contains a clue to the mystery?

Then again, I have the same feeling now that I did when we were deciding whether to question Guinevere LeCavalier about her husband's son, Preston. I have a sneaking feeling that this fight is something I *shouldn't* bring up with Ivy, even if I want to. Ivy might get mad or shut down. And sometimes, Mom says, knowing when to step away from a suspect is just as important as knowing when to trudge on.

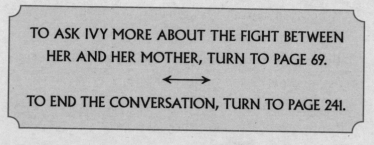

TO ASK IVY MORE ABOUT THE FIGHT BETWEEN HER AND HER MOTHER, TURN TO PAGE 69.

←——→

TO END THE CONVERSATION, TURN TO PAGE 241.

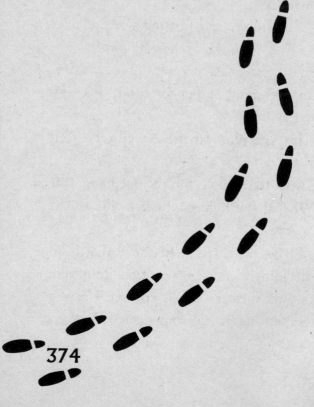

I DON'T THINK I should try anything.

A moment later, the opportunity passes. When Otto looks up from the treasure chest, he is mad. Steaming mad. Head-in-the-broiler mad. He turns kind of purplish.

"WHAT IS THIS?" he roars.

He kicks the treasure chest across the cave, and hundreds of feathers fly out of it, along with a single piece of paper. I pick it up and read out loud:

Congratulations! You've solved the treasure hunt! In this chest, you have found my collection of the best tickling feathers in the world. Trust me, they're ticklelicious!

I snort.

"Well, Guinevere *did* say her husband was eccentric," Eliza groans.

"Still," I say. "At least we caught the culprit."

"You haven't caught me yet," Otto growls. "In fact— I'll catch you first!"

He lunges, grabs my head like a football, and runs down the hall with me. My arms and legs are flailing behind. We run through caves and caverns I've never seen, with wet, drippy walls and slimy ceilings. I squirm, but Otto's holding me too tight.

"Where are you taking me?"

He doesn't answer; he just yanks me around a corner. My head is going to pop off my neck if he doesn't let go soon.

We finally reach a long ladder that goes so high, I can't even see the top. Otto pulls me up the ladder by my neck. I swear, by the end of this day, I'll be a giraffe.

The exit leads right into a toolshed . . . I think. It's a tiny one-room space with gardening tools littered everywhere. The walls are covered with pictures of Guinevere—some with her eyes scratched out, some with devil horns, some normal, but they cover every single space on the walls in a creepy collage.

Otto's level of obsession is *clearly* unhealthy. And terrifying.

"Let me go!" I shout, hoping someone from Guinevere's house will hear.

But Otto opens a drawer and stuffs something into my mouth . . . marshmallows! And . . . yes, peanut butter! It's so sticky and fluffy that I can't talk.

Otto hides me under a blanket and carries me. I try to kick, but it doesn't work, and when he finally takes the blanket off me, I'm in the passenger seat of a car. Otto hops into the driver's seat, presses the gas, and we zoom down the road.

By the time my mouth gets unstuck, we've arrived

at Otto's house. Or as I like to call it: his EVIL LAIR.

I spend the next two years being Otto's evil minion, doing all sorts of wicked super-villain tasks. By the time I'm finally reunited with Mom and Eliza and Frank, I don't even know how not to be evil anymore. Otto has passed on all of his dastardly ways. *Muahahahahahahaha.*

CASE CLOSED.

I ENTER THE words in the keypad, and the box clicks open. Inside, there's a diary.

Eliza opens the diary to the first page and begins skimming. She's turning the pages so fast it's like she's playing with a flip-book, not reading the words.

"Anything interesting?" I prod.

"She keeps talking about her secret lover schmoop-sie-poo—her words, not mine—but she doesn't actually name him. Useless. And she has two entries in here about soap. Useless and boring— Wait!"

Eliza pauses and pulls the diary closer to her face. As her eyes go back and forth across the page, they grow wider and wider.

"What? What did you find?!"

"GIMME!" Frank says, yanking the diary out of her hands. It flies across the room.

"Frank!" Eliza and I cry.

Eliza retrieves the diary and places it gently back in the box. "You'll never guess," she says, sounding all excited. "But Patty has an entry about Smythe."

"Smythe! Is he her secret boyfriend?"

"Ewwwwwwww, cooties!" Frank says.

"I don't know. But Patty says Smythe is so mad at Guinevere that he wants to leave her employment, after thirty years of working with her. Smythe asked Patty to hire him as a butler!"

I blink, which is not the reaction Eliza wants,

because she sighs loudly.

"*Carlos!* Smythe taking a job with Patty would be, like, the ultimate slap in the face to Guinevere."

"Oh. Right."

"Patty says Smythe feels mistreated by Guinevere."

We knew Smythe was mad, but mistreated? I wonder what that means. Did something happen between the two of them? Did they get in a fight?

"We have to get more information out of Smythe," I say. "This feels like a big clue!"

"At least now we know that he's mad for a *reason*. We just need to find out what that reason is!" Eliza says. "We should go confront him."

"Fight, fight, fight!" Frank chants.

"Or . . . ," I say, and I tell Eliza and Frank all about the paint I found in the garage. How it looks exactly like the paint used in the second death threat. Patty looks just as suspicious as Smythe with this new clue.

So which lead do we follow up on?

TO EXAMINE THE SCENE OF THE SECOND DEATH THREAT, TURN TO PAGE 153.

←——→

TO CONFRONT SMYTHE, TURN TO PAGE 264.

"CAN WE TALK about the death threats, Mrs. Guinevere LeCavalier madame ma'am your highness?" I say, trying to be as respectful as possible.

"Of course. The first threat was made from cut-up magazine letters. Hold on . . . *Smythe!* THE FIRST THREAT!"

Smythe marches into the room, his big footsteps making the floor rumble. His droopy eyes are fixed in a glare at Guinevere.

"Here," he grumbles as he pulls a piece of paper out of a drawer right next to Guinevere. She reads it aloud:

> *"The treasure does not belong to you.*
> *It belongs to me.*
> *You have seven days to find it.*
> *Or else."*

Eliza frowns. "Can we keep this threat? Just in case we need to revisit it later?"

Guinevere nods. "And you should have this picture I took of the second death threat." She slides a photograph and the ransom letter over to me, and I tuck them both into my pocket

"What's the second death threat?" I ask.

"You might've seen it walking in. Three days after I got this letter in the mail, I walked into my house and found my library destroyed. On the wall, in red paint, was a message."

"What did the message say?"

"It said, 'You are running out of time. Find that treasure, or MEET YOUR DOOM. HA HA HA HA HA HA HA.'"

A shiver goes up my spine.

"Oh wait," Guinevere says. "I actually think there were more *HA*s than that. How about this? *HA HA HA HA HA HAHAHAHAHAHA*."

"Okay, we get the—"

"Wait!" she says, holding up her hand for silence. "I'm not done." She clears her throat. "*HA*. Okay, now I'm done."

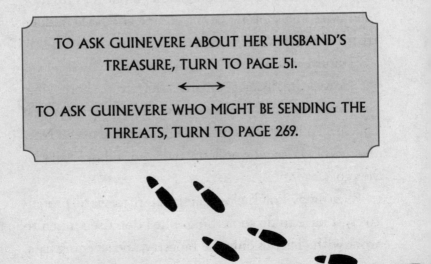

TO ASK GUINEVERE ABOUT HER HUSBAND'S TREASURE, TURN TO PAGE 51.

←——→

TO ASK GUINEVERE WHO MIGHT BE SENDING THE THREATS, TURN TO PAGE 269.

"WHY, OTTO?" I say, taking one step closer. "Why are you doing this?"

I hold the lantern up and peer into his face, which looks dark from the shadows or anger . . . or both.

"My name isn't Otto," he says harshly. "It's Preston LeCavalier."

Preston LeCavalier? Mr. LeCavalier's son? My heart skips a beat. "Y-you're him?"

"Ah," Preston says, "I see you've heard of me. That's surprising, as this one"—he shakes Guinevere—"likes to pretend I never existed."

"I . . . didn't . . . mean . . . ," Guinevere peeps.

"Oh, but you *did* mean," Preston says. "You meant to erase me from my family. And you were successful at it. Except for one thing: you can never erase the memories I have of my father talking about the hidden treasure beneath the house."

Guinevere squeaks.

"Now I finally get to give Guinevere here what she deserves, *and* walk away with my treasure. Of course . . ." He studies us through squinted eyes. "Now that you kids know who I am and what I did, I can't let you go."

Eliza hugs Frank close, and I step forward protectively. I have to do something. But I don't see much to work with. There's only the tapestry, the sleeping bats, the lanterns, Eliza's backpack . . . Wait a minute!

Suddenly, clear as crystal, two plans form in my head. Both involve creating a distraction for Otto while we escape with Guinevere LeCavalier. The first plan is where I set the tapestry on fire. And the other plan is where I throw raisins at the sleeping bats to wake them up.

Which one would be a better distraction?

TO SET THE TAPESTRY ON FIRE,
TURN TO PAGE 152.

←→

TO THROW RAISINS AT THE BATS,
TURN TO PAGE 237.

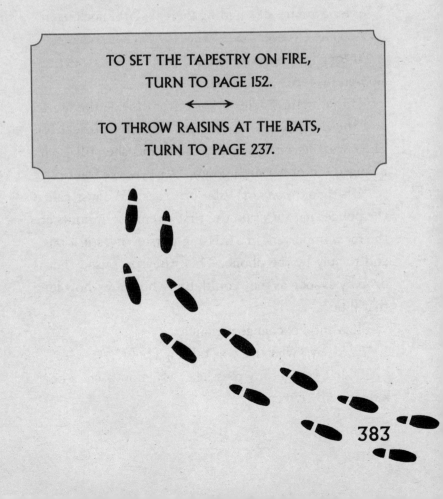

I DECIDE THAT maybe we should check in with Guinevere LeCavalier after all—just to let her know that we're on the case. And maybe, while we're there, we can tell her all we know about Patty and Maddock.

I let Frank ring the doorbell, and he presses it over and over, a billion times, *ding ding ding ding ding!*

Finally Eliza has to grab his hand and pull him away from the doorbell.

After a minute of standing there, I start knocking like crazy. Where is everyone? What the heck is going on?

At long last, Smythe opens the door, a sour expression on his face.

"Is that them?" cries a voice from inside the house, and the door swings open even farther to reveal Ivy. She's wearing curlers in her hair, and she still hasn't changed out of her nightgown. Her eyes are frantic.

"Oh thank *goodness*!" she breathes. "We just called the police, and they said the first twenty-four hours are the most important in a missing-person investigation—and to stay by the phone. Then they promised they'd drop by as soon as they could, but who knows how long that'll be?"

Eliza and I exchange a glance.

"Er," I say, "what are you talking about?"

"Didn't you get my message? My mom—she's been kidnapped!" Ivy cries.

384

"B-but," I say, my brain trying to wrap itself around this new information. "But we told her to go to a hotel!"

"She *was* at the hotel," Ivy says, her voice all shaky. "With me. But then she woke up in the middle of the night, missing Mr. Wubbles."

"A stuffed animal?" Eliza asks.

"No, her diamond necklace," Ivy says. "She texted me, saying she went home for it, but I didn't get the text until I woke up in the morning. And when I got to the house, she was gone! And there was a note on her pillow." Ivy opens her palm and hands us a small piece of rough, rolled-up paper.

I uncurl the note and look at the big block-lettered writing.

SHE WILL FIND THE TREASURE WITH ME . . . OR PERISH AT SUNDOWN.

A shiver goes down my spine, and my stomach drops like it's falling down an elevator shaft. Oh man oh man oh man. We really *shouldn't* have taken this case. At first it was all kind of fun and mysterious, but I don't think we took the third threat seriously enough, and now there is ACTUAL danger. It's more than my mom's fate on the line. . . . I mean, if we can't solve this, then Guinevere might die. And if we get too close to catching the criminal, we'll be in danger too.

Oh, man, what was I thinking?

"What does *pear-ish* mean?" asks Frank, pointing at the note.

"Perish. And it's not good," Eliza says.

Ivy snatches the letter back from my hands and waves it frantically. "WHO?" she crows. "Who would kidnap my mother? *You've* investigated this—who do you think is guilty?"

I think for a moment. We've found out some interesting things about a whole bunch of people. I could tell Ivy all we've learned—everything we know about every single person. But then again, maybe I don't want to go around pointing fingers too soon.

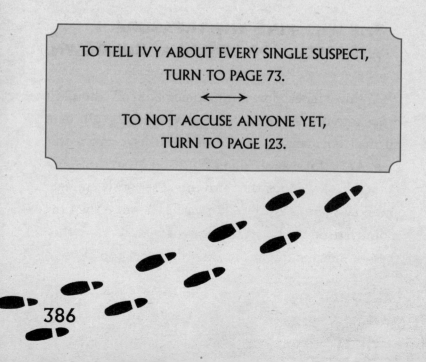

TO TELL IVY ABOUT EVERY SINGLE SUSPECT,
TURN TO PAGE 73.

←——→

TO NOT ACCUSE ANYONE YET,
TURN TO PAGE 123.

ELIZA HELPS FRANK climb onto my shoulders.

"Feel around up there, Frank!" Eliza calls. "Try up high, near the ceiling."

Frank feels around for a while. Meanwhile, I'm dying under his weight.

"Ugh, Frank!" I groan. "You're heavier than you look."

Frank huffs. "Of course! I'm a BIG KID!"

My shoulders start to ache.

"Ooooh! A vent!" Frank says. "Taller, please!"

"I can't get any taller!"

"Wait!" Eliza says. "Carlos, lift your left foot." I lift my left foot, and Eliza slips an enormous platform shoe underneath it, which boosts me up five inches. "Now the other!"

"Awesome!" Frank says as he pulls on the vent's screen and sends it clattering to the floor.

"Watch it!" Eliza says. "That almost hit my head!"

"Sorry!" Frank pulls himself up into the vent, and an enormous weight is lifted off my shoulders . . . literally.

At first, I can hear him climbing around. There are clattering sounds from the vent. Then the noises start to get far away from us. In the end, I can't hear Frank wiggling around at all.

"Do you think he made it?" I say after a while.

As if the universe was waiting for me to ask that question, the closet door opens, and Frank stands there grinning.

"Great job, buddy!" Eliza exclaims, and I clap Frank on the back.

We run around the halls, looking for Otto. But he's gone. My stomach drops to my toes—we *need* to find him. Without him, my mom's life is ruined.

"We have to hurry! He's getting away! Any ideas, Eliza?"

"I have two. Didn't Otto say something about how the treasure is buried beneath the house? We could go into the basement and see if there's a way in down there."

"Or?"

"Or we can ask the LeCavaliers for help. Maybe they'll know how to get in. It's *your* mom on the line, Carlos. You choose."

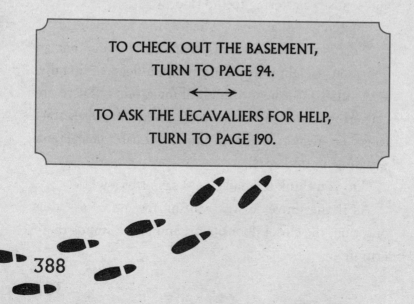

TO CHECK OUT THE BASEMENT,
TURN TO PAGE 94.

←——→

TO ASK THE LECAVALIERS FOR HELP,
TURN TO PAGE 190.

I **DECIDE TO** follow Maddock. He *does* give me a weird vibe. . . .

We tiptoe down the hall behind Maddock, being as sneaky-stealthy as we can be. We creep behind him as he bounds down the hall. We slither down the stairs. We inch across the living room—

"What are you doing?" Maddock says, whipping around to face us.

Oops! I guess I was so busy being sneaky I didn't notice that Maddock was onto us.

"Er . . . nothing," I say.

"You're following me, aren't you?"

"Whaaaat?" Eliza says. "Who? Us? No! What?"

I smack my forehead. Could she *be* any more obvious right now?

"I demand you stop following me at once!"

"HEY! YOU SKUNKY SKUNK FACE!" Frank shouts. "DON'T BOSS US AROUND."

Maddock runs a hand through his greasy hair and smirks. Then he leans so close to us that I can smell his stinky breath. "If you don't stop following me, I'll slap you with a lawsuit!"

"You can't sue us for walking around," Eliza says.

"Yeah! It's a free country."

Maddock smiles. "A free country, hmm? We'll see about that."

He brushes past us and runs out of Guinevere's house, but we stick to him like my abuela's dentures stick to her gums. We follow him all the way down to his office, where he drafts up something called a restraining order and gets a judge to sign it. This piece of paper means we're not allowed to go within five hundred feet of him or we can get fined, sued, or put in jail. Which is *crazy*, because I can't afford to be fined, sued, or put in jail!

Maddock drives back to Guinevere LeCavalier's house. We wait outside on her lawn for *hours*, but Maddock doesn't leave. As long as he's in there, we can't be.

In the afternoon, Maddock opens a window and sticks his tongue out at us. "I'm not leaving . . . ever! How does it feel to be shut out of this case?" he gloats as he slams the window closed.

CASE CLOSED.